THE FANT
OF BURNEO...

David H. Keller's "The Flying Threat" is a story of science gone mad. It certainly parallels H. G. Wells' "The Island of Dr. Moreau," in that it features a small party of civilized people who are trapped in a far off, danger-filled land and faced with the terrifying threat of a mad scientist and his horrible monstrosities. It was also a most unusual tale for its time (1930) because it featured a lead female character who was—unlike the typical trembling beauties that filled the pages of the pulp magazines of the day—an intelligent, independent, strong-willed woman, unafraid to look adversity, even stark horror, straight in the eye without blinking.

But if you're afraid of bugs (especially big ones!) don't read this story, because Dr. Keller has a field day slowly nurturing the terror of an army of giant insects that are soon to be unleashed upon an unsuspecting mankind. It is another example of the kind of taut, well-written science-suspense yarns that Dr. Keller was famous for.

FOR A COMPLETE SECOND NOVEL, TURN TO PAGE 135

CAST OF CHARACTERS

DR. ANNA ROCK
A middle-aged millionaire who could have anything she wanted, yet she was possessed with the study of entomology.

TIMOTHY JONES
Who was he really? He claimed to have escaped from the perilous jungles of Borneo and told a wild tale of monsters and madmen.

HERMAN SCHEERMANN
At one time he was considered a most brilliant scientist, but thirty years in the jungle can turn even the most learned man a bit loony.

HELEN BROWN
Almost a spinster but not quite, she had led a most sheltered life; but a trip into the wilds of Borneo cured her of all naivety.

STERLING POWERS
He had retired at a young age and was independently wealthy— and a perfect match for someone who loved entomology.

PROFESSOR PACKARD
As a man of science his mind had to be objective, but the lurid story of a giant silkworm was just too much to swallow.

SAKIO
He was polished and polite, but his lack of any sense of true morality had led him into a bargain with the devil.

THE FLYING THREAT

By
DAVID H. KELLER, M. D.

ARMCHAIR FICTION
PO Box 4369, Medford, Oregon 97504

*For more information about Armchair Books and products, visit our
website at…*

www.armchairfiction.com

Or email us at…

armchairfiction@yahoo.com

CHAPTER ONE
Two Peculiar Eggs

THE telephone bell rang. Dr. Anna Rock, considerably annoyed, placed her book on the table and picked up the receiver. She listened to the voice at the other end of the line and then replied sharply, "Tell him that I refuse to see him. I have told you repeatedly that I see no one except by written appointment. Tell him to leave or I will have him arrested for trespass."

Then she slowly replaced the receiver, picked up her book, and started to read. She had a great deal of studying to do and only a limited number of years to do it in. Consequently, she felt that there was no time to be lost in endless conversation with unimportant persons, particularly of the male sex.

Dr. Anna Rock had inherited a considerable estate from her parents. To this she had added for many years from her income as a physician. At the age of thirty-nine she had ceased to practice and had decided to devote the rest of her life to a very intensive study of insect life. She was not interested in the insect world as a whole; there were large sections of it that she despised and detested. The very thought of some bugs and ants made her shiver. Consequently, she was decidedly distinctive and selective in her desires to become an expert in entomology.

In making her plans for the rest of her life she had to have a suitable place to live, definite programs for each year of her future life and sufficient leisure to devote to study. She not only had to have a quiet place to live in, but that place had to have the necessary requirements to support the particular life she was interested in. Weighing all these points carefully, she bought a ten-thousand-acre tract of land in New Jersey, bordering on the Delaware River, which included the mountain range forming the eastern barrier of the Delaware Water Gap.

Being accustomed to precision all of her adult life, it was but natural that the first thing she did following the purchase of this land was to have it carefully surveyed. Her next act was to build a ten-foot fence around the tract, the upper three feet being composed of barbed wire. Thus she was able to give adequate protection to all the wild life that for centuries had lived in these almost inaccessible mountains. A carriage road from the ferry at Shawnee made her cabin accessible, but this road was securely barred by a gate, to say nothing of a trusty Irishman, who lived at the Lodge for no other purpose than to admit only desirable persons.

The ten-thousand-acre tract included two interesting natural wonders. One was Mount Tammany, the eastern half of the Gap; the other was a lake of peculiar beauty, located on the very top of the mountain range, a few miles north of the Gap. This lake, three-quarters of a mile in length and less than that in breadth, was evidently fed by some peculiar subterranean spring, as no stream of water flowed into it. The shore was sharply defined with masses of gray sandstone; white birch and spruce bordered its edge and were reflected in its crystal waters; perch, undisturbed for centuries, formed a piscatorial colony. Often for hours at a time the only moving thing on the lake would be the reflected image of clouds in the sky. Then, usually at dusk, the perch would come for flies, and later the moon would bathe in the limpid waters. It was a lake of beauty, made more beautiful by solitude.

On this lake Dr. Rock built her home, which she called, ironically, a cabin. In its nineteen rooms were located every convenience necessary to make life comfortable. There were fifty electrical servants, a library, and a workroom. Two women, one a widow, the other the wife of the gatekeeper, cared for the cabin, kept it clean and cooked the meals. Thus, the physical existence of the doctor was well cared for. Her social life included one friend, made years before, a lovely vivacious woman, who satisfied in every way the longing for intimate friendship possessed by every individual.

Amid these surroundings the doctor studied the *Lepidoptera*. Her love of the beautiful found expression in the study of the multi-colored moths and butterflies of North America. Her special scientific interest was in the silkworm, and the fact that mulberry trees grew rapidly on the Kittatinny Range, was one of her lesser reasons for selecting this site for her permanent home.

On this special morning she was waiting for Helen Brown. They had made an appointment to spend the day together, to hunt for some orchids, which they were sure ought to be in the woods, but which, so far, they had never been able to find. While waiting she read over again the pages of Malpighi's treatise on the silkworm; published in 1669. Naturally, she was irritated to have O'Malley call from the Lodge about a matter that he should have settled easily himself. She was more provoked when he called the second time about the same person.

"I am sure enough sorry to have to trouble you, Dr. Rock," he said, "but this party down here says that he just has to see you. He says that you will be glad to see him when you know his business."

"Well, what is his business?" asked the doctor, sharply.

"He wants to sell you some eggs."

"Eggs? You know well enough that I have nothing to do with the buying of eggs. Have him wait and see your wife."

"He wants to see you."

"Tell him I will have him arrested if he does not leave—and O'Malley, Miss Brown is going to come soon. After you let her in lock the gate and come up with her, I have some important mail for you to take to the post office at North Water Cap."

"And you will not see the man?"

"Never."

The doctor again picked up her book on silkworm culture. Fifteen minutes later Helen Brown rushed into the doctor's room to drag her out into the woods. The doctor picked up some letters and went to see the gatekeeper before she started on her orchid hunt.

"Get rid of your pest?" she asked O'Malley.

"At least, he left, Doctor," was the respectful reply. "He said that you would buy the eggs if you saw them."

"Well, what was so wonderful about them? An egg is an egg, isn't it?"

"A hen egg is, but there are lots of different kinds of eggs, and, from the way he talked, I fancied that these were not just ordinary hen eggs."

"What did he look like?"

"He was a foreigner of some kind, Doctor, with a longish beard and he had the eggs in a basket with a white cloth tied over the top. He had walked up from the ferry and he was hot; said he was used to cooler weather where he came from."

"Did he leave?"

"No. Still sitting on a rock outside the gate, sort of thinking and sucking his thumb."

"Keep him there. Take these letters to the post office, and when you see him tell him to leave and not come back."

Ten minutes later O'Malley was on his way to North Water Gap, while the doctor and Helen Brown were already in the dark spruce woods, hunting wild flowers. They did not return till it was time for dinner. As soon as they entered the cabin the doctor was met by Mrs. O'Malley.

"The phone has been ringing, Doctor. You are wanted on 207-J."

The doctor went to the phone and called that number. On being connected, she listened for a few seconds and then said, almost harshly, "No! I do not want any eggs!" and hung up. Then she turned to Miss Brown.

"This phone is going to be the death of me, Ellen," she said. "I am either going to take it out or have a private number, not listed in the directory. Here is a wonderful example of the way it works to keep up my blood pressure: A pest comes to the gate to sell a few eggs. He insists on seeing me, and bribes O'Malley to phone to me and find out if I won't see him. Of course I refuse. Now he goes to a pay station and calls me up. Won't I at least look at the eggs? What did he think my time was worth? Why should I look at a hen egg unless I am ready to eat it?"

"Perhaps it was another kind of egg," suggested Miss Brown.

"Let's eat," was the reply. "Perhaps your stupidity is the result of hunger. Perhaps it was a rooster egg or a turtle egg or an ostrich egg."

IT was late in the afternoon before Miss Brown returned to her summer bungalow across the river. She frequently spent the night with her friend in the cabin on the Lake of the Mountain, but this evening she was expecting company of her own. The doctor ate a light supper and then went out on the stone terrace to watch the approach of night. Just at dusk an airplane hummed noisily over the lake, and a few minutes later she heard the sound of splintering glass. The noise came from her small conservatory. Running there, she found a man trying to shake off the folds of a parachute, and at the same time make his way out of the broken frame of the hothouse. The doctor watched his efforts in silence.

Finally, the man unstrapped himself and took off his hat with a polite bow, as he said, "Are you Dr. Rock?"

"That is my name," replied the doctor.

"My name is Timothy Jones. I have been trying to see you all day."

The doctor shook her head. In spite of the gathering dusk, she was beginning to see daylight.

At last she said, "You are the man who wanted to sell me eggs?"

"Yes, Madam. I am that man. Your gatekeeper said you would not see me; so I telephoned to you and still you refused— Then I went to the Commercial Air-Field at Sciota and hired a plane to take me over your place, and at the right time I jumped. I am sorry about your hothouse, Madam. But I was so worried about not breaking the eggs that I didn't think of anything else; and it was the first time I had ever used one of those umbrella things."

"So, you brought the eggs with you?"

"Yes, Madam. I knew that you would not want to see me without the eggs."

"All right. I will buy them. How much a dozen?" The man placed the basket down on the ground and started to take off the cloth cover. He looked up.

"I only have two eggs, Madam, but they are nice ones," and he placed one in the doctor's hands.

It was too dark to see clearly, but she felt that she was holding a round object, at least eight inches in diameter, with an exterior that was almost as smooth as glass. She took a sharp breath.

"What is it, Mr. Jones?" she whispered.

"Just some kind of an egg," was the reply. "If you want to buy the two of them and will let me sit down somewhere, I will tell you about them. That is, I will tell you all that I know about them."

"I'll buy them. Put this one back in the basket and come with me to my library. Have you had supper?"

"No, Dr. Rock. I left the Water Gap early this morning and I have been so busy trying to see you that I forgot about eating since breakfast. I just couldn't rest till I showed you those eggs."

The doctor ordered supper for the man, and while he ate, she sat, silently looking at the two eggs. Perhaps one was a trifle larger than the other, but otherwise they were identical. The shell was smooth, and slightly elastic, like the egg of a reptile, while the color was almost a dead white. At last the man stopped eating and the doctor rang for the maid to come for the dishes. Then she started the fire in the open fireplace and told him to make himself comfortable and begin with his story.

"It is not much of a story," he said. "I told you my name—Timothy Jones. Before the war I was a grocer's clerk, working in an Atlantic and Pacific Store, and I was happy and content at my work. Then came the war and I saw some very hard service over there, and when I came back I was not the same as I was before. I had no pleasure in selling sugar and oleo and writing the advertisements for the Saturday Specials. It seems that I had been in such big things, Madam, that the life of a grocery clerk seemed impossible; so I started to see the world, and there is no doubt that I saw it. I would go to some place, like Benares, where they have cows in the churches and have the most peculiar way of doing their stable work. There I would hear of some dead city in Siam, and forthwith I went there. I continued, just like I could not rest, and finally I landed in Central Borneo and found a white man there who wanted me to work for him. He didn't say what the work was, but I found out soon enough, and though he watched me very closely, the time came when I made my escape. Finally I landed in New Orleans. I bummed my way up north, but all the time I carried the eggs with me, and at last I got to Port Jervis. That used to be my hometown. I had charge of the first A. and P. store opened there. I had been away for years and everything was different. The girl I used to go with, she was married and had grown children; so, I started to walk down the river valley. All the time I thought I would sell those eggs sometime, especially if I could find someone to listen to my story and believe me. Up at Milford I met a man who said you were interested in butterfly study, so here I am."

"You mean to say?" asked the doctor, but for some reason she did not have the courage to finish her sentence.

"I mean to say," replied Jones, "that these eggs are butterfly eggs. At least, I think so; though they might be something else."

"Did you ever see butterfly eggs?" asked the doctor.

"Not to know them."

The doctor left the room for a few minutes and then returned with a small leaf in her hand.

"Here," she said, "are some of the eggs of the tent caterpillar. You can see them with the unaided eye, but they are just like little dots. They are about the average size of butterfly eggs. I do not pretend to be the world authority on butterflies and moths, but I know a great deal about them. These large things you brought here are not butterfly eggs. Why, if butterflies were produced from such eggs, they would be enormous. I can hardly tell how large they would be. That is my answer, Timothy Jones. You put those two things back in the basket and the cover over them and I will have O'Malley come and take you to the gate."

"In other words, you think I am a liar?"

"Something like that."

A change came over the ex-soldier. Somehow, he seemed to sit straighter and have a little more intelligence in his face. His voice became hard, decisive.

"I can hardly blame you, Dr. Rock, but at the same time, it is a fortunate thing for you that you are not a man. I may have been a grocery clerk in an A. and P. store, but no man ever called me that and got by with it. The trouble with you is that you just cannot imagine something you have never seen. Now, with me, I do not have to imagine what those butterflies are like, because I have seen them. Yes, Madam, I mean just that. I have seen the butterflies that laid these eggs, or some just like them. It is because I saw those flies and moths and other things that I decided to leave that man and come back to America; because I became afraid."

"What were you afraid of," asked the doctor coldly, unsympathetically. "I should think that a soldier who had been through the World War would not know what fear was."

"That is just what made me afraid. I have seen men killed in every way in war and stood it, because it was just a part of the game. I would like to tell you what I saw in Borneo, but what is the use? You would just think I am insane or shell-shocked or something like that. But you can take them or leave them. They are just what I said they were—butterfly eggs. I am going to keep on until I sell them, because I need the money. If you had faith in me, I would like to stay here and talk to you some more and perhaps stay and work for you until the eggs hatch out. I saw a lot of that the two years I worked for that man in Borneo."

DOCTOR ROCK looked at the man. There was no doubt in her mind that he was in earnest. She hated to make a fool out of herself, and at the same time she dreaded the thought of his taking the eggs to one of her rivals in the field of entomology. She did not want to employ the man, but she did want him available for at least a year.

At last she said, "Suppose I give you five thousand dollars for the two eggs? That seems to me to be a fair price. Then I will set you up in some kind of business in Shawnee, the understanding being that you promise to stay there till the eggs hatch. How about it?"

"That is fair enough. I will take that offer."

"I suppose you will want to open a grocery store?"

"No, not exactly. I want a lot of leisure and something that is different. I was pretty tired of selling groceries, especially butter substitutes. I thought I would open a hosiery store, if I could finance it. Silk stockings are going to be popular again someday."

"No," said the doctor, "everybody is wearing cotton again."

"That is because the silk ones wore out so quickly and were so expensive. But how about it, if the silk thread was heavier and practically everlasting? That may come some day. Perhaps you may have something to do with it, Dr. Rock."

"What makes you think I am interested in natural silk production?" asked the doctor, eagerly.

"That is what the man up at Milford said. He thought you knew more about it than almost anyone in America."

"Well, suppose I do? What has that to do with these eggs and your opening a store to sell silk stockings?"

"Simply this: These eggs are, or at least I think they are, the eggs of the silkworm. Not the kind they have in Japan or China or anywhere else at the present time, but a giant silkworm that this man bred in Borneo. I tried to get the egg of a male and a female, and if you can breed them, you may be able to make some natural silk right here in America that will revolutionize the industry. That is what the man went to Borneo for in the first place, but after he had been successful with the silkworm, he started in other things. I hated him when I realized what was in his mind. I hated him and was afraid of him too, and it was just God's providence that I was able to escape alive."

The ex-physician scientist never replied. She simply started to write a check for five thousand dollars. This she handed to the ex-service man.

"You stay here all night as my guest, Mr. Jones," she said. "Tomorrow we will go over to Shawnee and see about a location for your hosiery store. If what you say is true, I will see that you are well taken care of for the rest of your life. But you must promise me that you will stay near here to help me raise these eggs. Do you realize that you have only told me a little part of your story?"

"I know that, Madam, and I have tried to tell you why. The time I was with that man in Borneo I saw some very peculiar things, and most of them no one would believe, especially not a hard-headed business woman like you are, not meaning any offense, Dr. Rock, in calling you hard-headed. Some day when it is raining hard and you cannot do anything else, I may come up here and tell you all about it, but just now I think that the less said about the ideas of that man in Borneo the better."

The doctor had Jones shown to his room and then she took the basket, placed it on a chair in front of her and sat and looked at the two eggs. Now and then she felt them. Her fingertips, delicately trained by long years of examination and treatment of the human body, vibrated at the peculiarly smooth, polished surface. She took a flashlight, placed the lens against the further side of an egg, turned out all the lights in the room, and turned on the flashlight. The trans-illumination was nearly perfect; the whole egg glowed softly. Turning on the lights, the scientist placed the basket of eggs in her safe and called O'Malley on the phone.

"O'Malley," she said. "Sorry to bother you, but I want you to take me across the river right away. I have to see Miss Brown. Bring the car around as soon as you can."

And to herself she said, "This is the largest, most wonderful thing that has ever happened to me, or perhaps to any entomologist. I want to talk to Helen about it. She may not be able to follow me, but at least she will stimulate my thinking by serving as an audience for my monologue. Eggs! Two eggs! If they really are a variety of silkworm egg, the entire industry will be revolutionized."

CHAPTER TWO
The Silk Worm

HELEN BROWN was sleeping soundly in her little two-room bungalow on Topcrest, on the Pennsylvania side of the Delaware, just about opposite to her friend's palatial cabin on the Lake of the Mountain. She had entertained company for supper, but they were gone, the dishes were all washed and she had at once retired for the night. Her first deep sleep was rudely disturbed by an insistent pounding at the door. The clack-clack-clackedy-clack of the doorknocker was in the code used only by her friend, Dr. Rock.

Miss Brown lit a candle, opened the door, and at once returned to her bed and comfortable blankets and quilt. It was early spring and that meant cold nights on Topcrest. The doctor, without saying a word, raked the ashes in the little open fireplace, put in an old copy of the *Morning Sun* and some kindling, and when the time was ripe, a fat piece of pine. Then, making herself comfortable in a Morris chair, she started to talk.

"Somewhat of a surprise, Helen," she said, "you were not expecting to see me, were you?"

"Nothing you do surprises me, Doc," was the sleepy answer. "You tell me to go to bed early and get all the sleep that I can, and then you come and make night hideous for me. Just because you have insomnia is no reason for pestering me, is it?"

The entomologist laughed at her friend's tirade.

"You will forgive me, old fellow, when you hear my story. But first, let me ask you how much your stockings cost you a year, and why?"

"Those stockings are a nightmare," was the reply.

"I pay anywhere from two to four dollars a pair and they last just about three washings on an average. They develop runs faster than I can buy them."

"Why?"

"Rotten silk, I guess. I asked a New York stocking buyer the same question one day and he said that it was hard to get the best grade. It seems that all the good silk is kept in China and Japan and we just get the leavings. He said that real silk of the best grade was almost everlasting."

"I believe him," said the doctor. "I have my grandmother's wedding dress. The material is just as good today as the day it was bought. Her father brought it with him from Japan. Do you know anything about the silk industry? I judge not. I won't worry you with the bug side of it, but let me tell you about the silk. Each cocoon furnishes from 500 to 1200 meters of a silk thread, but unfortunately, this thread averages only about one-sixteen-hundredth of an inch in diameter. Of course, this is too fine to use as a thread; so, singles are made, consisting of one strand of twisted silk composed of filaments from eight or ten cocoons. A thread is then made out of two or three of these singles, and in making the actual material, the silk dress goods, the woof (crosswise yarns) is often made out of several threads. That is the way real silk is made. But there is a great deal of material

17

that the Orientals think is worthless. This is called silk waste. Take a cocoon with the chrysalis inside. It weighs about 50 grains. Only one sixth of this weight is really pure cocoon, and of that sixth, only one-half can be reeled off as silk. For centuries the Orientals have thrown the waste away. Now they are spinning it and selling it to the rest of the world. That is why your stockings wear out as rapidly as they do."

"That is all very interesting," said Helen Brown, sarcastically, "but hardly worth while being awakened for. How is it going to help me save money?"

"Simply in this way. Suppose we were able to produce cocoons that gave a thread a mile long and large enough to weave directly instead of taking twelve to twenty filaments to make one thread. Suppose we could grow cocoons like that in America, what then? We could force the Orient to send us their best silk or none at all. In fact, it would make no difference to us whether we bought from them at all. The silk would be permanent. Of course, I can see an objection to that, because women are always wanting to change styles and colors, but it would be so satisfactory to be able to buy a pair of hose and wear them the whole year. A woman who could do that would save time, money, and nervous energy, no matter what the perfect stockings cost her a pair. Think what a satisfaction it would be to go out in the morning perfectly clad and know that not a single runner would appear the entire day...or the entire summer?"

"That would be very nice," said Helen Brown, lazily, "but how do you do it?"

"I believe I can produce perfect silk. Perhaps the cocoons will be twelve or fifteen feet high."

The sleepy woman sat up in bed.

"Anna Rock! Are you drunk?"

"Not at all, but I feel intoxicated with the idea. I bought some eggs tonight. The man was pestering me all day; you remember that I told you about him? Well, he called on me this evening. Dropped down from an airplane and landed on my conservatory. It ended in my buying his eggs."

"Hen eggs?"

"No, Silly! Silkworm eggs. Beauties. You will go wild when you see them. For the life of me, I cannot identify the species, but the man insists that they were laid by a mulberry-feeding moth. I am going to have you meet him tomorrow. He is a man with a past. You have always said that if you ever met a man with a real past, you would marry him. He told me just enough to make me die with curiosity to hear the rest. He won't tell me now, because the poor fellow is shy and thinks that I will look on him as a liar. I have the two eggs safe up in the cabin; he is sleeping in my guest room, and tomorrow I am going to set him up in business in Shawnee."

"And you wake me for this? That means that I shall have to be his main customer, and that implies the sale of another bond to pay the bill."

"My dear child," said Dr. Rock. "Take my advice. When you buy hose from Timothy Jones, you buy one pair a trip and the cheapest he has and buy them often, because I feel that he is a real man and he will not remain a bachelor for long at Shawnee in that business. If you do not marry him, someone else will."

"I don't want to marry, Anna," pled the younger woman. "So long as you live, I never am going to marry. It just means cooking and bills and babies, and I am satisfied with life as it is. If I was sure of finding a he-man who was also a gentleman and had a past, I might take a chance; but these bifurcated animals who call themselves men just nauseate me."

The scientist stood up and put on her coat.

"Just think it over. Come up and see us tomorrow. Have dinner with us. I have to go now. I guess O'Malley is dead to the world and nearly frozen out in the car. Think it over. This may be a great day for both of us. Me finding a giant silkworm and you a perfect husband."

"The door is over there," said Helen Brown. "When you go out, shut it softly so as not to awaken me, for I am so little interested in your remarks that I will be asleep by the time you reach the door. Yes, I will be over for dinner, but not to meet my future husband; rather to serve as a chaperon. Hell's bells! You probably will end up by marrying the man yourself. I never heard of your sleeping a man up there before."

"He is safe, and so are the eggs. I am going to ask him to shave twice over, and he is going to have some new clothes before you see him."

"Have him dress like Adolph Menjou. I just adore that kind of man—on the screen," was the sarcastic reply.

Dr. Rock returned to her cabin on the shore of the Lake of the Mountain. Before retiring she opened the safe and looked longingly and lovingly at the two eggs.

CHAPTER THREE
Hatching the Eggs

THE next morning Timothy Jones and the entomologist had breakfast together. Immediately afterward the Doctor announced that they were going to Stroudsburg to buy the former grocer clerk some clothes.

"If you are going to sell hose in Shawnee," she said, with a very definite air of authority, "you will have to be one of the best dressed men there. Of course, we cannot get a complete outfit for you in Stroudsburg, but we can buy enough to last till we go to New York to buy your stock. I am anxious for you to make a success in your new store. For some reason you have a rather definite inferiority complex. If you can overcome that, you will make a success out of life. Nothing makes a person feel better than to be well dressed. But we have to hurry because I am going to have company for dinner and you must have on your new things when they come."

Timothy Jones looked at the woman in a certain mild astonishment.

"That man in Borneo was a hard man to work for, Doctor."

"Yes. What of it?"

"Oh! Nothing. Only I ran away from him. Since the war, after I saw so many people killed, I have had a longing for freedom. That is one reason why I did not want my old job back in the A. and P. store. The inspector came around every week and gave me orders. I was rather fed up on orders by the time I left the army, Madam."

The woman laughed.

"I will admit that I was rather dictatorial in what I said about the clothes, but it was really for your own good, Mr. Jones."

"I know. That is what the inspector used to say if I argued with him. But we will buy the clothes this morning. I am always willing to try anything once, and a promise is a promise. I told you that I would stay around here till you hatched out the eggs and got the hang of raising the worms, so I will stay. But I will just be asking you this one thing, Dr. Rock, and that is to make the staying as easy as possible for me. You see, you really need me to help you raise those silkworms."

"Oh! I know how to raise silkworms," said the doctor.

"You never raised any worms like these," Jones replied.

However, the morning was spent in buying clothes in Stroudsburg and getting a haircut and, on the way back, renting a store in Shawnee. It was after oneo'clock, therefore, before Timothy Jones was ready to walk downstairs in his new clothes and join the ladies who were waiting for him in the library. Clothes cannot make a gentleman, but if a man is already one, they certainly add to his appearance, and the ex-service man almost looked like a banker as he entered the room to be introduced to Miss Helen Brown. To say the least, that lady was surprised. She had expected to meet a tramp; instead, she was introduced to a globetrotter, whose very air of diffidence added to his appearance. The doctor at once led the way to the dining room and absolutely refused to talk shop of any kind during the meal. As luck would have it, however, the subject of orchids was introduced at the very beginning of the meal, and Mr. Jones was asked if he had ever seen any in his various wanderings around the world. At once, he brightened and actually talked for over ten minutes about these parasitic plants. He had no particular, definite, scientific knowledge of his subject, but he was able to present his experiences in an interesting way, he ended by saying:

"It might be interesting to you ladies to hear of an experience of mine down on the Amazon River. I had heard a lot about the man-eating plants and naturally, I wanted to see one. I was that way for a good many years—if I heard of anything new, I wanted to see it myself. After a hard trip, which was financed by a rubber company—you see, I was employed as a scout to find new rubber forests, but I was allowed to go about where I wanted to, and was to be paid when I came back—and many of the boys never did collect their back pay—well, anyway, that is how I happened to be in the Amazon River district, and when I heard about these man-eating plants, I wanted to see one. They are an orchid; I guess there is no doubt about that; at least they look like some of the others, only they are bigger and have a habit of eating meat. As far as I could see, it did not make any difference what kind it was, just so long as it was meat and fresh. They are curious things to look at and all around them are piles of white bones. They suck all the juice out of the bodies and then throw them out on the ground, and the ants pick the bones. One of them saved my life, and that is one reason for my being thankful to them. I was being tracked by a cat. Yes, Madam. Of course it was not an ordinary house cat, but a wild one, like a panther or cougar. The cat was so interested in hunting me that he lost his caution, and the first thing I knew I heard him screaming and saw him up in the tree, being pushed right down into the middle of the flower. I made sure that there were no more plants like that in the neighborhood, and then I sat down to see what was going to happen next. The poor cat just cried once or twice and then everything was still, and in about an hour his body was thrown out on top the pile of white bones and the ants and beetles got to work on the hide and bones. Now, that plant could have taken me just as easy as it did the cat, but the cat was handy; so, I am here telling about it. Lots of times things like that happen to me. Once in the war, a chap in our squad went to the Corporal and asked him to have my place in the front rank, because he could drill better than I could. The Corporal put him there and me right behind him, and one day when we were marching, he was killed by a stray bullet. Just another example of how things work out for me."

"Before you talk anymore," said Dr. Rock, "let's adjourn to the library. I want you to tell me how to start hatching those eggs. Is it the right time of the year? And what do they eat?"

After they were comfortably seated and the eggs had been brought out to show Helen Brown, the former grocery man started to tell what he knew about the eggs.

"I suppose you have mulberry trees up here?" he asked.

"Certainly," answered the doctor. "Ever since I came here, I have been raising silkworms—in fact, that is one reason why I bought this land. There are a number of old mulberry trees on it, and I have set out several thousand more."

"What time do they start with their new leaves?"

"About two weeks from now."

"Just in time. You get an incubator of some kind and place those eggs in it and keep it rather warm, about real summer heat—say ninety. In about ten days the worms will break through the eggs and be ready for their first meal. After that, all you have to do is to see that they are kept at a temperature of about seventy, because they might be chilled with your cold nights. When they get some size, you need not worry. Just turn them loose in the woods and have a man stay with them and watch them. Perhaps you will need several men. Down in Borneo the man used a whole tribe of natives. The worms will moult about four times: on the sixth, tenth, fifteen and twenty-third day after they are hatched, and then they will start spinning their cocoons. I have seen a lot of them do that and it is most interesting. You see, they are so big they can be watched easier than a little caterpillar. If the temperature is kept at seventy, they come out as moths in about fifteen days, and then they get married and lay about five hundred eggs and die."

"Do you mean," interrupted Miss Brown, "that one female moth will lay five hundred eggs as large as the two you sold Dr. Rock?"

"Yes, Madam. That was about the average."

"That is impossible!"

"I knew that you would not believe me and that was why I did not want to talk so much about it. There are a lot of other things I saw when I was with that man in Borneo, but if you think I am lying about the silkworms, you never would believe the rest of it."

Dr. Rock joined the conversation. "I have an idea, Helen, that Mr. Jones is telling the truth. At least, he thinks that he is telling the truth. And that is the same thing. Now, there is just one question I want to ask him and that will determine some things in my mind that are at present rather questionable. Mr. Brown, your story, and your eggs and caterpillars and moths are all very large. In fact, they are unusually large. How did he control those moths when they were ready to fly, and what did he do with his surplus?"

"I CANNOT tell you all about it, but it seems that he had been working down there for a good many years. He found some large silkworms to begin with, and he fed them for size. Gave them some drug, and later on used some kind of X-ray on the eggs. He claimed that this killed some, but the rest were stimulated. You understand that he went to Borneo in the first place to grow a better grade of silk? So, a lot of the cocoons were used for silk, and in those instances the pupa was killed, and the cocoon spun into silk. He saved two or three of the best cocoons and let them develop into adult moths. They are sure enough big when they come out of the cocoon, but seem lazy and stupid for a day or so, and during that time the man had them chained to trees. He used a heavy chain, not as heavy as they use on elephants, but pretty strong. He chains them to trees near each other and after they lay their eggs, they die, and then he has them thrown into the river, and the fish and turtles eat them. He keeps the place cleaned up all the time. He moves his camp every week or so, and in that way has lots of food. Of course, he has a main camp where he has his workshop, but the caterpillars range over a lot of country when they are growing. They eat a lot."

"And the natives like to work for him, herding the caterpillars?"

"No. They do not like it," was the serious reply, "but they like it better than being killed, and that man has them in a state of terror all the time. They are so afraid of him that they are willing to do anything he tells them, just to keep on living. He gets lonely at times and employs a white man to stay with him, but the time always comes when they want to return to civilization and then he kills them—to keep his secret. I managed to get away from him, and I suppose he was rather mad about it. He told me once that he would destroy the human race if his secret was betrayed. He is sore at everybody anyway; ever since the Germans lost the war he has been angry; at least, that is what he said; mad at the Allies for winning and the Germans for not winning. I had the idea that there was something wrong with his mind."

But Dr. Rock was not satisfied. She had to ask one more question.

"How did he kill those white men?"

"He did not really kill them himself. He just fixed things so they were killed."

The scientist shrugged her shoulders. "Why not come right out and tell the whole story?"

"My usual reason. I know that you will think I am a liar. I suppose you think that now. The only way that I can show you I am telling the truth is to have the eggs hatch and that will take time. Till then I would rather not talk too much."

"All right," said the doctor. "Helen, will you go with us to New York to buy that incubator and the stock for the hosiery store? We are leaving at once. I am not going to rest in peace till I have at least tried to hatch those eggs. We will have O'Malley drive us, and we will start in half an hour."

"But I haven't any clothes."

"If I might interrupt," said Timothy Jones, "there are a lot of stores in New York City where the lady can buy clothes. When I was there, I was really astonished—to see how many ladies' wear stores there were."

It is hard to tell whether it was this profoundly true statement of the ex-soldier or just woman's natural curiosity, but when O'Malley started out in the automobile to New York, Helen Brown was one of the passengers.

The next two days in New York City were most peculiar ones for all three of the party. It was no unusual thing for the two ladies to spend several days in New York. Sightseeing and theater going, but it was a distinct novelty to both of them to have a man in the party and especially such a man as Timothy Jones. There was no doubt about the fact that Helen Brown was jealous. She was accustomed to come first in the mind and attention of Dr. Rock, and to have that lady give over half of her time to a man was a very difficult fact to face and live with. Dr. Rock, for the time being, was of a one tracked mind, and on that track ran little else but silkworms. In the theater, wholesale hosiery houses, sales rooms for scientific apparatus and restaurants, it seemed that there was nothing of interest to her but silkworms. She was enjoying the experience. At the same time, she was watching the attitude of her friend toward the new masculine element in their lives.

Helen Brown tried to ignore Timothy Jones. But he was a hard man to ignore. In the metropolis, under the careful tuition of the entomologist, he had effected a metamorphosis, as wonderful in its way as the changes that took place in the silkworm. In an evening suit that was one hundred per cent perfect, Timothy Jones looked the part of a typical man of affairs. It was only when he talked that the real man appeared, and even that real man, though he had been grocery clerk, soldier, and tramp of fortune, was a male that was unique in his way and in every way well worthwhile. He had had many strange experiences, from all of which he had emerged with credit. Consequently, it is not in the least remarkable that he was able to spend these hours in the city with two ladies who knew every detail of correct behavior, and satisfy their idea of correct behavior in their masculine escort.

Their shopping ended, the trio went back to the Delaware Water Gap. Dr. Rock urged her friend to visit her for a few days, but she refused to do so until she was sure that the new hosiery salesman was safely out the way, and selling ladies' wear of one kind or another in the little store at Shawnee. She bluntly told the doctor that she had stood all of Timothy she could for the time being, and while she was not averse to talking about silkworms, she would appreciate a few minutes of her friend's time, hunting orchids or something, or just visiting with her—the two of them alone in the library.

Dr. Rock was so interested in her incubator that she was poor company for anyone; so the two women came near quarreling and Helen Brown withdrew to her own amusements at Topcrest. The adventurer was busy unpacking his stock and arranging a window display in his store. The season was early, as far as the summer boarder was concerned, but it was not long before every woman in the vicinity, and even a few from Bushkill, visited his store and made a purchase. One of his peculiar ideas in regard to this new type of salesmanship was to wear a Tuxedo morning, noon, and night. This one fact brought him more customers than anything else. The news spread, and many times a day he was forced to give his explanation.

"'You see, it is this way, Madam," he would say. "Before the war I was a grocery clerk in an A. and P. Store. No matter how hard one tried, it was difficult to keep clean. Now I am in a business where I can dress nicely, and I feel that I am going to have many customers who will appreciate it. Of course, it means that I am going to have to shave twice a day, but I can easily do that during the lull of noontide. I do not know whether this is the correct dress to sell hose in, but it is a very comfortable one to wear."

ON the tenth day of the incubation Dr. Rock telephoned hastily to the hosiery salesman and then to Miss Brown. She thought, from the appearance of the eggs, that they were going to hatch and she wanted everyone there when it happened. Helen Brown lost no time in making the trip across the river, but it was several hours before the ex-soldier appeared. He made no effort to give the reason for his delay.

"You see, it was this way, Dr. Rock," he said. "Just as you called, one of my best customers came in. She comes every day and buys several pairs of hose at each visit. Must be some reason for her doing that; she surely does not wear them out so quickly. In fact, I asked her one day and she said that so long as she paid for them, what she did with them was her own business."

"So, she comes every day?" asked Miss Brown.

"Yes, Madam; she has not missed a day since I opened the shop. She comes at odd times when there is no one else in the store. I asked her to come to my afternoon teas, but she always says she prefers doing her shopping when we can be alone."

"Are you serving tea?"

"Yes, Madam, and if you had done me the honor of calling at my shop, you would have known of that fact. When I was in the war, I was with the British for a while, and I liked their idea of drinking tea in the afternoons. I am serving tea and cake at four, and it is well appreciated by all the ladies."

The lady from Topcrest turned to her friend.

"Show us your eggs or your bugs and let me go. If I stay here much longer, talking to Mr. Jones, I will explode. It seems he must be a social lion in Shawnee. That dame must be a centipede. Why does she have to pester the poor man that way? Have you told her that you used to be an A. and P. clerk, Mr. Jones?"

"I did."

"And what were her comments?"

"She said she did not believe me. Thought it was a joke. But let us look at the eggs. They are doing very well, Dr. Rock. They will be out in a few minutes."

His prophecy was correct. Even while they were watching, the shell of one broke, and a decidedly nasty, wormy-looking worm started to sprawl over the floor of the incubator. The three looked at it. Once out of the shell, it was over a foot long and several inches in diameter. Dr. Rock rushed for one of her drawings and compared it carefully with the liberated worm. At last she looked up.

"This is very similar to a young silk-worm!" she exclaimed. "It has some points of difference, which makes me certain that it is not the worm of *Bombyx mori*, but it is in the same family. If this is a worm just hatched, what would the larva be like, or the moth? What do you suppose is the matter with the other egg, Mr. Jones? Why should it be late hatching?"

"I do not know, Dr. Rock. I think that it is the same kind of an egg. Perhaps it is not. Suppose we wait and see?"

Two hours later the second egg hatched, and there was no doubt that this worm was different. The three studied it carefully.

"Is this the male?" asked the entomologist.

"I doubt it," was the reply of the ex-soldier. "I have something in my mind, but why worry you with it? Suppose we take them out to one of the mulberry trees and turn them loose? You will have O'Malley guard them for a few days. After that, he will need some help."

"I suppose they will eat a good deal?"

"Certainly. Later on they will eat a tree, limbs and all, but just for a few days they will only eat the leaves. Perhaps it would be better to have the young branches cut and brought to them. It would keep them more contented and satisfied. They do not know much, but in a week or so it is a wise thing to keep them satisfied, and there are some other things I want to advise you about, but I will do so when the proper time comes. Suppose we carry them out by that clump of mulberry trees by the side of the lake, and you can arrange at once for someone to watch them? I notice you have deer come to the lake to drink. It wouldn't do to have these worms stepped on. They are tender now, but you need not worry about that, for they will get tough soon enough. Yes, Madam, some of those worms I saw in Borneo were real tough."

So the two worms were carried out to the shore of the lake and mulberry leaves were placed on the ground in front of them. The worms started to eat at once. The small one ate rapidly, but the large one was not overly pleased with the food.

"They are going to eat a lot of leaves?" said Helen Brown.

Timothy Jones looked around the forest, and then down at the worms before he replied to Miss Brown's implied question.

"I think that there will be lots for them to eat, and all I hope is that they will not want to eat anything else but leaves. Dr. Rock, you have these worms watched carefully and I will come up every day and look at them with you and give you any help that you need. Now I will have to go back to my store. That little Ford car is certainly helpful in my business.

Are you going back with me, Miss Brown, or are you staying?"

"I think that I will stay, Mr. Jones. I do not want to interfere with your business, and I am afraid that your regular customers would not like it if you were seen riding around with a lady."

"Oh! They would not mind it. Several of them have been out with me in the evening after I close the shop. We study the sunset and they say that it helps them decide the right shade for their hose."

"Oh! They do, do they?" and that was the end of the conversation.

It was a puzzled Irishman who was left in charge of the two worms under the mulberry trees.

CHAPTER FOUR
The Worms Grow

DOCTOR ROCK realized that the work of guarding the worms would be tiresome; so she at once arranged for a division of that labor. She relieved O'Malley four hours a day, and secured the service of two more Irishmen for night duty. Electric lights were strung, so that the worms could be carefully inspected in an emergency during the night, but the nocturnal guards were told to use nothing but a flashlight under any circumstances.

For three days the two worms ate constantly. One ate as though enjoying the leaves, the other as though driven by hunger. They both grew, but the one with the better appetite gained in size more rapidly. On the fourth day one was nearly three feet long, while the other was a few inches less. These four days passed without any particular occurrence of interest. On the fifth day both stopped eating. Jones, when informed of this over the telephone, said that they were probably preparing for their first molt. Dr. Rock had lost sight of the fact that their behavior would be the same as that of the commercial silkworm, and she needed this statement from the adventurer to bring her sharply to the consciousness that she had on her hands two silkworms and nothing more; of course, they were enormous worms, but the probability was that their life history would be similar in every way to that of the *Bombyx,* which she had studied by the thousands.

She went to bed on the evening of the fifth day, determined to get up early and watch the worms shed their skins. However, she was called early in the morning, about two o'clock, by one of the night watchmen.

She stood at the landing at the top of the stairs and he called up from the foot. There was no doubt that he was excited.

"Dr. Rock. You had better come down right away. One of those things has gone into the lake."

"Into the lake?"

"Yes. We were eating our lunch and that one that does not eat very well, he started in to be restless, and Bill said to me, 'Let him walk around a while, he needs the exercise.' And then the first thing we knew he headed for the lake and we tried to catch him and he knocked Bill over and bit him on the arm and went right on into the water!"

"How about the other one?"

"That one is all right. The hide is cracking over the back and I guess she is going to shed by daylight. Just like a rattler; seems to twist a little, but stays right in one place."

"What time is it?"

"A little after two."

"Tell Bill to come up here and I will tend to the wound. You stay with the other worm and if you let that one go into the lake, I guess I will have to make you swim in after it."

By the time the doctor had dressed, Bill was waiting to have his arm treated. There was no doubt that he had been bitten, and it was not a mosquito bite, either. A piece of skin and muscle, nearly one inch in diameter had been cut out of his arm as neatly as it could have been done with a knife. The retired physician sewed the wound, put in drainage, and bandaged it. She was not afraid of ordinary infection, but she did feel that there was a danger of poisoning. In fact, she was just afraid without knowing why.

The morning came at last. A little cold, foggy, and raw. Dr. Rock joined O'Malley and the two night watchmen on the edge of the lake. The worm was just finishing the shedding of its former skin, now made useless by its rapid growth. It looked very much as it did before, only larger, and not really larger; it just looked as though it could grow larger. A heavy fog hung over the lake and beneath that fog, under that watery surface the other worm was living. The entomologist hoped that it was dead, or that it would come out and behave itself as did the one on land, but all the time she was afraid that it was very much alive.

Telling O'Malley that from now on she was going to have an extra guard to share the responsibility of the day watch with him, and assuring Bill that his arm would soon heal, the worried doctor walked back to the cabin to eat her breakfast. Under ordinary circumstances she would have given anything for a good long talk with Helen Brown, but there were some matters to be gone over that she felt would not be thoroughly understood by her friend. Helen Brown knew her botany, she loved flowers, she could make anything grow, even the *Heleborus Niger* under the snow; but she did not care at all for the insect world, and had expressed herself in a most decided manner as to just what she would do with those worms if she could have her own way. The breakfast was not much of a success; in fact, it would have been a total failure had not the hosiery salesman just happened to come on his daily visit at that time. The doctor welcomed him as she would have a long lost friend and insisted that he stay and have breakfast with her. He consented, and the grapefruit had hardly been served when she told him her troubles.

"One of those worms went into the lake last night, Mr. Jones."

"Is that so?"

"That is so. And he not only went into the lake but he bit Bill on the arm when the night men tried to stop him."

"I was afraid of that."

"Afraid of what?"

"That he would go into the lake. You see, it is this way—but suppose you let me finish my breakfast and then talk? I have been up a long time."

"Doing what?"

"Swimming. That lady that buys so many things from me—you know I told you and Miss Brown about her—well, she wants to go in swimming early in the mornings, and so I have to go with her. She says that it is better to go in the morning—not so many people around."

The rest of the meal was passed in silence. At last the appetite of the early swimmer was satisfied, and he announced that he was ready to talk. They walked into the library and sat down in front of the open fire.

"Before we talk about worms," said the doctor, "let's talk about the lady. Who is she and what is she and is she good looking?"

"She is good looking," was the answer. "Though I am not as much of a judge of female beauty as I used to be of butter substitute or the freshness of pig's liver, I think that we can say almost positively that she is good looking. Have you seen the ladies swim nowadays? I used to see them in the Pacific and there is not much difference in the amount of clothes they wear. Now to business. This man in Borneo kept his eggs on long shelves like a wareroom has. He only used the largest and the best eggs. But he grew other things besides silkworms and I had an idea that sometimes he got the eggs mixed. The night I escaped I went into that storeroom in the dark and picked out two eggs, and I could have sworn that they were eggs of the silkworm but I know now that I made a mistake. One was a silkworm and the other was something else. I was afraid of that when I saw the way he nibbled at the mulberry leaves. He ate them to keep alive and not because he liked them. I suppose that he stood it as long as he could and then he made a rush for the water. That is going to be his home for a while. You need not worry about him for a few weeks, though I guess he will eat all the plants and most of the fishes and turtles in the lake. When he gets bigger, I think it would be a good thing to buy some old horses and cut them up for him. When he is bigger, he is very fond of fresh meat."

"Then he was not a silkworm after all?"

"No. And that is the bad part of this entire affair. The old German really went to Borneo to grow silkworms. He wanted to grow better and bigger and healthier worms. He did that and then he started to experiment, and when a man starts to do that with nature, trouble begins. He was more successful with his experiments than I like to think, and after the War he must have gone insane. No really sane man would have had the dreams and made the plans he made."

"Do you know the name of the mature insects that will grow from that thing in the lake, Mr. Jones?"

"No, I am not a scientist. Up to the time of the war I was just a salesman in an A. and P. grocery store—"

The doctor interrupted him. "If you say that again, I am going to scream. My nerves are frayed as it is. What do I care about your being a clerk in a grocery store! Listen to me! What kind of a thing grew out of those other eggs? When it came out of the water, what was it like?"

The ex-soldier looked at the worried woman very kindly indeed.

"Now, listen, doctor. You have enough to worry about besides thinking about that worm in the lake. If I told you all I knew, you would think that I was a liar. Sometimes you believe me and sometimes you don't, that is why I am not going to tell you who went swimming with me this morning. You ladies are all right in a way, but you worry too much about little details. That was one reason why I wanted to stop selling groceries. Take tomatoes, for example. One woman would come in and wonder if they were fresh and she would poke one with her finger, and then another one would come in and poke one, and by the time they had been thoroughly poked, they were not fit for anyone to eat. Why couldn't those women have taken my word for it? This business of selling hose is far different. If I tell a heliophile that a certain shade just matches her tan, she believes me."

"So you refuse to tell me?"

"Just for now."

"Suppose I go elsewhere for advice?"

"I wouldn't. Suppose this gets into the newspapers. How would it be to have a lot of reporters around? Suppose they write up a wild article about enormous insects at the Gap?"

"Well, what of it?"

"It would either kill the business or ruin it with crowds. The buses would run Saturday excursions and so would the railroads. It would be a mess. No! The less we say about this the better. We have a nice quiet place to raise these things, and so far we are able to keep the help from talking. I do not want any publicity—at least not now. I am afraid of a good many parts of this experiment, but I am especially afraid of this man from Borneo."

"But what am I going to do?"

"Raise that one worm. Get all of the pleasure and happiness out of it you can. You are a scientist. Make lots of notes. Take pictures and measurements and when it is all done with, you will be able to write a very interesting book. That silkworm is just as harmless as a kitten. You will be thrilled when you see how it turns out. The thing in the lake is different. I am glad he went there of his own accord. I was watching him carefully, and if he had not gone, we would have had to kill him. They are dangerous. Well, I guess I will have to be going. That lady will be wondering why my store is closed. She is a hard one on stockings, and at times I think that she is purchasing agent for some fashionable orphanage of some kind. Did I tell you that I had to hire a girl to help me run the store?

"I am learning to play golf and it takes my time. But I don't have to pay for the teaching. Seems the ladies around here are kind to a lonely man. Did you burn out that hole in Bill's arm? Better wash it out with permanganate of potash. Goodbye. If you happen to see Miss Brown, tell her to drop in some afternoon at three and have tea with me. She will meet a lot of fine ladies there. The place is gradually becoming the social center of the town."

The scientist followed him out to his Ford car. Just as he was ready to start, she said, "Mr. Jones, how large is this silkworm going to be when it stops growing?"

"Right large, Madam. Yes, they get right large," was the reply.

CHAPTER FIVE
The Butterfly Horde

MR. STERLING POWERS, retired broker, was lazily smoking at his desk. He had private offices on the twentieth floor of a fifty-story building. Here, as he had no business, he played.

The game that he played at was butterflies. He was writing a book on the butterflies of New York City. He ran a permanent advertisement in several daily newspapers, offering nominal sums for any butterfly captured within the metropolitan limits and brought to him in a satisfactory condition. He did not understand how so frail a thing as a butterfly could exist in the great beehive of industry, but there they were, and he found great pleasure in studying them. Every newsboy knew about him, and practically every taxi-man. He paid from one to ten cents for duplicates of his collection and as high as twenty-five dollars for novelties.

It was the middle of April, and the buying of butterflies had just begun. Powers knew, from past experience, that the first few warm days of spring would bring lots of dirty-face boys to his office, ladened with tin cans and pasteboard boxes. Under ordinary circumstances the owners of the building would have cancelled his lease. As he owned the building, he could entertain whomever he pleased. In addition to the money, the boys received candy and the older men cigars. He not only secured butterflies, but also a lot of data of human interest. He had been a philanthropist for years, and now, after talking to hundreds of the common people, he was on the verge of becoming a sociologist.

This special morning one of his regular customers came rushing into the office. Mikey the Rat was only eleven, but in those few years he had secured a wide experience with life in general. Powers wanted to take the Rat and make a man out of him, but so far the little waif had fought shy of any suggestion curtailing his liberty. This morning he lugged in a hatbox.

"Gee, Mr. Powers. Put some dope in here and kill this bird before he breaks his wings."

"Is it worth anything?" said the butterfly buyer, as he reached for his cyanide bottle.

"It ought to be. Gosh! It's big, Mr. Powers. It's bigger than a bird."

And it was bigger than some birds. The man waited, for the butterfly to die and then cautiously opened the box, took out the *Lepidopter* and slowly fastened it to a cork base and spread out the wings. Then he scratched his head, went to his bookcase, and started to read. The passing minutes made the Rat restless. He went over and pulled at the man's sleeve.

"Ain't it worth anything, Mr. Powers?" The man rubbed the boy's head.

"It certainly is, Mikey, but this moth never grew in New York City. This is a very fine specimen of the *Anosia Archippus,* or at least similar to it. That is the closest I could come to it. Perhaps it is a moth and then again it may be a butterfly, but we don't care which it is, do we, Mikey, old chap? All we know and care about is that it is rather pretty. How's finances? Have you paid your board bill for the month? Here is a ten-dollar bill. If you see any more, bring them in and tell the boys that they are worth fifty cents apiece for the first dozen."

Mikey thanked him and rushed out. In the next few hours other boys and men came bringing the same kind of *Lepidoptera.* It seemed as though there was a shower of them. Soon Mr. Powers was giving only five cents for them, and then he locked his door. He did not have to buy any more. All he had to do was to open his office window. For they were flying in the air in abundance. At times he could see ten or twelve outside of his window. It was a rather unusual sight. He determined to take his finds around to the Academy of Natural History and see if he could have them identified.

Once on the street, he saw that the blasé New Yorker was yielding to a new excitement and was catching butterflies. They were in abundance. The canyons of the metropolis were filled with the flying beauties, almost as plentifully as they were filled with papers and confetti the day Lindbergh rode up Fifth Avenue. Many were flying in the air, momentarily free, but hundreds had been captured and destroyed by curious hands, and the pavements were filled with torn fragments of dead and dying insects that but a little before had floated in iridescent beauty in the April sun.

At the Academy, Powers found that he was but one of several excited entomologists who had rushed there for information. They were gathered around the man in America who knew more about insects than anyone in the world, except his teacher, the great Lubeck, of Vienna. The Master was speaking, and though he knew Mr. Powers well, he gave no sign that he was aware of his presence.

"What we are witnessing, gentlemen, is nothing new in the scientific world, though it is, no doubt, most unusual in a large city like New York. Here are the facts. H. W. Bates reported that one day in South America he saw an enormous number of butterflies, all males, and over eighty different varieties. Sir Emerson Tennant, in Ceylon, saw some white and yellow butterflies, which were evidently migrating. He said that there were so many that they darkened the sun and took many days to pass over his station. Were there millions? Nonsense! Such a horde was composed of billions. He did not know where they came from or where they were going. They were all of the same kind. Darwin saw a butterfly shower that was so thick that even with a telescope he could not see a spot that was not filled with them. Gatke states that migrating moths travel under the same conditions as migrating birds, and often in their company, usually in an east to west direction, in numbers that exceed all ability to even estimate, but always in the millions. Tutt says that the *Deiopeia Pulchella* has been seen one thousand miles from its usual habitat and at least that far from land. This variety that has selected New York City for its objective is a new variety. To my knowledge it has never been described. I feel that we should determine where it came from and why. Perhaps the where is easier to answer than the why."

THE discussion that followed the short lecture of Abraham Packard was interesting but so technical that it would be useless to record it. When it was over and the various scientists had returned to their homes, not one of the questions raised had been answered. All that anyone was sure of was the fact that a most unusual migration of *Lepidoptera* was taking place. Sterling Powers stood for a moment on the steps of the Academy. The shower of butterflies was continuing. In fact, it was growing denser. The automobiles were moving with the greatest difficulty on streets, slippery with the crushed bodies of millions of insects. Pedestrians were walking carefully, partly from the dread of stepping on soft bodies and gorgeous wings of the fallen butterflies. Powers stood thinking.

"This is most unusual," he mused to himself. "How stupid mankind really is. We pride ourselves on being Lords of Creation, but what do we know after all? Practically nothing. We go in circles, on circular tracks, and beyond our little region of intellectual effort we are hopelessly lost. Now, here is a physical wonder; a most remarkable scientific curiosity. Professor Packard knows everything; at least, I thought so, but he said that we had to determine where these insects came from and why? Did he answer his question? Not at all. And the reason he did not was because he *could* not. Perhaps back of it all is an answer. These pitiful beauties are obeying some urge of nature. Shall I say a Divine command? If so, what a waste of beauty! Each one lovely as a sunset in autumn, with colorature that would make an Asiatic harem faint from sheer delight, and yet how wasted and unappreciated here in New York City! Already they are an obstruction to the traffic. Tomorrow's papers will tell how much this has cost and time lost, accidents, additional laborers. How many will see the pity of it, the useless expenditure of beauty, where beauty is not wanted! In a thousand so-called city homes these little things are dying, impaled by pins on a Lears and Lowbuck catalogue, or pressed between the pages of the family Bible, for the first time opened in twenty years to sacrifice the life of a little thing that has never known what sin is. They are being crushed beneath the wheels of rumrunners, taxicabs, and stately chariots of the rich. Shop girls, factory workers, messenger boys, workers and idlers, rich, poor and plain folks, chorines and waitresses will soon be crushing them beneath low heels and high, and wondering whyenell the city does not clean the streets."

Even as Powers was talking to himself, Professor Packard was dictating a statement to a reporter from the New York Times. This article, which appeared the next morning, said in part:

"Nothing happens by chance in the world of nature. There is a reason for everything. All natural occurrences are the result of some natural law. The flight of an unknown species of _Lepidoptera_ or butterfly, which has taken place in the city, is unusual for this locality but is no novelty to science. The migration of life, the simultaneous determination of a certain species to move to another home, is one of the earliest historical novelties known to man, (Here followed a detailed account of some of the great human migratory movements and their supposed cause.)

"Today animals, like the caribou migrate; birds migrate, often thousands of miles, separating their sum-

mer and winter homes. Fish, like the salmon, go enormous distances to their spawning streams. The eel has a journey that nearly takes it around the world.

"This appearance of millions of butterflies is but one of the migratory movements that takes place all around us. The reason we are especially interested is because it has caused so much annoyance to millions of human beings at the same time.

"The interesting point in regard to this phenomenon of nature is that practically one hundred per cent of the butterflies are males. Are they seeking the female of the specie? That often happens. One female of the *Endromidae,* imprisoned in a wire cage on top of a building in Washington, has been known to attract males from Philadelphia. It may be that something like this is the secret behind the appearance of our unusual visitors."

This last paragraph from the article of the scientist was not intended to be humorous. He wrote it with no idea of comedy. Yet it was at once seized upon by the columnists and gag writers of a city that has to have novelty at any price. At once a girly-whirly show put on a butterfly dance, in which dozens of winged males whirled madly around the feminine butterfly in the wire cage. One girl, meeting another on the street, would ask, "How many butterflies have you on your string?" or, "I have a new butterfly. He is going to give me a pearl necklace before he burns his foolish wings in the flame of my candle."

The insect shower lasted for two days and then came to an ending as sudden as the beginning. For two more days New York talked about the unusual happening and then turned to another novelty. The sacrifice floated down the sewers of the city or started to turn to dust in forgotten places. Everything was as it had been and the city was looking for something else to talk about and suddenly it found it.

It was a paid advertisement in one of the picture papers. A full page was taken, and while it was a startling news item, still there was no attempt made to feature it by the use of large type. In fact, the type was small and the margins so wide that it attracted attention by the unusualness of the page appearance as much as by the context. The paper on its editorial page commented on this paid advertisement and assumed no responsibility. The management simply stated that the space in the paper was for sale and that anything was printed so long as it conformed to certain requirements. Every reader was privileged to form his own conclusion as to what the paragraph meant.

And this was the paragraph:

"I was directly responsible for the recent appearance of the millions of butterflies in New York City. This is but a mild manifestation of my power over the insect world. I demand the abolition of capital and the freedom of the worker. A new government must be formed in the United States first, and then all over the world, a government in which all are equal. I also demand the apprehension and punishment of the American who stole from me two eggs and the immediate return of those eggs. Unless all this is promptly attended to, I will send another shower of insects, in number and size sufficient to destroy the city. I would advise the immediate return of the eggs and a revision of the form of government. For all this I will wait till January first, of the next year."

This reading notice attracted the attention of many different persons in many different walks of life. The Governmental leaders were sure that it was the work of an insane person. When Professor Packard was asked for an opinion, he simply stated that up to the present time there was no scientific proof that such a migration of butterflies could be the work of a human being, and though under very extraordinary circumstances it might be accomplished deliberately, he was of the opinion that a crank was simply trying to gain the credit for something with which he was in no way responsible. Alienists were convinced that the paragraph was the work of a paranoiac who was deteriorating. Otherwise, why should he be so concerned over the theft of two eggs?

During these days Dr. Rock, as was her normal habit, carefully read the New York papers. Whatever conclusions she reached were carefully kept from the entire world, including Miss Helen Brown and Timothy Jones. That worthy made his daily trip to the Lake of the Mountain to confer with the doctor in regard to the rapidly growing worm. Perhaps he read the papers and perhaps he did not. At least, he did not mention the paragraph in regard to the arrest of a certain thief and the return of two eggs. During this period the worm had rested one day and then once again shed its skin. It was now seven feet long, a perfect caterpillar in every way only of a size that made everyone, even the doctor, wonder what the end would be. This worm ate not only mulberry leaves but also the branches. It was most interesting to see it slowly and successfully masticate a limb two inches in diameter. In spite of its size and rapidly increasing strength, it had a calm and placid disposition. So long as it had enough food it was content to stay in one place. O'Malley became attached to the strange thing and called it Peter. He said that this was appropriate because it was such a pumpkin eater. He would play to it in the afternoons on his Jew's harp, and insisted that it enjoyed and appreciated his music—much more than his wife did...

Except for a constant disturbance of the fish in the Lake of the Mountain, as shown by their everlasting leaping out of the water, there was no definite sign of the worm that had sought a watery home. The doctor finally yielded to the advice of the ex-soldier, and every day from fifty to one hundred pounds of meat was cut up and thrown into the lake. The doctor wanted to row out and see if she could see the worm eating, but Jones begged her not to.

"It is too dangerous, Madam," he said.

"But, why?"

"You would not believe me if I told you."

"Mr. Jones," she replied, "I believe you a little more than I did."

CHAPTER SIX
The Perfumed Path

A FEW months before, a stranger had landed at a lonely seaport of British Guiana and had, without the loss of a day's time, gone into the interior. Here, in some mysterious way, he had secured the services of a tribe of natives. There was no doubt he paid them well. For days they roamed over the surrounding territory, carefully hunting for a certain type of cocoon. In the meantime the stranger had built a cage, four feet in size each way, out of fine copper wire. He also brought to the native village, and assembled there, an airplane that was the last word in modern construction.

In his laboratory, crudely constructed and yet admittedly suited to his needs, he labored day and night with chemicals. At last he obtained a combination that pleased him. Once the formula was obtained he made many gallons of the peculiar scented liquid and stored it in a tank of the airplane. The construction of this tank and its outlet was such, that when the plane was in motion, a few drops were thrown in a fine vapor every few seconds. In fact, it was nothing but a gigantic atomizer. On the tail of the plane he securely lashed the four-foot wire cage.

It was springtime in the tropics. That meant something different from springtime in the colder zones. Still, it was a season of renewed life, the birth of another generation. Birds were laying, so were turtles and alligators and snakes. Flowers were blooming with renewed vigor. Here and there gorgeous butterflies flew their short life through the sunshine. The stranger carefully selected a hundred of the cocoons that the natives had so painfully gathered and started to incubate them. By supplying them with artificial heat, he was able to gain a day or two on those that depended on nature for their incubation. His skill was shown by the fact that these hundred cocoons supplied over seventy females. These he carefully placed in his wire cage.

He was now ready for the termination of his experiment. He was doing something that had never been done before; something that had not even been thought of before. He was about to replace God in the economy of nature. He was going to force the duplication of one of the most remarkable phenomena that had ever been observed by man. For centuries the butterfly had migrated for reasons unknown and unguessed by mankind. Now one of the human race was going to lead millions of these butterflies on a peculiar Odyssey, which would end in their total destruction. That final debacle did not worry the man, however. All that he was striving for was a very definite psychological effect on a great nation and finally, on an entire world.

He had given the native tribe the final payment of cheap jewelry. He had the seventy new females in their wire cage. His tanks were full of gasoline and the special perfume. Then he started on his journey to New York. But first he flew in a large circle that covered parts of all of the Guianas—French,

Dutch, and British. He flew slowly and as closely to the top of the forest as he could with safety. As he flew, the atomizer sprayed the perfume in an extremely delicate flood behind the plane. And as the plane sailed over the forest, the appeal of that perfume, combined with that thrown off by the seventy captive females, inflamed the imagination of millions of male butterflies just emerging from their cocoons. Thus it was that when the airplane finally left the flight over the forest and started north over the ocean, it was followed by a constantly enlarging stream of amorous males.

The man had done one thing. He had started a migration northward. He had manufactured a perfumed path, along which thousands of one particular kind of *Lepidoptera* were flying gaily to their deaths. He hoped that their leaving South America would induce others to leave out of a desire to imitate or a thirst of curiosity. Perhaps in the primary stream there would be sufficient females to perpetuate the migratory current.

Arriving at a flying field in New York, he established headquarters in a centrally located hotel. There in the privacy of his room, he transferred into individual cages the females who had survived the journey. He gave them each an opportunity to feed on sugar water and then he engaged hotel rooms in different parts of the city—as many rooms as he had living females, and on the window of each room he placed a small wire cage. He took the remaining perfume from the tank in his airplane and sprayed each windowsill. He did all this as rapidly as possible, because he knew that the advance guard of lovesick males was on its way. He had hardly placed the alluring bait before the first wave of butterflies arrived, and in a few days he had the satisfaction of knowing that he had made a thorough success of his undertaking. He had brought the butterflies to New York.

But he had done more than that. He had made a great city conscious of the fact that there was such a thing as a butterfly. He had psychically prepared them for the next step in his carefully prepared plan. Paranoidal he might be, but he certainly had no lack of brains, and the entire history of his thirty-year adventure in the field of experimental entomology showed conclusively that Johnkin Peters might have taken his place among the Masters of Science had he only been able to control his soul as well as his intellect.

Thirty years before he had gone to Borneo to solve the secret of the production of a perfect grade of silk. It may have been the isolation, the constant separation from the rest of the civilized world, the tropical sun, the brooding introvertive silence; it may have been all these or none or perhaps heredity or an unfortunate love affair. Whatever it was, he was led into the paths of magic and uncanny working with the mysteries of nature. In his longing to become more of a God, he had become more of a Devil.

During all these years in Borneo he had employed many white men, and all had died when they became either useless or dangerous to the final success of his plans. At least, all had died save one, and that one had escaped. He had not only escaped, but he had taken with him, in his mad flight through the Borneo jungles, two eggs. The escape was not so bad. Johnkin Peters knew that not one hundredth of his tale would be given credit. Many men had gone into the waste places of Earth and been called liars when they started to tell what they had seen and heard during their wanderings. But the theft of the eggs was a hard blow. They could be hatched. The man could tell his story and be called a liar, but when the eggs hatched, men would be forced to believe him. He had traced the thief to North America and there the trail became cold, hopeless.

Before this he had always promised himself that he would wait for the psychological moment before he would throw his final gesture at the laughing world. Now he felt that the time had come and he treated New York to a miraculous display of living pyrotechnics. After that he placed his advertising paragraph in the paper. Let *them* catch the thief! They would have to return the eggs. The nation was responsible for the action of one of its citizens. Now was the time for the establishment of an ideal state. Let them make it any way they wanted to, if only they made all men equal!

He put the paragraph in the paper and waited. Instead of reforming over night, the nation noticed, laughed, and forgot. For a day or two the popular gag was over eggs; then something else took the forefront of national attention. Peters had thought to make a new nation for eternity; all that he accomplished was to make a nation laugh for a few days. Instead of recovering his two stolen eggs, he lost several months of life working in South America. He had made millions of insects follow him, but he could not secure the support or even the curiosity of a single American.

Furious, he returned to Borneo and prepared for the final step.

CHAPTER SEVEN
The Cocoon

ON the fifteenth day after the worm had crawled out of its egg, it moulted for the third time. It was now fifteen feet long, and had an appetite in proportion to its size.

Dr. Rock and Timothy Jones went to see it the day after it had its new skin. In order to save the appearance of the lakefront, the doctor now had mulberry trees cut down in the back forests and the limbs hauled to the insatiable worm. O'Malley was almost tender in his constant care of the creature and seemed to possess some kind of a psychic influence over it. At least he talked to it as though it was a child, and to a certain extent it seemed to understand and react to the conversation.

Neither of the chief actors in this drama had so far mentioned the peculiar happenings of the last two weeks in New York. Whatever they thought, they had very cleverly concealed from each other. Both had made secret and rapid trips to New York during this period. There seemed to be a deliberate motive back of this desire to avoid the discussion of the serious problems that were rapidly approaching a point at which they would have to be solved. The doctor spent much of her time in study and thought. Jones played around Shawnee, made his daily trip to the cabin on the Lake of the Mountain and the rest of the time sold hosiery and wrote. He told the two ladies that he was writing an autobiography.

"And when it is finished," he said, "I may have it published. It is going to be most interesting. Three periods, one in the A. and P., the next in the A. E. F., and the third a vagabond around the world. I am going to devote particular attention to these delightful weeks at Shawnee. In all my experiences, I have never met more beautiful ladies than these Shawnee ladies."

"You mean the New York and Philadelphia ladies you are meeting at Shawnee," interrupted Miss Brown, rather acidly.

More days passed slowly. At least, they seemed to pass slowly for the anxious doctor. And now the time came for the final moult. The worm was twenty-three days old and when it cast its skin for the fourth time it emerged, a full-grown caterpillar. In appearance it was very similar to the larva of the *Bombyx mori*, except that instead of being three inches long, it was over thirty-five feet. It was hairless, ashy gray in color and rather slender for its length. The second thoracic ring was humped, and there was a spine-like horn, or protuberance at the tail. It remained quiet so long as its hunger was satisfied; when hungry, it often reared fifteen feet in the air and waved its head around in the quest for food.

In another week it ceased to eat. Jones had warned the doctor about this symptom. A stout pole had been placed in the ground near the feeding place of the worm. This stick of timber, fifty feet high with a few branches left on it, was to provide a place for the larva to spin its cocoon. With almost human understanding, it showed its appreciation of this arrangement and one week after the last moult, began to climb this tree. The piece of timber was just tall enough for the caterpillar to reach the top before it started to spin. It began to eject from its silk glands, not a microscopic thread that would rival that of a spider, but rather a thick cord, almost the size of wrapping string. Jones visited it and assured the doctor that everything was progressing normally. As far as the doctor could determine, the progress of cocoon making was the same as she had observed hundreds of times in her laboratory on a small scale. For three days the larva kept its head going in rhythmic routine movements and at the end of that time it was enclosed in a cocoon, seventeen feet long and over ten feet in diameter. A final inspection was made, and then Dr. Rock and Jones adjourned to the library for one of their regular conferences.

"How do you feel about everything, Mr. Jones?" asked Dr. Rock, rather casually and at the same time with a good deal of anxiety in her voice. The last month had been a hard one for the retired doctor.

"I guess it is working out all right," was the ex-service man's reply. "I think that we are going to obtain a living butterfly. Whether it will be male or female I cannot say and I do not know that it makes any difference, because it will not have a mate either way. Even if both of those eggs had been silkworm eggs, they might have been of the same sex.

Anyway, you will see one beautiful moth. If you donate it to some museum, I guess they will be proud to call it after you. That is a habit they have when a new kind of bug is found. Even that German wanted to name one after me, but I had an idea that it was to be a memorial to a dead man, so I refused the honor. The A. and P. did name a cereal after me. There was a contest, Madam, between the different stores to see which one could sell the most butter substitute and I won, and so they started to sell Jones' Johnnycakes, and for a time my picture was on the package. For a time I thought that it was an honor, but during the war I found that life had greater things in it for me, and so it had. There was a year that I reigned as King on one of the Solomon Islands, but I found that they changed kings frequently and ate the old ones, so I lost interest and left. I guess my twenty-seven wives are still wailing over me—nice girls they were. Would seem all right now. Women are funny. Millions of dark ones spending their money on bleaching powder to turn white and

millions of white ones spending their money to secure tan, artificial or otherwise.

"How about the one you go in swimming with?"

**Illustrated by
LEO MOREY**

*It remained quiet so
long as its hunger
was satisfied*

"She is real nice. She says that she likes the idea of my being an A. and P. clerk once in my life. Makes me human."

"How long before the moth will come out?"

"In about two weeks. Maybe a day or so more or less. Now, let us be serious. You have a big problem on your hands, Dr. Rock, in regard to that thing in the lake. Are you feeding it enough?"

"I should think so. Two hundred pounds of fresh horsemeat every day. How about it?"

"That ought to be enough. We won't have to worry about it for another week or so. I think that you will have a quiet week. Take my advice. Put O'Malley back at the gate. Dismiss the other guards, give them a bonus, and tell them that you will make it more for every month they keep their mouths shut about the happenings here. Take Miss Brown and go on a little trip and just forget that there ever were two eggs. Come back in nine days, and then you will be rested up and ready for work. If you have a chance, see someone in New York and find out how to kill a moth with a fifteen-foot body without spoiling it or breaking its wings. I will come up here every day and go over things with O'Malley. How about it? It seems to be the thing to do. If you do not take care of yourself, you will be sick. How would it be for you to get one of those household moving-picture cameras and then when the moth comes out you can take some pictures? It is a wonderful sight, Madam, to see one come out all wet and shrunken and gradually dry and grow in the sunshine. If you took a trip like that, it would be a nice thing for Miss Brown. That poor girl is jealous, and this last month has not been a pleasant one for her. She needs a change as much as you do."

"I will do that," replied the doctor. "As you suggest, I have a lot of things to attend to. I will go to New York and take Helen with me. Can I do anything for you there?"

"Yes. Suppose you go and see some bug expert and find out how he reacted to those butterflies in New York? Did you read about them?"

Dr. Rock shook her head in the affirmative.

"You did? Well, you never said anything about it. If you read about them, perhaps you saw this in one of the papers?"

He handed her a page of a small, illustrated New York paper. She glanced at it, then handed it back."I saw that, too," she commented.

"You did? And all the time I thought that women could not keep quiet. Let me tell you something. When those butterflies came to New York, I was hoping that it was just a coincidence. Then when I read this little paragraph about the thief and the two eggs and making over the Government. I knew that it was all the doings of the man from Borneo. He was here. Right here in New York, hunting for me. He knew that I had the eggs. If he had the eggs, his secret was safe. If I was dead, he was safe. For a while I was frightened. I am not afraid of any right-minded man, Madam, but this man from Borneo is different. He may be in New York now, but I do not think so. But I do know, *that hell is going to pop open* on or about the first of next January. Unless someone tied down the lid, Dr. Rock. However, it is early in the year and there is lots of time. You go on your vacation and have a good time, and if you can find out anything that will help us, look into it. I am going to try and rest a bit myself. I have been so busy swimming and playing golf that I have not put the time into my business that I should. Worries me sometimes."

"The next evening the two ladies landed in New York and registered at the new Astor. As they were undressing the doctor looked at her friend curiously. She remarked, "My word, Helen, but you are certainly tanned."

"I guess I am Anna," was the reply. "I have done more swimming and golfing in the last month than I have ever done before."

CHAPTER EIGHT
The Specialists Consult

THE first day in New York the ladies went shopping. The second day Dr. Rock asked her friend to excuse her, as she was going to spend the day seeing some of her old friends in the medical profession. Consequently, Helen Brown headed for the Metropolitan Museum, while the doctor, instead of calling on a physician, went to see Sterling Powers. She knew of this man by reputation; she had read his various articles on *Lepidoptera* of New York City; she knew that he was a retired broker and wealthy. For these reasons she wanted to consult with him concerning the events of the past month.

She had no trouble in being admitted to the office of the retired magnate. In a way, her admission was due to a mistake. She spoke in such a way as to make the office girl think that she was there to sell butterflies, and that was the statement that the said office girl had given to Mr. Powers. He looked up pleasantly enough and said, "Got something good to sell me?"

The middle-aged woman smiled.

"I certainly have," she retorted. "I have something that you never saw before, but it is not for sale, at least, not now. I am Dr. Rock. Doctor Anna Rock, late practicing physician and surgeon in Brooklyn, but now retired and devoting my leisure to the study of silkworms. You can look me up in "Who's Who" or Dunn and Bradstreet. A month ago I ran against something big. I thought that I could handle it myself, but it seems to be too big for me. I need help, advice; that's why I am here."

Sterling Powers was primarily a gentleman and after that a scientist. He lost no time in assuring the visitor that his time and talents were at her service. They sat down, one of them on one side of the desk, and the other in an armchair at one end. Dr. Rock unwrapped a number of pictures and placed them in two piles on top of the desk in front of the lover of butterflies. Then she started to tell her story:

"Over a month ago, Mr. Powers, I was fortunate enough to be able to purchase two eggs. I incubated those eggs and they have hatched. I took pictures of the worms at regular intervals. One of the worms went into my lake and from that time I was only able to take pictures of one of them. Finally, that one spun a cocoon and I am now waiting for the pupa to emerge as a moth. These pictures are in chronological series, numbered one to fifty. You will observe that in every picture I placed some familiar object near the egg or the worm so that the relative size of them could be more easily determined. I want you to look at these pictures and tell me what you think of them. In the meantime, I will glance over the morning paper. Take your time. You never saw a series of pictures like this before and the chances are that you never will again."

Without an audible answer, Powers started to look at, the pictures. They were large, seven by twelve inches in size. First, he looked at them hastily and then, starting all over again, he spent long minutes over each, till finally it was eleven A.M. At last he placed them all on a pile and started to wrap them up. The doctor put down her paper and looked at him.

"Well?" she interrogated.

"Dr. Rock," said the entomologist gravely. "You are a very clever photographer. There is only one question I want to ask you. Why, when you are capable of such great things, do you stoop to such chicanery?"

"In other words, you think I'm a liar?"

"That is a name I have never called a lady."

"Suppose I asked you to come and see the cocoon?"

"I would come."

"You would have to. Now, one thing more. No doubt, you know about the butterfly-shower and the peculiar paragraph that appeared in a newspaper after it? Suppose I tell you that these eggs, the ones you have just seen in these photographs, were the two eggs that the writer of that advertisement wanted returned to him? What would you think then?"

Sterling Powers unwrapped the pictures. For another hour he looked at them. Then he took down the telephone and called Professor Packard at the Academy of Natural Sciences—

"Is this Professor Packard? Yes? Well, this is Sterling Powers. Can I come up and see you right away? Important? Certainly. I have something to show you that will make you scratch your head."

He turned to the doctor.

"Packard knows more about bugs than any man in the world except Lubeck of Vienna. I want him to see these pictures. You come with me. He may want to question you. If anyone in the world can tell whether these pictures are faked or not, it is Packard. We will not tell him a word about them—simply hand them to him and ask him for an opinion."

Thirty minutes later the Master was looking at the pictures. He, as Powers had done, took his time. It was two before he even looked at the woman and man seated near him. Then he simply said, "Who took these pictures?"

"I did," answered Dr. Rock.

"You are the person we have been looking for. You have the intelligence and the ability to do what we want. Name your salary. The work will be to make large papier-mâché models of small insects for our museum."

Sterling Powers shook his head knowingly. He had an idea that this would be the decision of the Master.

THE doctor flushed. Thoroughly mad, she took the bundle of pictures and started to wrap them up. "Those pictures are not faked!" she cried.

"Sit down," he commanded. "In science, two and two make four. Art only can vary. The Greeks made the heads of their statues smaller than normal to secure the proper artistic effect. The scientist has to observe nature as he sees it. You hand me a series of pictures, showing the development of a species of silkworm from the egg to the worm, to the cocoon. The caterpillar, about to spin the cocoon, must be over thirty feet long. I say that no caterpillar ever was that long. Yet, what would I say if I saw that cocoon? The observations of a lifetime would be discarded for a single new fact. I could say that you made the cocoon. Suppose I saw the moth come from it? Ah! You could not fake that. Yet, how great that moth would have to be to retain its relative proportions to the egg and the caterpillar and the cocoon. I am a Christian; yet I would sell my soul to the Devil to place that moth in our Museum. Nowhere else in the whole world would there be such a moth. What a sensation it would create! But the most remarkable part of these pictures is the other worm. What happened to him?"

"He crawled into the lake. At the present time he is eating several hundred pounds of horse meat a day."

The Master jumped from his chair, and almost ran over to the part of the room that the doctor was sitting in. He pleaded with her:

"Please, lady, tell me that you are lying to me. Assure me that this is all a silly joke. It cannot be true. Oh! God! It must be a dream. For, if these pictures are true; if it really went into the lake and is there now, growing and eating meat, then it is nothing else but the larval form of the dragonfly, known as the *Protodonata*. But this type lived in the Carboniferous age, and we know of them only by fossil remains. These remains have been found in Commentry, France, and C. Brongniart has given us a wonderful description of them. He sent us some of the fossils. But there is a great gulf between our age and the Carboniferous. We have not thought it possible that any have survived. So please spare an old man and tell me that I am simply dreaming."

But the doctor shook her head. "Those are real pictures, professor."

He looked at her, and wiped the sweat off his face with his hand, and then with his handkerchief. "What do you think, Mr. Powers?"

"I do not know what to think."

"Nor do I. But I know this—I will not rest day or night. I cannot eat till I see for myself this cocoon, hanging on a fifty-foot piece of timber. Once I see it, I will stay there. Day and night I will stay there till the moth comes out. And I will stay at the edge of the lake you tell me of. If you do not feed me, I will starve, but I will not go from there till I see that thing come out of the lake. And when it comes out, we had better be ready to kill it—real quickly—for it will be hungry."

"I'll tell you what I will do, gentlemen. After a short stay in New York, I am going back to my home. When my adviser thinks that the time has come, I will telephone you and you can visit me as my guests and make any scientific observations you wish to. How will that suit you?"

"That will be heavenly!" almost shouted the professor. "But who is this adviser you speak of?"

"His name is Timothy Jones."

"I cannot place him. What has he written?"

"Nothing. He used to be a grocery clerk in an A. and P. store."

"And now he is telling you how to care for these worms?"

"Yes. You see, he was the man who stole the eggs."

"What eggs?"

"The two that were mentioned in that mysterious advertisement."

The professor looked at the retired broker. Then he sighed.

"Here is something big, Mr. Powers. I thought at the time it was all humbug, but perhaps—perhaps Dr. Rock, will you let me go and see this Timothy Jones person?"

"He is too busy selling stockings to talk to you," was the reply.

Soon after that the conference came to an end, Sterling Powers took Dr. Rock to lunch, during which meal they found that they had more than entomology in common. Arrangements were made for a visit to the Lake of the Mountain when the moth came out of the cocoon. It was dark when the doctor returned to the hotel and rejoined her friend. They argued as to the spending of the evening, but this was all unnecessary. Mr. Powers called on the phone: "Will you see a show with me?"

They would and they did.

It was two in the morning when they returned to the hotel. A telegram was waiting for them. It was from Timothy Jones.

Dr. Anna Rock:
Astor House, New York City.
All quiet here. Nothing new. Am attending to business. Have not golfed or been in swimming since you left.
                    —TIMOTHY JONES.

"That," remarked the former physician, "is one strange man. There are so many things about him that I cannot understand that I feel at a loss to fathom his least movement. Now, why should he stop his sports just because we came to the city? Why should he take the trouble to wire me that he had done so?"

"Perhaps he wants us to know it. It may be that the woman he was with so much has left Shawnee, and this is his way of telling us."

"I think he is some kind of a fool. What were you doing all day, Helen, while I was talking to those men?"

"Buying things for my hope-chest."

"Your hope-chest! A woman like you with a hope-chest! What in the world do you want a hope-chest for?"

"What does any woman want a hope-chest for?" was the sleepy reply.

CHAPTER NINE
The Cocoon Breaks

FOURTEEN days after the completion of the cocoon, the inhabitant thereof began to show signs of activity. An interested group of scientists were gathered around the silken ball. Dr. Rock had kept her promise and sent for Sterling Powers and Professor Packard. These two gentlemen had lost no time in making their arrival at the isolated cabin. There had been long hours of anxious waiting, but now that was all over. There was no doubt in the minds of any but that the moth would come from the cocoon.

Conferences had been held with Dr. Rock. Timothy Jones had been closeted with the two New Yorkers, and when they did emerge, they were convinced either he was insane, or they were. His rambling talk, his constant reference to past experiences was almost too much for the scientific and accurate mind of the expert from the Academy of Natural Sciences.

'The party was seated around the cocoon that afternoon. It was an unusually hot afternoon and the reflection of the sunlight on the clear water was almost unbearable. Dr. Rock had served dinner out on the shore, as she knew that no one would want to go inside while such a remarkable event was nearing completion. She had a slow-motion moving-picture camera, which was filming the gradual escape of the moth from the cocoon. Timothy Jones simply sat there and lazily smoked a pipe. Of all those present he seemed the least excited. He had made only one suggestion; that a keg of sugar water be available for the moth's first meal. Obviously, none of the flowers on the mountaintop—none, or for that matter, not all of them—would be sufficient to supply such a moth its meal of nectar. Helen Brown lazily worked on a fine-linen handkerchief.

The moth came out, slowly, but certainly and surely. It was a rather wretched, wet-looking, pitiful creature, uncertain either of its strength, beauty, or purpose in the world. Finally, it had pulled its body entirely out of the cocoon and had crawled part of the way up the tree. There it clung, breathing heavily and trying to stretch its wings. Its body was at least fifteen feet long. What the wing expanse would be could not be determined until the wings were thoroughly expanded and dried. It found the keg of sugar water that had been hung up near the top of the piece of timber, and thrusting in its proboscis, drank eagerly.

Professor Packard put his cigarette on a stone, stepped on it, and went over to where Dr. Rock was watching the camera.

"My dear Doctor," he exclaimed, "I want to apologize to you for doubting your honesty. What I have seen today is an unexplainable wonder. I cannot understand it and yet I am sure that it must be so. Entomology has gone backward today. We are not in the twentieth century. We are millions of years before the birth of Christ. This butterfly is, for some reason, a survival of ancestors whose existence we have only suspected. Mr. Powers and I owe you a debt that we can never repay. I know men that would have given thousands to see what we have been asked to see for nothing. I assure you that I will say nothing of this until you give your permission, but I must ask one thing. This moth is a female. Without another moth, her eggs will be infertile. Why not sell it to me for placement in our Museum? Any price you name will be paid you. We should not delay. At any time it may sail away and either be lost or damaged."

Timothy Jones had been a silent spectator to this scene. Without intending to, he had overheard the conversation, and in a quiet manner, he joined in it.

"I would advise you all to leave the poor thing alone till tomorrow. They do not gain their full size for at least twenty-four hours and for that long they remain quiet. I am sure this moth will be far larger and finer in every way if we wait. Tomorrow afternoon will be time enough to kill it."

Everyone, especially the men from New York, looked at him. Mr. Powers walked over to where he was lazily smoking.

"Mr. Jones," he exclaimed, "you know a great deal about this that you are not telling us. Why not come clean and give us the entire story?"

"For a very good reason, Mr. Powers."

"And what is that?"

"If I told you all I know about it, you would not believe me. Ever since I came to this part of the world people have been looking on me as a liar. Naturally, I am sensitive. No one believes me anymore. Even the ladies who buy hose from me doubt me at times. But you can take my word for one thing: This butterfly or moth, or whatever you want to call it, will still be here tomorrow. They stay rather quiet for at least a day."

"Suppose we assured you that we would believe you?"

"You might say so, but you wouldn't feel so. You people are so scientific that you won't believe anything unless you see it. You are just a lot of doubting Thomases. Why, Dr. Rock told me that even when you saw the pictures you accused her of manufacturing them; and she is a lady. Instead of talking to me, why not look at that beauty? It'll be a long time before you ever see anything like that again. See those wings move and begin to glisten in the sunshine as they dry."

The men saw that nothing was to be gained by talking to Jones; so they began to take notes on the moth. With the aid of a long ladder they made careful measurements and noted carefully the size, anatomy, and color. They were especially impressed by the close resemblance to the *Bombyx*, the silkworm of commerce. They did not stop their examination till the onset of twilight.

It was hot. It was unusually hot for that time of year. Everybody was tired, weary, not so much from work as from the excitement. Nerves were frayed, and Dr. Rock, always the physician in spite of her resignation from active practice, suggested that they all go to bed so they would be ready for the more serious business of the next day, the killing of the moth and the preparation of its body for shipment to the museum. For she had finally agreed to give it to the Academy of Natural Sciences. The professor had, in gratitude, asked for the privilege of naming it after her. Thus, everybody was satisfied, happy, and tired.

Helen Brown did not want to stay all night. She said that she had special reasons for leaving at once. Timothy Jones said that if that was the case, he would go with her, because he did not think a woman should go without an escort at night, and O'Malley had better stay on guard. He promised to return early in the morning. There were a few hints, he said, that might be of use to them in the preparing of the moth for shipment.

By ten o'clock, all in the cabin were safely in bed. Not asleep, however. The heat was intense. Sheet lightning filled the sky. There was no rain, but a constant rolling of thunder. Just before going to his room, Professor Packard made a last trip to see the moth. O'Malley was on guard. Everything seemed as it should be. On the timber, far above the ground, the enormous moth rested, apparently asleep.

The storm continued most of the night. The heat seemed to grow more intense. Toward morning a cool wind came over New Jersey from the ocean and sent all in the cabin into a deep sleep. Consequently, it was not till eight that anyone wakened, and then, it was by force. Mrs. O'Malley was shaking Dr. Rock by the shoulder.

"For God's sake, Doctor, dress and come down to the lake with me! There has been some kind of hell raised there last night, and I think the old man is dead. At least, he is bleeding badly and I cannot rouse him."

Ten minutes later the doctor, Packard, Powers, and a few frightened servants were down by the lakeshore under the cocoon. O'Malley was on the ground breathing deeply and bleeding from a severe cut in his chest. Part of his clothing was torn off. The moth was gone, but scattered over the ground were tattered pieces of wing, pitiful evidence of the fate that had overtaken the iridescent beauty.

Dr. Rock started to take care of O'Malley. He was carried to the cabin, the hemorrhage stopped and the wound bandaged. After helping the doctor as best they could, the two disappointed New Yorkers went back to the beach.

"This is the fault of no one but Jones!" thundered the irate professor. "He should have let us put this moth in a safe place."

"He may have been at fault," agreed the retired broker, "in giving us poor advice, but he certainly had nothing to do with the killing of the moth. What would have been his motive? And why should he have tried to kill O'Malley?"

"I simply do not know, but in my opinion he is simply a damned rascal!"

Just then the very man they were talking about walked toward them.

"Good morning, gents," he said as he came near. "O'Malley is conscious and waiting to tell his story. I see the moth is dead. Poor thing. Born for a day. Why should it have been born if only to die so soon? Come, let us listen to O'Malley."

But O'Malley had little to say. He simply said that he had been rather nervous, what with the storm and the responsibility, and the first thing he knew he had been knocked down. He thought some large animal must have tried to kill him. He was then thrown under some large bushes and that was the last that he knew till he found himself on the couch in the cabin. Dr. Rock gave him a sedative and told him to go to sleep. The scientists went out on the walk in front of the cabin.

CHAPTER TEN
Big Game Hunting

TIMOTHY JONES left the party and went over to his Ford car. The New York men watched him, and there was no doubt that they were not only angry at him, but also very suspicious of the part that he had taken so far in this drama. He, however, seemed absolutely unaware of their emotions. At least, if he did realize how they felt toward him, he did not show it by his action. He went to the car, took out a large package and walked back to join them.

"Can you men shoot?" he asked.

"Shoot what?" asked Dr. Rock.

"Big game."

The professor acknowledged that he had once hunted bear. The ex-broker admitted that he had been in Canada after moose.

"Good enough," answered Jones. "At least you will be able to pull a trigger and not be gun-shy. I have here three elephant guns, loaded with explosive bullets. If you hit the right place, that would seem to be enough to kill anything. I want you to take these guns and become thoroughly acquainted with them. How to load them and all that sort of thing. Then I want you to stay here with me. We will build a shelter out of some plank and brush. We are going to stay here till something happens, and we will stay here forever if we don't hit the thing we are shooting at, Dr. Rock. You send all the help down to Shawnee and tell them to stay there till we let them know. You see that we get some coffee and sandwiches. If you want to help with the shooting, you can take that little rifle you have in your library, but my advice is to stay indoors."

"But see here, Mr. Jones," protested Professor Packard. "You are doing a lot of ordering and no explaining. Just what is all this excitement?"

"You won't believe me if I tell you. But you have to do as I say or get out. You don't have to stay here and get killed, and I am telling you that unless we shoot straight and fast, we are going to be. Be sensible, man, and do as I ask you to. Mr. Powers, you trust me? I must have someone to trust me. Dr. Rock said that you were a sensible man. You'll stay here and take orders from me, won't you?"

Sterling Powers looked at Anna Rock. Something telepathic, mystic passed between them, and the rich man said slowly, "Hand me a gun, Jones, and show me how to load it. I will do anything you say."

And a few minutes later the professor had the courage and manhood to acknowledge that he had been overhasty in his speech. At once the three men started to get to work. Hours passed and it was noon. More hours and it was four in the afternoon. It was another hot day. The three men sweated in their shelter near the side of the lake. Jones lay on his back, smoked his pipe, and watched the sky. During that whole time he only said a few words, but again and again he examined the mechanism of the three guns.

At last he saw what he was looking for. Silently, he pointed into the sky. An airplane was driving, full speed, through the clouds. Behind it was another plane, of peculiar construction. It seemed as though the one was chasing the other. Rapidly the large one came up to the small monoplane and overshadowed it.

"That is wonderful," exclaimed Professor Packard. "They must be doing that refueling trick."

And then the two planes, firmly united, swung around and came back toward the lake. They were at least six thousand feet in the air and twenty miles away, but the visibility was perfect. Jones stood up and whistled shrilly.

"I promised the doctor I would call her," he explained. "I would rather have her stay in the house, but she insisted."

And the doctor came running down from the cabin with her pet rifle in her hand.

She seemed to ignore the two men, but sat down near the broker, and when she spoke, she talked right at him. "Do you think," she said, "that I would leave you here alone?"

"I do not think you would. In fact, I know you wouldn't," was the soft reply. Jones simply kept on watching the double airplane. The professor frowned as though something were happening that he could not understand. He was a scientist, not a sociologist.

Then on and on came the two planes, and as they came closer, their appearance was more peculiar. At last, with a rush, they landed on the lakeshore, fifty yards from the ambuscade. Then it was all too easy to see what had sailed down from the sky.

One of the planes had, in reality, been nothing but a large dragonfly. Large? Yes—there is no doubt of that; for in its anterior legs it held the monoplane firmly, while with its mandibles it was rapidly tearing it to pieces.

"Let's all shoot for the head," whispered Jones. "Then load as fast as you can and aim for the upper thorax. Dr. Rock, can you see that eye? You ought to. It is as large as a barrel. Aim for that."

At the signal, the three elephant guns roared. The dragonfly rose in the air and then fell, kicking and twitching with the released, uncontrolled energy of one hundred feet of insect body. Again the guns spoke and, in a short time, once more. That was the end—the vital parts of the insect, blown to pieces by the explosive bullets, the rest of the body was harmless. The four ran up to the body. Gradually movement ceased and, as luck would have it, the enormous trunk rolled to one side, uncovering the monoplane. A frightened aviator crawled out from the wreckage, dripping with juice from the insect, but otherwise unhurt.

"My word!" he exclaimed. "I went through the war, but this beats all that I ever saw there. Is this your private pet?"

"Private pet? What do you think we are?" exclaimed the doctor. "You trespass on private, property and then insinuate that we keep hundred-feet dragonflies for pets! Man, you had a narrow escape from being eaten by that thing we just killed. Won't you come into the cabin and wash? My name is Dr. Rock. These gentlemen, whose accurate gunfire saved your life, are Professor Packard of the New York Academy of Natural Science; Mr. Sterling Powers, an authority on New York *Lepidoptera,* and Mr. Timothy Jones, owner of a hosiery store in Shawnee."

"And I," replied the man, acknowledging the introduction, "am Captain Lewellen, of His Majesty's Royal Air Corps. I was doing a Montreal-Mexico flight when this beastie started to chase me."

"Could he fly fast?" asked Jones.

"Fast? My word! I was easily making two hundred miles an hour and he had no trouble at all. Just as soon as he got me, I cut off the gas. I did not want to irritate him by tickling his belly with the propeller. I do not think the old boat is injured much, but we will not be able to tell till we can get rid of his blasted carcass."

He walked over to Jones.

"Did the lady say your name was Jones?"

"Yes, Timothy Jones of Shawnee."

"Seems that I have met you before."

"Shouldn't wonder. I used to be a grocery clerk in an A. and P. store. Lots of folk came in there that I did not know by name."

The doctor took the captain indoors. Jones took the guns away to the kitchen to clean them. The two scientists were walking around the dead dragonfly, taking measurements and pictures, and talking matters over. Finally, the entire party gathered in the sitting room. It was growing colder and a mist was falling. The captain was washed and tried to look dignified in a Roman toga, made out of several Indian blankets and safety pins. Jones was twiddling his thumbs. The doctor and the New York men were whispering together in a corner. Finally, they all settled themselves around Timothy Jones. Sterling. Powers acted as spokesman for the group.

"We have been talking this thing over, Mr. Jones," he said, "and we have decided that we have a right to ask you to be honest with us and tell us what you know about the events of the last two months. I think that you can rely on us and, if you want secrecy, we will promise you to keep anything you say to ourselves. But we feel that after all we have been through, we are entitled to the facts."

Timothy Jones looked a little more inane than ever. "Of course," he said, "you know all about my working in an A. and P. store?"

"Yes," replied the doctor. "I believe that we do."

"Then I judge that you do not want to hear about my experiences there? How I won the district prize? After that I was in the war, and after the war I was a wanderer. I finally landed in Borneo, and went to work for this German. His name was Scheermann. He was an authority on bugs, and when he was drunk used to brag that a man by the name of Lubeck had been his pupil."

"STOP a moment," ordered Professor Packard.

"Lubeck is the world's authority on insect life. He has repeatedly stated that he owes everything to the instruction of his Master. Herman Scheermann. But Scheermann died over thirty years ago. He sailed for the East and his ship was wrecked."

"He did not die," retorted Jones calmly. "He simply took the opportunity to let the world think that he was dead. He went to Borneo and I worked for him there. Over a year. He always had one or two white men working for him, and when they grew tired and wanted to go back home, they died. I am sure that he knew bug life, and he knew human nature. He was a king in the wilds of Borneo, where he had his little city.

"I worked for him just long enough to secure a little idea of what he wanted to do to the world. He had, at first, the idea that he could grow better silk. Then, as he grew older, he found that he could do the same thing with other insects that he could with the silk moth. So he started to play with insect life, and I guess it made him insane. Perhaps he was insane before he came to Borneo. Anyway, he had an idea that he could make the world a great brotherhood by frightening them. He thought he could grow beetles and dragonflies so large that they could conquer any army sent against them. Not so silly an idea, after all. What would our air force do against ten thousand dragonflies like this one we killed this morning? Anyway, I became frightened, and when I found that all the white men ahead of me were dead, I made up my mind to escape. But I wanted to take something with me—something I could show the world and make them realize the danger that threatened humanity.

"That is why I took the eggs out of the storeroom. I went out of Borneo and I went fast and kept on going, hunting for a place to hatch the eggs. Dr. Rock was the first one who seemed to have the ideal mind and the proper surroundings. She has done very well indeed with her part of it. I did not realize that there were two kinds of eggs till the one worm went into the water. Even then I did not visualize the danger. In Borneo I was never allowed to go into the dragonfly valley. All I knew about them was what Scheermann would boast of when he was drunk. I knew that they ate meat and I suggested to the doctor that we put horsemeat into the lake, and for over ten days that creature has been eating nearly an entire "horse" every twenty-four hours. I had an idea that it would stay under water for a long time. I was wrong there. It must have come up the night before the storm, crawled through the brush, climbed a tree, and shed. I suppose we would find its case if we looked. During the intense heat of the storm it became hungry and killed and ate the harmless sugar-eating moth. Then it sailed off for new game. I was not greatly worried, because I knew something about the habits of the ordinary dragonfly. They have a favorite resting place, and when they capture their prey, they return to that place to eat it. I knew after it killed the moth that it would come back. In the air it met Captain Lewellen and thought his airplane was some kind of bug, caught it, and brought it back here to eat. Had we not been prepared, the captain would now be somewhere inside of the fly. That is my story.

"I can say this much. Scheermann was behind those butterflies in New York City. I do not know how he did it, but he was responsible. He was the one who put the paragraph in the paper. He wanted me and he wanted the eggs. He must have had some idea that I came to America. Anyone but an insane person would have gone at it different, but he thought he could frighten the nation. I think that he has gone back to Borneo. Perhaps he is preparing for trouble. You remember the paragraph put the time limit as the first of next January. Now I think that you know the danger. You have seen a giant dragonfly in action. In the cold storage that Scheermann has—yes, actual cold storage in Borneo—he has literally tens of thousands of eggs, and all he has to do is to take them out and put them in the sunlight. What are you going to do about it?"

"The Government should be warned of the danger!" said the professor.

Jones laughed. Up to this time he had not even smiled, but now he laughed, and it was some time before he could control himself enough to say. "But don't you see, my dear professor, that no one will believe you? Suppose you go before a number of Senators and tell them my story and what you have seen and ask them to communicate with Great Britain for a joint expedition into the wilds of Borneo? Do you know what would happen? *They would not believe you.*"

"There is only one thing to do," said Sterling Powers firmly. "I do not know what the cost of such an affair will be, but whatever it costs, I can finance it. Suppose I go over there and settle this matter?"

"I think that I had better go with you," chimed in Dr. Rock.

"I would die of chagrin if you did not ask to go with me," cried Professor Packard. "What a wonderful thing it would be! There is no telling what that man has done in these thirty years. Perhaps if he is approached in the right way, he can be reasoned with."

"Now, see here," said the English captain, "I am not on regular duty. In fact, I am retired. You folks will need someone who can fly; so, why not ask me to go with you? I have a little money and will pay one-third of the expenses."

Dr. Rock was accustomed to rapid action. She showed this trait here. Without the loss of a minute, she went for paper, pen, and ink.

"I think we should draw up an agreement. Suppose the captain, Mr. Powers, and I agree in writing to share the expense of a trip to Borneo to free the world of this menace? We will ask the professor to go along as our guest, because his scientific knowledge will be of the greatest value to us. I am going to ask Miss Helen Brown to go as my guest. We are great friends and have never been separated. And I want Timothy Jones to go with us as guide and adviser."

"I am sorry, Madam, but I cannot go," was the ex-soldier's astonishing statement.

"You mean that you won't go?"

"That is what I mean. I have a business that is a pleasure to run. If I leave it for six months, it will be ruined. I want to stay in Shawnee and sell hose to the beautiful ladies and play golf and swim. I have been in Borneo; I know that place, and I know that German. I feel that I am happier right here. When I awake in the morning and see the Water Gap, it makes me happy, but I never was happy when I was walking through Scheermann's private graveyard. I will draw a map for you, and tell you just how to get there and all about it, but I do not think that I will go. My nerves are not as strong as they used to be."

They could not make him change his mind. Even when Miss Brown positively accepted the doctor's invitation, he sadly insisted on remaining in Shawnee.

Busy days came. The dead dragonfly had to be cut up and disposed of. This, in itself, was no little job. Lists of supplies had to be made, plans gone over, maps studied. Through it all, Jones moved like a sad, sorry shadow of his former self. But nothing could make him change his decision, not even the fact that O'Malley was going with Dr. Rock.

At the last he announced that he was not going to New York to see the party off. Miss Helen Brown so far forgot herself as to go to the hosiery store and say goodbye. He gave her a picture as a farewell gift.

A few days later the party sailed for Europe on the *Brennin*.

CHAPTER ELEVEN
Borneo!

TIME was passing slowly, as far as General Wood, the governor of North Borneo, was concerned. For some time his work had been purely administrative. Few visitors came to Sandakan, the capital of his province, and those few had lately been decidedly uninteresting. It was, therefore, a relief to him to hear that a new steamer had entered the harbor and that one of the passengers desired an interview.

He was more than surprised to find that the visitor was a middle-aged lady, evidently an American and apparently a physician. The governor, therefore, dressed with more than his usual care and made a dignified and imposing appearance as he welcomed Dr. Anna Rock, late of Brooklyn, New York State, U. S. A. to his office.

After refreshments had been passed, he asked the doctor what he could do to make her visit to North Borneo a pleasant one. He said that he would try to make it pleasant but could not promise comfort, as the weather was apt to be hot and sultry with frequent tropical rains.

"Do you want to see my papers?" asked the doctor, passing him a bundle of official documents. The governor took them and looked them over hastily.

"These seem to be all right, Doctor," he said. "I will not take your time or mine examining them in detail. What are your plans and in what way can I help you?"

"We are a party of scientists, Governor," said the little lady. "The group is composed of Professor Packard, of the Academy of Natural Sciences, New York City; Mr. Sterling Powers, retired broker and amateur student of entomology; Captain Lewellen, retired captain in the British Air Corps; Miss Helen Brown, a friend of mine, and myself. I am a retired physician and interested in orchids and silkworms. We wanted to spend a little time in your country, gathering specimens for the Academy in New York City. I have an Irish servant, O'Malley, and that concludes the list. We will need a few natives and some boats and local supplies."

"Have you any idea where you want to go?" inquired the governor. After hearing the purpose of the company he had lost interest. After all, they were simply one more group of bug-and-plant hunters who would want to spend some weeks in the interior and at the same time enjoy all the comforts of civilization. He could furnish guides and natives in plenty for such an expedition. What he longed for was something to break the weary monotony of his existence.

"Yes," was the doctor's unexpected reply. "We have a very definite objective. I understand that in your territory is a mountain called Kinabalu. It is the highest mountain in Borneo. To be exact, it is 13,694 feet above sea level. East of it is a plateau. This plateau can be reached by going up the Kinabatangan River, first by a small steamer and then in native boats. Perhaps the last hundred miles will have to be done on foot, unless we can secure some of those little native ponies the travel books rave about. Our scientific work will be done on that plateau.

"No it won't!" cried the governor, almost jumping out of his chair.

"Why not?"

"Because that is the worst spot in all Borneo. White men have gone in there now and then, but they have never come out. I can sit here and tell you stories of that district that will make you wish you were back home. There are a few tribes up there. We call them the Dusans. They used to be headhunters, and I guess they are yet, though no one has been up there to find out for years and years. Savages? Well, that would not be so bad if that was all they were, but they must be worse. You ask a hundred of our guides and local natives to take you up there and one hundred of them would refuse. They would say that they were sick or busy or going somewhere, but the real reason would be that they were afraid to go. Strange demons haunt those mountains. Gods of terrible shape. Personally, I do not credit all those tales, but I do know that it is no place for a white woman. You can go out in my back yard and find all the pretty plants and bugs you want, and you are given my permission to take any to

New York that you want to take, but you are not going up to the Kinabalu district."

"Again I will have to ask you why not?"

The governor was decidedly irritated. He jumped up and walked excitedly up and down the room.

"I cannot talk to you, Madam. I cannot swear in the presence of a woman. I have told you as plainly as I can that no one has gone up in there for the last thirty years and come back. They die up there. Some time when my native constabulary is civilized enough to overcome their superstition, I will go up there and clean the place up. Degenerate foreigners, bloodthirsty natives, perhaps a gang of half-breeds, robbers, fugitives from justice! I do not know what there is up there, but it is just Hell. Must be. And you and your party are not going! *You are not going!* I would be writing letters of explanation to the United States Government for the rest of my life, trying to explain why I allowed you to go when I knew that it was certain death. You send Captain Lewellen to see me. He is English and I can make him understand."

"That is final?" asked the woman, standing by her chair.

"Absolutely! What are you going to do about it?"

"We are going."

"I forbid it. You will have no help. If necessary, I will place you under arrest and communicate with your country, explaining the matter."

"General Wood," said the doctor quietly. "I come from a land that does not know the word, 'failure.' We have put a lot of time and thought and money into this trip. We have maps, equipment and the necessary brains and cash. I do not want to appear conceited, but I will say that our group is unusually well prepared to take care of themselves. The only weak spot is my friend, Miss Helen Brown, and even she is rather clever with a gun. All I can say is that I will go back and confer with my party, and we will let you know our final decision in a few days."

"That is more like it," replied the governor. "All of you come in and have supper with me tonight."

"Sometime, and thank you very much, but not tonight. We will be too busy. To use an American phrase, we will have to go into conference."

THAT was all the explanation the governor could get. She left him fuming and sweating.

"Dammit!" he cried. "Here I am all wet and excited over some silly Americans. What fools we were in 1776! If we had just been sensible and kept those colonies, at the present time the English people would be Lords of the World. What people those Americans are! I think they call themselves Go-getters. Little woman. Little old woman! Sat there and said she would let me know. Wanted to know why? Told her she was going to certain death and she wanted to know why? Hell! Up goes my blood pressure. Guess I will have to call on them. Officially. Pay my compliments to the other lady and the men. What did they do to that captain? Must be in love with the girl to go on such a blasted, silly, bloody trip."

And that is what the governor did. In his official launch, with an escort of his lesser officers, he called that evening on the scientists. They received him, as best they could, on their little steamer, which was well loaded with supplies of all sorts. He met Miss Helen Brown and the rest of the party. He was introduced to Captain Lewellen, and as soon as he could do so, he took the Englishman to one side.

"I cannot let you go up to the Mount Kinabalu district, Captain," he said rather firmly.

"So Dr. Rock told us."

"What are you going to do about it?"

"The doctor has not decided."

"My word! Does she rule all you men?"

"Just about. She is a very remarkable woman, capable, brilliant, fearless, and never married, talked it over, and decided that she ought to be head of the expedition."

"But you will be killed if you go there."

"Is that so?"

"That is bad country for over twenty-five years. White men, tramps, soldiers of fortune, beachcombers, have gone in there by the dozens and none have ever come out alive."

"Not one?"

"Not a single one!!"

"I understood that a man by the name of Timothy Jones came out."

"Never heard the name. There may be white men up there now, but if there are, they are the scum of creation, men who have gone native, refugees from the law. It is a bad place to go. Stay away."

"From what you say, it is a bad place. Well, the best we can do is to talk it over and see if we can find the same bugs and plants elsewhere. You will refuse to send us up country on the Kinabatangan River?"

"I will not only refuse, but I will arrest you if you try to go without my permission. I will have you all declared insane by my medical adviser and send you back to England via Calcutta."

"That would be harsh treatment."

"Not as bad as letting you all get killed."

For a few days after this visit the governor received no definite news from the steamer. At last, worried over their calm and non-committal way of taking his ultimatum, he decided to make another call. He, found a few sleepy sailors, a sleepier captain and first mate and O'Malley, who, clad in white pants and straw slippers, was lazily fishing over the side of the vessel, seemingly oblivious to his surroundings.

"O'Malley!" called the Governor sharply. "Where is Dr. Rock?"

"I don't know, General Wood. For the life of me, I don't."

The general almost ran up the rope ladder and took the Irishman by the shoulder and shook him.

"Where did she go?" he shouted.

"She and the rest of them went up country in captain's hydroplane. That is what makes me so mad. She said to me, 'O'Malley, someone has to stay here to look after our supplies and answer our radio, and you are elected for the job. You are married and I never would be able to look your wife in the face if anything happened to you.' That is what she said to me, sir. Right after you called on them they had a meeting and started to put the plane together and lower it on the water, and off they went, early this morning, bound for that mountain. Three men and two women and their guns and a little food. Enough gas to get them there and back; at least, they thought so. Doctor said all she wanted was to get there. Said water ran down to the ocean and they would come down on the river."

The governor sat down on a pile of rope and wiped the sweat off his face.

"They will never come back, O'Malley."

"Then I am here fishing for a year. The doctor has hired this steamer for that long and she said that I should keep it right here till they came back, or the year was up. I would like to have my hands on Timothy Jones. He is the guy who got the poor little doctor into this mess."

"I never heard of him," replied the governor as he recovered his dignity and walked slowly back to the rope ladder.

CHAPTER TWELVE
Mount Kinabalu

THE machine that Captain Lewellen had selected for this adventure was a beautiful hydroplane. He had selected this type of aircraft for two reasons. First, he thought that he might have to start from water, and second, he thought that in an uncultivated country, largely forest, the only safe landing place would be a lake.

The hydroplane might have been larger, but it could not have been more complete. Naturally, when the party found that the governor absolutely refused to help them, their only thought was of making the journey by air, and the captain was sure that this could be done, provided no effort was made to take supplies with them. They loaded the gasoline tanks to capacity, filled part of the space with their guns, ammunition, and a little food and then just about found room to squeeze in the pilot and four passengers. The plane had been assembled on the side of the steamer away from shore. In that way perfect secrecy was obtained, and the party was able to leave in the early morning without any of the officials being aware of it.

Their destination was Mount Kinabalu, or rather, the plateau that nestled on its eastern shoulder. Careful measurements on a large-scale map showed them that it was just one hundred miles from Sandakan. Just one hundred miles of air travel. A distance that could easily be made in less than two hours. One hundred miles by air, and according to the governor, the distance from Heaven to Hell by land. By air, a pleasant journey, simply far enough to get the motor running sweetly, but otherwise, a trip almost impossible for any but the strongest to make: Twenty miles up the Kinatabangan River, in a little steamer that at times made a mile an hour or less against the sluggish current, twenty miles of puff and blow and churning of the weeds and frightening of the snakes and fighting of the mosquitoes. Then more miles in native canoes, two natives and one white in each canoe, and death on every side, grinning at fate. Then the long walk through swamps and jungles and forests, so dark that the sunlight never reaches the ground and Death still with the party, and fate shaking dice with him to select the next victim. Snakes so small that they are never noticed till they bite and then so powerful that the blood turns to water in three minutes. Insects, a thousand varieties, ten million individuals; plants that sting, roots that trip, leaves that cut to the bone, and back of the tree, hid by the rock, covered by the mimicry that is the most ancient art in the world, the head hunter, waiting for one more trophy before he goes to buy another bride with a basketful of dried heads. Could men go to Mount Kinabalu on foot? Certainly. Men, since there were men, have gone everywhere, but most of them *never came back*.

One hour and thirty-seven minutes after leaving the steamer the hydroplane settled with the grace of a swan on the waters of a little lake that was, millions of years before, planted by a giant hand, at the very foot of Kinabalu. To the west the mountain reared, partly wooded, but the top was bare and forbidding. Tradition States that Buddha stepped there as he journeyed, and that the footprint is still in the top of the rock. But who has been there to see?

The plane came to a slow pause near the rocky shore of the lake.

"So far," said Dr. Rock. "The description given us by Timothy Jones has been deadly accurate. He said there was a lake on the east of the mountain and here it is. This is almost like a scene from the Arabian Nights. The governor said that this part of Borneo was Hell on Earth. How did he know? He was never here. Must have listened to a lot of fairy tales.

However, we better take our guns with us when we land. The place seems deserted."

"Not exactly deserted," whispered Captain Lewellen. "There is a wharf and a powerboat, and that slope there looks like a grass lawn. What a miracle to find all these right in the jungles!"

"Of course, anything is possible," interjected Sterling Powers.

"And here comes the owner," whispered Helen Brown, "and a Chinaman behind him, carrying an umbrella."

The captain anchored the hydroplane and the party went on shore. They were just a few rods from the wharf, and soon they were met by the white man and the Chinaman.

He was a small man, somewhat old, but immaculately dressed in white linens. Clean-shaven he was and his hands and nails showed the culture and refinement of years of careful living. He talked with a slight accent, but his words were well chosen and his tone soft and pleasing.

"Allow me to welcome you to my home," he murmured. "I have been expecting you. I think that the governor was wise in advising you not to make the river trip. It would have taken you days and caused you untold hardship. Now, in a plane, it is a matter of a few hours. I always go westward over the mountains, but I believe that the eastward route is also very pleasant and, if you stay in the air, uneventful. I am so glad you wanted to come and see me. Life here is un-eventful. Occasionally I go to Shanghai or Calcutta, but at my age the pleasure is not what it used to be. Dr. Rock, allow me to escort you to my home where breakfast is ready for you. Gentlemen, care for Miss Brown. Yes, I have everything all ready for your entertainment. The radio service I established some years ago is very useful. What do you think of my lawn? Creeping bent grass. Hard to establish and care for, but worth all the trouble it causes. It adds a touch to the place. I have it cut often; makes me feel better—like shaving once or twice a day."

The astonished party made only general answers to his rambling discourse. It was not till they were on the wide gallery of his house, which was well hidden in the forest that they realized that they had left their guns in the hydroplane. Each of the party carried a small revolver and some ammunition in his belt. Otherwise they were unarmed. Seated in comfort on the gallery, drinking iced lemonade served by white-robed Chinese servants, they looked perplexedly at each other. There was neither time nor opportunity for anything like a conference. Soon small bamboo tables were placed in front of each guest and breakfast served; then tobacco.

I WOULD advise," said the old gentleman, "that you allow me to put you up in my home while you are in this vicinity. The hotels here—are impossible, and there is some element of danger. Will you be my guests?"

"I am afraid, sir, that it would be too great an imposition on your hospitality," said Sterling Powers, suavely. "We came out here to rough it, and if you make things too pleasant for us, it will take away much of the anticipated enjoyment of the trip. Besides, it hardly seems proper to accept this much courtesy from a man who, so far, has not seen fit to give us his name."

"An oversight," cried the old man. "An unintentional, but at the same time, an almost unforgivable breach of social etiquette. Will you pardon me? Especially the ladies? I have been away from ladies for so long that I forget. Besides, I am growing old. My name is Herman Scheermann, and I have lived here for so many years that I feel that I never had any other home. I know you all through my radio agencies. Now that that is done, may I renew my invitation for you to be my guests?"

"We will accept, Mr. Scheermann," was the rather unexpected reply of Dr. Rock. "We have come a long distance and spent a good deal of money for no other purpose than to have a long talk with you about some matters which we thought might be of mutual interest. I admit that we thought to find you under different circumstances, but evidently we were either misinformed or made a mistake in judging human nature. So, if it is not too much to ask of you, we will stay as your guests till we have talked these matters over and arrived at some mutual understanding of our difficulties."

"Everything I have, doctor, is yours for as long as you want it," said the old man, bowing. "May I suggest that I show you to your rooms so you can remove the trace of travel and prepare for dinner? The gentlemen will find white linens and the ladies may find in their suite a few things to gild the lily of their beauty. Chang, show the gentlemen their rooms, and tell Nida to care for the ladies. Dinner will be served at one. For the present, you will have to excuse me, as I have engagements that will keep me busy for several hours."

He remained in the room till the visitors had left. Then he gave orders for dinner with plates for six. After this he walked leisurely out to the wharf, where he held a lengthy conversation with some natives who had come up the lake in their canoes.

The two women waited till Nida, who seemed to be a Malay type, left the room. Then the doctor whispered, "How does all this impress you, Helen?"

"At present, it is a dream, *but*—"

"I agree with the but part. It may end up as a nightmare. Think of all the things told us by Timothy Jones! Remember how we prepared for this man from Borneo; compare all that with the actual man. Either Jones was a terrible liar or Scheermann is one of the cleverest villains I have ever heard of. Think of it! He knew we were on our way. He prepared for us. Instead of a native hut, he has a country palace. Where does General Wood come in? How is it that the general does not know about this place and this man? He said that no man ever came in here and left it alive. Jones said the same thing. Does this old grandfather impress you as a murderer? I am sorry about our rifles. Sorry that we are separated from the men. When you dress for dinner, and evidently he expects us to put on these beautiful silks, put your gun and belt on underneath. I am sorry I brought you here. You should have stayed in Stroudsburg with your folks. I wish that Jones was here. He was a fool, but he always gave me the idea that he was capable. If only he were not such a liar! He must have lied about this old man."

"Anna Rock," the younger woman declared earnestly. "I do not believe that Timothy Jones ever really lied to hurt anything. He may have twisted things at times to make matters easier for himself, but they were white lies. At times he seemed to be a perfect fool and at other times he gave flashes of being something different. I do not know why he did not come with us. I cannot tell why he let me come without a word of protest, if he thought it was dangerous. But I do know that he is a gentleman and I would feel a lot safer if he were here. Captain Lewellen is a perfect dear and no doubt as brave as brave can be, and the other two men are brave too. They will do all they can, but Timothy would do a little more. I tell you how I feel...I am scared. Plenty scared. My advice is this: Have dinner and then casually walk down to the hydroplane and get back to the ship as soon as we can. Once there, see General Wood and tell him the whole story and let the English Government tend to the business—that is, if there is any business to attend to."

The eyes of the little doctor flashed, as she hurled her reply.

"So far, I have never been a quitter. I came here to solve the problem of the flying threat, and I am going to do my best to solve it before I leave. The governor would not believe us. He might fly up here, and then he would be sure that we were lying. The only thing I can do is to stay. You can have the captain take you back if you wish to go."

Helen Brown sighed.

"Don't let's quarrel, Anna. Life is too serious. I came of my own accord and I am going to stay as long as you do; only I think that if Timothy were here he would tell us to be careful."

One o'clock came and the party reassembled for dinner. The service was faultless, the cooking perfect, the conversation sparkling. Everything was as it should be. Herman Scheermann was a perfect host. The doctor realized more and more that it would be hard to tell the man just what their business was. Yet, it had to be done. Meantime, the old man talked on, at times rambling, at other times clearly, but always in an interesting manner. It seemed that he collected insects, orchids, and live animals for the export trade. He also raised some fruit, did a little mining, made a good living, and was Godfather Bountiful to all the natives. Head hunting had ceased in that part of Borneo. He served as the local judge. He had done his best to lessen the mosquito pest and reduce malaria. All of his men and women had to be protected against smallpox by vaccination and he had hoped some day to open a small hospital and install a doctor and a few nurses. He thought that Governor Wood was very capable. There was a future in the silk industry, if only the worms could be made bigger and thus obtain a heavier silk thread. He had done the best he could, but was growing old and needed young blood and more capital. He had tried to interest some young men, but they had wearied of the solitude and left.

Dr. Rock listened to him as though in a dream. She closed her eyes and visualized the governor as she had seen him. She could hear him speak in his office: "…No man has gone up there for thirty years and lived to come back. Degenerate foreigners, bloodthirsty natives, half-breeds, robbers, fugitives from justice. It is just Hell! If you go there, it is certain death…"

And, in confliction came the low voice of the old man, "I hope someday to make this a country that will be an earthly Paradise, where life, property, and happiness will he as safe as it is in Germany or England."

CHAPTER THIRTEEN
The Real Herman Scheermann

FOR some reason the old man's voice grew far away and the Doctor was unable to keep awake. As she shut her eyes for the last time, she stupidly glanced around the table. Scheermann was still talking in his monotonous monotone. The Chinese servants stood motionless at one end of the room. The three men had fallen forward, fast asleep on the table, pushing aside the dishes with somnolent arms. Helen was trying to say something even as she fell backward in the chair.

Then came oblivion, followed by the headache of the morning after.

The Doctor awoke in the room that had been set apart for her use. Before the dinner it had been shared by Helen Brown. Now, Dr. Rock was alone except for the presence of a sleek, muscular Malay woman. The woman was evidently a guard. The Doctor looked at the windows; they were barred. Her head hurt; sitting up in bed gave her vertigo.

"Drugged…" she whispered to herself. "Perhaps Jones was right!"

In the meantime, Helen Brown was rousing in another room that was similarly guarded by a native woman and iron bars. The three men were not so fortunate in their choice of quarters. They had been placed in a dry well, over thirty feet deep, with smooth walls. The top of the well was covered with a lacework of iron bars. A clay jar on the floor was found to contain tepid water, while some fruit was the only food visible.

The three men met the situation in three ways that were typical of their former life.

The Professor took out his notebook, wound his watch, and started to make the necessary entries to keep his diary up to date. He did not say a word to the other men.

Sterling Powers smiled.

"I suppose," he said, "that we stay here or elsewhere till we can arrange for a ransom. Too bad the ladies are here. But I guess the old boy will treat them right. He probably is looking us up in Dunn and Bradstreet. How about it, Captain?"

The Englishman turned around. He had been carefully examining the walls of the well, tapping on them with a piece of stone.

"Ransom your eye!" he whispered. "Didn't Jones tell you that he was the only one that got out alive? How about the Governor's telling us the same thing? Ransom? Nonsense! This man is a killer. I don't know what he will do with the ladies, but we are dead men unless we get out and kill him first."

"We have our revolvers," chimed in the Professor. He seemed pleased to be the one to make this suggestion.

"Put that thought back in your subconscious," advised the Captain. "You have a gun, but what good will it do? Look at it. See how many shells you have in your cartridge belt. I have looked. The old man had us searched before he put us down here. Do you think he would miss a trick like that? Just as soon as I awoke, I found that out. Jehoshaphat! What a headache! And all the time he was telling us he wanted to make the place as safe as England or Germany."

"What do you think he is going to do with us, Captain?" asked Powers.

"Kill us."

"Not in cold blood?"

"Certainly. Do you think a man like that would hand us weapons and give us a chance to fight it out? Not in a million years. I suspected something like this, and I packed a few extra shells for my revolver in my shoe heel. He must have suspected it, because I am barefooted, whereas you two still have your shoes on. Here is a game of poker, gentlemen, with the aces wild and Scheermann making all the local rules. If you are able to do any constructive thinking, better start right in now."

The conversation was interrupted by the removal of the iron bars at the mouth of the well. A rope and bamboo ladder were lowered.

"That means come up," commented the Captain. "Let's go."

He went first. At the top he was met by Herman Scheermann, who had a pair of shoes in his hands.

"Put these on, Captain," the old man ordered. "We are going to walk over some rough ground and I do not want your feet cut. Sorry I had to take them off, but the heels needed repairing. Good morning, Mr. Powers. How are you feeling by now, Professor Packard? Well, I hope? Suppose we go walking...? I thought you would like the hours spent with me better without the immediate presence of my guard; but please remember this. Wherever we go, they will be near.

They have orders to shoot to kill at your first false move. So please avoid suspicion. I want to show you my silk factory first."

He walked on ahead, and without comment they followed. Fifteen minutes of slow travel along a forest path led to a clearing, where a large bamboo shed stood. Here a dozen Chinese women worked at wooden reels. The old man paused.

"When I came to Borneo thirty years ago, I had only one idea, and that was to grow a larger silkworm so I could furnish the trade a better grade of silk. I was finally able, by selection, feeding, glandular treatment, and a few other details—which I will not go into at this time—to produce a cocoon that varied from twelve to fifteen feet in length. Of course, I was not able to produce an infinite number of these cocoons, but I at once made a raw silk that was the envy and despair of the silk merchants of the Orient. They gave me fabulous prices for all I could make, and I can say with pride that the richest men in China, Japan, and India are wearing fabrics made with my silk. The individual filament I produce is so large that it has to be split before it can be used in weaving.

"When I first came here I had hopes of establishing my new breed of silkworm in Japan, but I saw later on, and the silk merchants realized immediately, that if I did so, the old business would be ruined, the former machinery would become useless, and thousands of laborers would starve from lack of work. The silk producers of the East are very careful in regard to the labor situation. I talked the matter over with them and finally they saw the wisdom of giving me a million dollars a year in gold, provided I agreed not to export any of the eggs and to sell them all the raw silk, which would have to be spun and reeled on my estate to preserve the secret of the source. The important thing was to keep all the eggs here.

"Whenever a producer secures a fine strain of silkworm, the other men try to steal the eggs. That happened in the year 550. Justinian was Emperor in Constantinople. The Chinese were willing to sell him silk but would not allow any of the details of its manufacture or any of the eggs to be taken out of the country. So Justinian sent two Persian monks over to China to teach the heathen Christianity, and when they came back to Constantinople, they brought with them a bamboo cane, and that cane was filled with graine, the commercial name for masses of silkworm egg.

"That was clever. The Japanese did not want my eggs to leave the country. Occasionally, rumor reached the Chinese, and they would send men here to steal the eggs. Of course, it was my bread and butter. What do you do with thieves in your country? I kept all those men here. They had to stay here, under the sod.

I will show you the cemetery later on. I only bury their clothes and private papers. The bodies are disposed of elsewhere. I will show you that too. See those cocoons the women are working on? Are they not beautiful? One of my females lays five hundred eggs. I just produce enough to supply the demand and earn the million. But I have thousands of eggs in reserve in my storeroom. Let us walk on."

Another short walk brought them to another frame building, carefully screened and immaculately clean. Opening the door, the old man asked them to enter. "This is my laboratory," he explained. "I do considerable work here with the help of two technicians whom I trained from early boyhood. The Japanese make good laboratory workers if they are trained. This place is necessary to keep my silkworms free from disease. If they developed muscardine or grasserie, the labor of a lifetime would be ruined in two seasons. My worms have to be kept healthy. I watch my mulberry forests very carefully.

"I would like to show you those forests and my natives feeding the worms and some of the worms spinning, but time will not allow. Are you gentlemen sensitive to the cold? No? Well, button your coats anyhow, because now I am going to take you into my cold storage. It is lighted with electricity, but at the same time it has other remarkable features. It is dry, and I have been able to so close it that all insects, birds, and rats are kept out. Of course, this was necessary."

HE led the way through the forest and came at last to a door in the face of the rock. This he opened and asked them to enter. Pressing a button, he turned on the lights and illumined a large natural cave of limestone. The floor was of fine dry sand. Countless rows of bamboo shelves ranked in regular order and every shelf was filled with eggs. The air was cold, not below freezing, but certainly nearly so. The old man started to talk again, and his tone was, as before, that of an interesting lecturer.

"Here I keep my egg reserve. Silkworm eggs and other varieties. I have always enjoyed the study of insect life and, in a way, regret that I was not able to remain in Europe. My pupil, Lubeck of Vienna, has done very well. I understand that he and Professor Packard are now the leading entomologists in the world. How singular it is, Professor, that you should decide to visit me. Now if only little Lubeck was here, we would have a scientific trio such as the world has never seen in one generation. I have read your articles, Professor, and admired your ability, but I have one criticism. You have never shown any constructive imagination. You have to actually see something before you will believe it, and even then you will have to see it twice.

"But let us go on with our sightseeing tour. I am going to show you some fossil rock that no other white man besides myself has ever seen. At least, I think so. Perhaps many natives have seen it. Yes, of course! Many generations of natives have seen it. We will go right through the storehouse and down these steps. This is my private entrance. The natives go through the forest and I am not sure that many know this passage. Please do not try to take advantage of my age as we go down the steps. If you look behind you, the armed guards can easily be seen following us. Let us have no unpleasant moments to mar the pleasure of the holiday. I wax facetious. Perhaps I develop the garrulousness of senility. At least, I still am able to control the situation, though I have failed so far in making America a real republic where all men are equal; but wait till January first of next year."

The men followed him down several hundred stone steps, broken routinely by wide stone landings. Electric lights furnished more than adequate illumination. At last they came out into an enormous natural pit, a terrific hole in the earth. Three hundred feet above, they saw the sunlight and the trees overgrowing the sheer precipice. The floor of the pit, which was over five hundred feet in diameter, was covered with a fine sand. Part of the rock wall was flat, the rest rudely circular. With a grandiose gesture. Herman Scheermann pointed to the flat rock.

At first the men thought that it was an ancient native carving. Then, the scientists saw that it really was a fossil, nearly a hundred feet long.

Professor Packard turned on Herman Scheermann, and whispered, "At least do me the professional courtesy of not telling me about this. Let me tell you, and then you can agree or not. This is a very remarkable and surprisingly complete fossil of a dragonfly from the Carboniferous strata. The celebrated Solenhofen Rocks in Bavaria have similar fossils, only none of them are over six feet in length. I have read that in Malay there is a genus of dragonfly, the *Euphaea*, that closely resembles the fossil type in Solenhofen; also in New Zealand the genus *Uropetala* is similar. This fossil appears to be a little similar to the genus *Aeschna*. Do you agree?"

"Nearly, I congratulate you on your knowledge. Only a few men living could have done as well. Doctor Hagan; who has made a special study of the Solenhofen rock, practically agrees with you. He came to the conclusion that most of these fossil genera had ceased to exist but that in parts of the Orient certain very similar types had survived. Is it not a beautiful fossil? Can you easily understand that men might look on it as a God? Let me tell you a secret. Back of the fossil's head is a cave, approached by winding steps from a room back of the storeroom. When I want certain things done by my natives and done well, I give them the orders from that cave and they think that it is the voice of the God talking to them. We have monthly services here. The worshipers gather on the rocks and then we let in a few of the God's living representatives and feed them. Quaint idea? A remarkable sight.

"I forgot to tell you, I breed giant dragonflies. I will leave you to find out how. Perhaps I found the eggs, centuries old, buried in the mud of the lake. Or I may have taken our local species and used the same technique to enlarge them that I used with the silkworm. Of course, my pets would fly away if I allowed them to; so I operate on them as soon as they come out of their pupa case. Cut the ligaments of their flying muscles so they can just crawl and eat. How they can eat!

"In the storeroom I carefully mix the eggs of the silkworm and those of the dragonfly. The occasional thief would, no doubt, take one of each kind. Then when they hatched, the one would eat the other; thus my secret would still be safe.

Every detail has been attended to. I am sure that I have overlooked nothing.

"You should see this place when the moon shines full into the pit. The food is tied in the middle of the sandy floor and then the dragonfly is sent in. And the food is eaten. Sometimes we let two in at a time and let them fight over the meal. It pleases the natives, and they feel that it is approved of by the God. At the same time it gives me a powerful influence over them. I am the Priest of the God. I interpret his desires to them. When they are restless and want to leave, they recall that all who have done this in the past have been made to serve the living images of the God. A most peculiar and final service. Let us go..."

He led the way up the winding face of the pit, and at last they stood on the forest floor. From there Scheermann walked through the forest till at last they came to a meadow on the side of the lake. There the grass was cut, so smooth that it gave the impression of being manicured. In regular rows were placed large rocks, each rock with an inscription on it.

"This is my cemetery," whispered the old man, and he took off his hat and stood with bowed head and folded hands. "All who die in my service are thus remembered. The natives are given space by themselves. How time passes! I come here and look at the inscriptions and it makes me feel old. So many white men have died here. There is only one stone that is peculiar. It is a stone without an inscription."

"Why is that?" asked Sterling Powers, softly.

"One man came and stayed with me a year. I was fond of him. As a man, he was lovable, an admirable organizer and a fine executive. I loved him and often, when slightly intoxicated, took him into my confidence. He would have been my heir, inherited all my wealth and my greatness had he remained with me. But he left. So the only thing I could do was to prepare a stone for him. For I will not die till I see him properly punished for his crime. He was a thief.

"I came here to grow a larger, better silkworm. I have ended by breeding giant dragonflies. I have their eggs by the thousands. All I have to do to destroy humanity is to place those eggs in the swamps and rivers of Borneo. They will breed and they will eat, and before the world realizes it, an insect plague will be upon the face of the Earth, on the bosom of the waters that will wipe mankind out as a boy wipes out a mistake he has made on his slate in school. I have given them a chance. I told the United States what I wanted, and they paid no more attention to me than if I had been a fool.

"I am going to take you back to your pit now. You have seen all I have to show, heard all I have to say. It is a pity that those so clever, so intelligent, so young should die; but death must come to all someday; even I will have to die on the appointed day."

Captain Lewellen looked the old man squarely in the eye.

"You have been mighty open and above board with us, Mr. Scheermann. I suppose you realize that if just one of us escapes, the entire force of the British Empire will hunt you down till you die in a corner like a rat?"

"None of you are going to escape!" shouted the old man angrily. "You are all going to die here. Dr. Rock is going to die, too, though I never have killed a woman before. That other woman I will marry to my first technician. He is a clever Japanese man and the only one that I can depend on since that fool escaped. He told me last night that he would be my man forever if I let him have that woman—Helen Brown, I think her name is? I know you want to kill me right now for saying all this, but I snap my finger at you."

He snapped his fingers, and from the rocks natives sprang on the three infuriated men and bore them to the ground.

Ten minutes later they were once again at the bottom of the dry well. It was past noon and there was just a trifle of shade. A basket of fruit and a jar of water were lowered to them.

"At least," said Powers, "he does not intend to starve us."

"No," agreed Packard, "he will not starve us. I think that he is just trying to scare us. As soon as we are ready to promise him not to betray him in any way, he will let us go."

The Englishman looked at his fellows.

"I think that you gentlemen learned human nature, by dissecting beetles and butterflies. That man is not going to let us go. He is going to feed us because he wants us to live till the full of the moon. I think he made that very clear. Didn't you understand him? I did. He has some of those giant butterflies. They are carnivorous. Part of the full moon religious festival is to feed them. We are what they eat."

"Oh! Surely not!" exclaimed Professor Packard.

"That man is a pure scientist, a lover of entomology. I never heard of an entomologist acting that way."

Lewellen took a banana, peeled it, and ate it leisurely, as he commented on the scientist's statement.

"Before you die, you are going to find out a lot of things you never knew before. The more I see of Scheermann, the more convinced I am that Jones told the truth. I only blame him for not making us realize that he was telling the truth. And letting those women come here! I think he is going to kill us, but I doubt his killing the doctor."

"They will have to kill me first," shouted Sterling Powers.

CHAPTER FOURTEEN
Ultimatum

HERMAN Scheermann walked, practically unannounced, into the room occupied by Dr. Rock. She simply looked at him without speaking. He bowed low.

"Good morning, doctor. I trust you have not suffered from the lack of exercise during these three days of necessary but tiresome confinement. I have been so busy attending to the details of my business that I have not been able to show you the hospitality that I would have liked to show under more fortunate circumstances. Will you honor me by walking with me? We will have Miss Brown go with us and thus you ladies will enjoy the outing more."

"I will be pleased to see something of the country. This outlook through barred windows is not pretty." There was no doubt about the sting in the doctor's voice.

Fifteen minutes later the two ladies and Scheermann left the gallery of the palatial residence and started to walk through the forest. There was a well-defined path, but the jungles closed in on either side. In front two natives walked, guarding against the ever-possible snake, while two more, with loaded rifles, brought up the rear.

The German scientist was at his best. Every few minutes he paused to show some lovely blossom to the ladies or to pick up a multicolored lizard to demonstrate its ability to camouflage itself. The path led up the side of the mountain, but so gradual was the ascent and so steady the stream of interesting conversation, that the ladies did not tire as they might have done under ordinary circumstances. While they were in the tropics, the elevation made the atmosphere cool. At last they came to a tiny plateau, hardly more than a shelf on the side of the mountain. Turning, they saw the lake in the distance and on one side the stately residence. Near the shore was their hydroplane. It was practically untouched.

"It is a very pretty view, Mr. Scheermann," exclaimed Miss Brown.

"It is. You should have seen it when I first came here, thirty years ago. The only feature we lack here is feminine society. We have native women, but they have not the charm of civilization—that is, not a particular kind of charm. In other ways they surpass. I brought you ladies up here so you could see what I own. As far as you can see is mine. A deed? No, of course not. But if you live on land and no other man comes there or dares to come except as your servant, would you not call that land yours? All over this land I have the power and the glory. The men and women who live here do so by my sufferance. I am not only their ruler and employer; I am their God."

"That is a great responsibility," said Dr. Rock seriously.

"And one that I would like to share. That is why I brought you up here. I would like you ladies to remain here."

"Under what conditions?"

"I have someone from Japan working for me. He is of the nobility, but he had to leave the islands on account of an unfortunate…murder. He is highly educated and a polished gentleman. I think that when I die he will inherit all my property and carry on my work. He wants to stay here, but he is lonely. He has lived with a number of the native women, but he tires of them. He longs for an intelligent companion. I would like Miss Brown to stay here as his wife. I also need company; and I think that you, Dr. Rock, would have much in common with me. We both love nature and science. I would like to have you stay here as my wife. The four of us could be very comfortable and might finally obtain a certain amount of happiness out of the arrangement. I am a rich man. I might say, a very rich man. You ladies could have anything you asked for in the way of luxuries."

The two women looked at each other. At last Helen Brown said, "Impossible!" And Dr. Rock followed her with a rapid, "Absolutely impossible!"

The scientist did not appear in the least crestfallen over the complete rejection of his proposal. He replied, "I was afraid that it would not interest you. Are you steady? Can you look down without vertigo?"

"I think so," was the older lady's reply.

"Then let us go on. We will resume our tour of sightseeing."

And now the road led to a narrow rock edge. At its best, it was hardly eight feet wide. On either side, precipitous crags fell to a thousand feet below. On the right side was a large natural pit, at least a mile in diameter and with sides so nearly perpendicular that nothing could possibly climb its straight, smooth walls. On the left side was a similar pit, but one section of its walls was flat. The scientist handed the doctor a spyglass and asked her to examine this flat surface. She did so slowly and carefully.

At last she exclaimed, "A very remarkable fossil, Mr. Scheermann. I would like to call it wonderful, but if we use that word here, what have we left when we come to describe God? Really, with all these great evidences of a Supreme Being around you, I should think you would constantly think of better things—than some of the things you do think of."

"I thank you for the prettily worded sermon, Dr. Rock. However, there is no God in this part of Borneo except Herman Scheermann. Now, take your glass and look into the other pit. It is time for the feeding. Hear that gong? It is the signal. Every day I have five living cattle driven over this rock. The first gong tells the pets that dinner is on the way, while the next signal tells my natives to drive the cattle over the edge."

It is to Dr. Rock's credit that here, at this most horrible part of her life so far, her hand did not shake as she placed the glass to her eyes. A spyglass was not really necessary. At the bottom of the pit five large animals were running wildly around and jumping up on their hind legs, balancing themselves on their tails, like kangaroos. Even Helen Brown could easily see them with her unaided eye. The doctor looked long and earnestly, and then she passed the glass to her friend as she commented. "Dragonflies. Gigantic dragonflies. But what did you do with their wings?"

"Just as soon as they were hatched, I operated on their flying muscles. You see—if they could fly—they would not stay here."

"How very clever. And you want them to stay here?"

"For the time being. Later, by hundreds and thousands, I will let these beauties fly over the world. I have over fifty thousand of their eggs in cold storage. And I believe that if properly distributed, the insects would overrun the world in two years or perhaps three. One of those, flying, could capture the average airplane."

"I think that it could easily do that. How long are they?"

"Nearly one hundred feet. I presume you note the close resemblance between them and the fossil—?"

JUST then the gong sounded and the frightened bellowing of cattle was heard. On the rim, a hundred feet from where the ladies were standing, five steers came breaking through the brush, saw the rim of the pit, and tried to run back. But a pitiless cordon of spears drove them on, and one after one they jumped into the void.

Far below, the dragonflies waited, and as soon as the cattle landed on the rock floor of their pen, they sprang on them and tore them eagerly to pieces. The doctor's hand shook a little, but she took the glass from her belt and again looked through it.

At last she exclaimed, "They eat hair, hide, bones, and everything!"

"Certainly. They are hungry. I keep their appetite on a fine edge. Now, take your glass and look on the other side. Over in front of the fossil dragon. See those stakes? Every month we have a service here in honor of the Dragon God. The God gives his orders through the fossil mouth. The people, safely seated high up on the sides of the pit, hear, remember, and obey those orders. For those who fail to obey there is but one punishment—death. I am really the God. There is a small cave back of the fossil mouth. I stay there, and through the orders of the God I rule the people— with a rod of iron. At the same time I am kind to them.

"We have a meeting once a month. I was raised in the Lutheran church, but our meetings are different from the kind I attended as a boy. We wait till the full moon. When it reaches a certain part of the sky, this pit is illumined, like daylight. The people assemble. The God talks to them. They worship him. Flowers are hung on his tail. Then all retire to a safe place. I forgot to state that the food is tied to those stakes. No, not cattle, but live men and women who have disobeyed the orders of the Gods and, if all have been faithful during the past month, then slaves that have been captured, or sometimes the old and sick of the community serve. A large door is raised, which allows the dragons to enter the pit of worship. Amid the pleasant songs of the congregation they eat their monthly offering. That is all."

"Is that all?" asked Miss Helen Brown.

"Not all. I forgot one thing. Unless you ladies agree to my proposal and stay here with us, the three men will be tied to three stakes at the next meeting. If you do agree, I will liberate them, provided they promise me to keep the various pieces of information they have gained while here a solemn secret."

"You do not ask for much, do you, Mr. Scheermann?" asked Dr. Rock sarcastically.

"Not much, but then you forget that I am God. I have even condescended in asking at all. Gods take; they do not beg—for women."

"I cannot see clearly with these glasses," whispered the doctor. "How many stakes are there down there? Five. Then you can save one for me, and if you can be considerate enough, you can give me the stake next to Mr. Sterling Powers, so that our last hours may be spent together."

"So that is the way the wind blows?" sneeringly asked the scientist.

"That is the way it blows. With death near, it blows away many of my doubts. It blows hard enough to even remove the effluvium from you and your life. I see you as just an old man, a pitiful old man, who might have been somebody, but who has sold himself to the devils of life. I think that you are insane, Mr. Herman Scheermann."

The German looked at her. His lips tightened till they became just one white line.

"You are a remarkable woman," he finally answered. "Had we met in our youth, we would have faced the world together and accomplished wonders. I like to do ladies a favor, so I will make it possible for you to be near Sterling Powers—at once." He shouted an order in the native language and from the brush two men sprang, seized the woman and carried her away.

Helen Brown took the opportunity to spring on him. It was her ambition to hurl the two of them over the side of the precipice. She nearly succeeded, but help came in time, and the dragonflies lost a meal. After a struggle, she was subdued and held tightly by two of the guards.

Breathing heavily from her exertion, she cried, "You can tie me on the last stake!"

Scheermann brushed the dirt off his linen suit. "What a devil you are, Miss Brown. How fortunate that my man, Sakio, is muscular. You will attend the festival of the full moon but you will not be tied to a stake. That night you will be married to my heir. The ceremony will follow the feeding of the representatives of the God."

"I will not live to see it!"

"Oh! But you will. Suicide? Nonsense! You are too young for that. Wait till you see Sakio. He's a nice fellow."

CHAPTER FIFTEEN
Days Pass

THAT evening Miss Helen Brown took supper with Herman Scheermann and his first assistant, Nogi Sakio. The gentlemen were dressed in immaculate evening dress and Helen Brown, having made a complete inventory of the clothing that was in her room, had selected a white transparent velvet that harmonized well with her sunburned skin. During the afternoon she had done a lot of thinking. She realized that the three men were somewhere, helpless; otherwise they would have made an appearance before this time. She also knew, almost certainly, that her friend, Anna Rock, was with the men. The German had sent her there and she realized now that much of what he said he meant.

Of the entire party, she was the only one at liberty and able to do anything. There were some avenues that offered help and possibly escape. Could she reach the hydroplane and send an S. O. S. over the broadcaster? How about Sakio? If he loved glory and wealth and power and had to wait till the old man died, then perhaps he might be induced to kill Scheermann and let the party go, provided they promised to keep his secret. Or it might be, if only she could get a weapon, that she could kill them both. Then she would have to find the rest of the party.

One thing she determined—that she would show no fear. She could kill herself at any time. If she had to see her friends devoured by those giant dragonflies, she would face it and then die. She was not sure how, but there would be a way provided. And once again she worried over Timothy Jones. If only he was here. He had deliberately stayed away. They had invited him to join the expedition, and he had decided to remain in Shawnee and sell stockings. He knew the danger. He must have known the danger that they were going to be in, and he had kept out of it—and let them go. Had he warned them? It seemed that he had, but they had not believed him. That was what had hurt his pride—their constant thought that he was lying to them. He was a peculiar man. At times capable and at other times a fool. She was a college graduate and he an ex-grocery clerk! And now those differences were all leveled away, and in a week she would be dead. Anna would be dead. So would Powers and Packard and the nice Captain Lewellen. And Jones would stay at Shawnee and sell hose and serve tea in the afternoon to ladies from Philadelphia and New York, who were hunting new thrills.

At the supper, her conversation was sparkling. No one would have known there was a cloud on her mental horizon. She was witty; she laughed at Sakio's stories. She talked botany with the German. At eleven, they left the table. Nothing had been accomplished.

The next day was a day of similar failure. She took a sudden interest in silkworm culture. She allowed herself to be escorted through the mill by Sakio. She finally asked Scheermann to take her over to the valley where the worms were fed. A picnic was planned. She was carried over in a hammock on the shoulders of sturdy natives. Sakio walked gallantly by her side. She flirted with him. In the valley of mulberry trees she saw the worms in various stages of growth. She saw cocoons being spun. On the way back they passed a party of natives, carrying the cocoons to the silk mill. Two men carried one cocoon, slung from a twenty-foot pole.

An extra wide path had to be cut through the jungle, to allow them lots of room. Sakio explained that the least injury to a cocoon resulted in the loss of many yards of silk thread.

They were alone part of the time and Miss Brown, without a tremor, suggested that Scheermann be killed and that Sakio reign with her as his Queen. He laughed as he replied, "I will anyway when the Master dies. Why be precipitous?"

He treated it as a joke. She laughed away the idea that she was in earnest. She even allowed him to kiss her hand. They came back happy. That is, Sakio was happy. Helen Brown had played one of her aces and lost.

Meantime, the four were existing in the pit. For one hour of the twenty-four the sun, shining to the bottom, made life almost unendurable. The rest of the time the temperature was comfortable. At night it was cold. Food and water was sent down twice a day. The four were sure that they were going to die, and each spent the time prior to that death in his own way. The Professor made a study of the ants, flies, beetles, and centipedes that lived with them at the bottom of the dry well. Captain Lewellen wrote a daily entry in his diary. It was his hope that in some way this would survive him and the news of the last days of the party reach the outside world. With death but a few days distant, Dr. Rock and Sterling Powers threw all formalities to the wind and openly confessed their love to each other.

Three hours each day were spent in discussing every possible angle of the situation and devising plausible means of escape. On the fourth day a message was sent to Scheermann, offering a compromise. There was no answer. Another message offered ransom and complete secrecy. There was no answer.

The men started to dig a tunnel. It was a country of caves, and they thought that they might possibly break through into one and make a night attack on the German; at least they might recover their weapons and escape in the hydroplane. They were still digging on the sixth day. They knew that this was their last one. Careful observations of the moon warned them that it was nearly full.

And then a ladder was lowered to the floor of the well and Scheermann himself asked them to come up. They refused.

"Come and get us," yelled Lewellen.

A dozen natives came down the ladder. They were unarmed. There was a fight. A dozen more went down and at the end the three men and one woman were hauled up by ropes, their hands securely bound behind their backs and their ankles tied together. They were placed on the ground; in a row, like so many pieces of wood.

"I hate to be rough with you," purred Herman Scheermann, "but you make it so difficult. Why not be philosophers and die like Gods? I will give you each a drink of opium if you want it?"

He was standing too close. Lewellen rolled over and bit him in the leg. The German freed himself and gave the Captain a kick in the face.

"No opium now!" he cried. "Pity is wasted on such swine as you." And then he had them carried to the pit and tied to the stakes. It was early in the afternoon.

The sun was still reaching the sandy floor of the Temple, with merciless heat. Above them the fossil dragon seemed to smile sardonically down on them.

Packard and the Captain kept quiet.

Dr. Rock looked over to the stake where Sterling Powers was tied. She smiled at him.

"I am sorry, dear," she cried in a low tone, "that my hand cannot hold yours in these last hours."

"At least, our love can leap across the sands between us," he answered bravely. "I regret all the lonely years when you were practicing medicine and I was a broker in New York

City. There was only the Brooklyn Bridge between us, but we did not know. It takes great events to rouse some people to what life and love really mean. It took this dragonfly and an insane German and even death itself in our case, but now that we really know, I feel that death is not too great a price to pay. I would rather be here knowing that you love me, than be in my New York home and be ignorant of what you might have been in my life. I love you, Anna, and the fact that we are soon to die makes me love you with even greater tenderness."

The two middle-aged lovers smiled at each other.

CHAPTER SIXTEEN
The Dragon Speaks

LATE that same afternoon four native women walked into the room that had served as Helen Brown's prison. One talked enough English to make herself understood. She told the American woman that they had come to prepare her for the wedding that was to take place that night in the Temple of the Dragon and that they had been told that all four of them would feed the dragons if anything happened to the lady from far away before the marriage took place. They started in to dress the unwilling bride-elect.

Still later came presents: A beautiful diamond coronet from Scheermann and an equally beautiful bracelet from Nogi Sakio. She was asked to wear both presents. A light supper was served her in her room. Then came six native girls, virgins, dressed in white gauze and orchid, who were to serve as a singing escort. The day was light when the procession started toward the Temple. Helen Brown was still in hopes that something would happen.

They reached their seats just as the tropical daylight melted into dark. She saw that the natives were beginning to gather and fill the natural rock benches that began several hundred feet above the sandy floor of the Temple. There was still light enough to see her companions tied to the stakes in front of the fossil dragon. Soon, a singing band of natives came with torches, escorting the Oriental who was to be her bridegroom. He was dressed in the robes of his country. He was garbed simply, in silk that was made on the plantation— silk that would last a thousand years. He wore some jewelry. His guards were armed with swords and rifles. They also, as befitted their station, were splendidly arrayed in a uniform only used on gala days.

It became dark. Strain her eyes as she might, Helen Brown could see nothing. Above her there were stars; below her, a void. She knew that nothing would happen till the full moon was directly above the crater, would illumine it with a glory that only comes from the Mistress of the Night. Till then she could shut her eyes and pray. But she could not keep them shut. The tension was too great. After what seemed hours, she opened them and asked Sakio what time it was. He replied that it was eight. Would the lady take some champagne or orange juice? Some was here for her delight, served on crushed ice. Helen thought of those people tied to the stakes and replied that she did not care for any.

In the darkness, the fossil dragonfly began to glow till it was entirely distinct, something separate from the rest of the rock. The two eyes beamed like electric lights in red globes. She mentioned this to Sakio.

"I think, Madam, that it is radium. Perhaps the eyes are emeralds. The God has been worshiped for many centuries. I have been here two years, but I have never cared to examine the Dragon God closely. I have no religion. I am what is called in your language an atheist. Had I the faith of my ancestors, I would not be here. I stay here, in this Temple, and watch the sacrifice, because I am a part of the machinery.

Perhaps someday the Master will make me the great part of the machinery. Meantime, I follow the customs of the community."

"Do you approve of all this?"

"What difference does it make? It is evidently necessary. By these means the Master has ruled. By such means I will rule when my time comes. The matter of belief, of approval, does not play any part. These men die tonight. If not tonight they die later. One of your religions says there is a program and that when your turn to die comes, you die. The God wills it. Is there much difference between such a God and this one?"

And now the moonbeams fell slanting on one face of the rock wall and a few of them reached the sanded floor. It was the time for the song, and after the song, for the words of wisdom, the orders from the Dragon God. The song that the natives chanted was very old. A few instruments kept the time and carried the melody.

Sakio, apparently anxious to entertain, whispered to Helen Brown, "Ancient stuff, Lady. Very ancient and honorably old. The Master has found signs of venerable life around here. Perhaps a hundred thousand years ago men sang here to the God. Perhaps he used the same music. Very interesting. We play a small part with our few years of life. Bah! I am a fatalist. Why fight and struggle against the inevitable?"

The song ended and a dark silence brooded over the Temple. Then, in a singsong low tone, the Dragon God spoke. All that he said was in the native tongue, a language equally well understood by the natives, Chinese and Japanese who heard it. For what seemed many minutes he spoke, and as he gave his orders, the moonlight flooded more and more of the pit till at last the entire enormous crater was illumined. Then the voice ceased.

"The God tells them to sing and be gone," whispered Sakio to his future bride. "He says that it is not the right night. That nothing shall be done till tomorrow night. The God says that he is displeased with the appearance of the sacrifice. They should have been washed and garlanded with flowers. He directs that they be taken from here and properly cared for. Peculiar? What difference does it make if they are to be eaten anyway? He says we are to be married tomorrow night, and that as the worshipers leave, they are to throw their flowers at your feet. I have seen several of these worships, but never have I seen this. Perhaps the God grows old?"

The natives began to sing the same old song as they left the Temple. One by one they passed the stone bench on which Helen Brown sat and placed their flower at her feet. Soon she was nearly covered with scented orchids, lovely passionflowers. They flowed past her and partly covered Sakio. Then the singing died away for sheer want of singers, and up to the two, sitting by themselves with their guards of honor behind them, came Herman Scheermann. He was dressed in white linen. His beard was perfectly trimmed. A snow-white turban decorated in front by an enormous sardonyx covered his head. The moonlight was intense. His face could easily be seen. He wore a worried smile.

Before Miss Brown he made a deep bow, and said, "I salute the happy pair. A marriage is made in Heaven; so you are really man and wife though the ceremony will not take place till tomorrow evening. What a capricious God our Dragon Deity is! He wanted his victims washed and perfumed and garlanded. Think of that, Miss Brown. Or should I address you as Mrs. Sakio? At the same time, the Dragon is a diplomat. I am but his servant. He bade me give out clothes, food, new rifles. He advised me to give a holiday and for one month to abolish my law in regard to head hunting. No wonder the worshipers were glad to delay their entertainment for one more day! Suppose we go back to the house Sakio. I am sorry to keep you from your bride tonight, but duty calls. I had a serious message from the coast today. It seems that one of our silk carriers is not true to his trust. I want you to take men with you and bring him here. Tomorrow we will feed him to the Dragon. I have written all details on this paper. Take it, and if you prize my friendship and the love of your bride, be sure to come back tomorrow evening—with your man."

The worried Sakio bowed and took the written order.

He kissed Miss Brown's hand and started to leave. Scheermann called after him, "You might as well take these men with you, Sakio. They are all good men. I will escort your bride to my residence—I and the band of singing girls. I have ordered torches sent to me."

So, with torchbearers in front, singing girls behind and Herman Scheermann by her side, Helen Brown walked back to the palatial residence by the lake. Her mind was a whirling swarm of questions. What had happened? What good would it do if it all had to be gone over again tomorrow? At last she arrived at a conclusion that seemed perfect to her. Scheermann had done all this to increase their torture. He was a man who delighted in doing these things and doing them perfectly. That was it. He simply wanted to drive them a little closer to the edge of total despair before the end actually came.

Once in the house, Scheermann dismissed the singing girls and suggested to Miss Brown that she go into the parlor and there wait for the rest of the party. A supper would be served later on. He had ordered it. It would take some time for the other four to wash and dress, but as soon as they were ready, they would eat, would she mind eating in her bridal clothes?

An hour later Dr. Rock walked into the parlor. The two women flew into each other's arms, but neither shed a single tear. The three men followed, dressed in the clothing that they had worn when they left the ship in the hydroplane. Around their waists were cartridge belts and their revolvers were in their holsters. They had shaved and washed, and although thin, seemed none the worse for the mental torture that they had undergone. Scheermann bowed to each one in turn and asked that they precede him to the banquet hall.

"You will excuse the supper?" he purred. "I thought there would just be three of us, but Sakio had to attend to some matters for me; so, even with the addition of the four of you, we will only be six. I think there will be food enough. I have asked that all the viands be placed on the table and have dismissed the servants for the night. This is a holiday night for them. They go to the forest and sing and dance and make merry and I do not want to spoil their happiness. So the six of us are alone. You gentlemen need not be afraid tonight. In order that you may feel at ease, I directed that your weapons be restored to you, also the necessary ammunition. Now, let's eat."

CHAPTER SEVENTEEN
The Explanation

THERE was very little conversation during the greater part of the meal. In spite of the absence of servants, there was a marked restraint on the part of the five guests of Herman Scheermann. The men kept their eyes on him. Now that they were at least armed with their revolvers, they were determined not to face death again at the stake. They were each of them willing to die fighting—but they did not want to serve as a meal to monstrosities without being able in any way to defend themselves. Scheermann seemed to be the only one who was really at his ease, though he did not say much till nearly the end of the meal. Then he pushed his plate to one side and asked for their attention.

"My position in this community," he began, "is a very peculiar one. For thirty years I have ruled probably the greatest aggregation of desperate men that the world has ever seen. One hundred percent of my men are fugitives from justice, having committed every possible major crime. They have come to me because they know that I will never surrender them to justice. In order to make them good servants I have provided them with women, some native, others imported from Asia. With this class for followers, I have done some very remarkable work here.

"But they are a hard class to rule. There have been attempts to overthrow me. Once I had a very difficult struggle to win out. After some experimentation, I decided to add to the colony a tribe of native headhunters. They wanted heads, and often I had heads to give them—heads alive and on the right shoulders. I was able to use them to keep discipline among my jailbirds. If any fugitive became too hard to handle, he became a victim for the headhunter. Clever?

"But it was the organization of the monthly festival and the development of the giant dragonflies that finally made my power supreme. All men lust after blood and cruel sights and I gave my followers their hearts' desire, in this instance, at least. They became fond of the sights which attended the feeding of the representatives of the Gods and finally I swore them to a blood vow—that all strangers entering the territory should be sacrificed. So when you came they expected that you should go the way of all strangers. Had I shown any weakness, any hesitation, I would have had difficulty in controlling them. I might have lost my head. Consequently, I used diplomacy and made them think that your death would be the usual one. And when the time came, I made use of the voice of the God and caused a postponement of twenty-four hours."

For a moment he paused and seemed to fumble at his belt. Then he pulled an automatic and fired three shots into a curtain, covering a doorway. Running up, he jerked this curtain loose and a dead Chinaman dropped to the floor.

"I saw the curtain move and guessed we had an eavesdropper. He heard what I said. Had it gone through camp, how long would you have lived? Fortunately, all the servants are on their monthly debauch. This dead man understood English. I think that he was doing it at the request of Sakio, whom perhaps I misjudge. Anyway, I have given you a few hours of liberty. I think that your hydroplane is in as good condition as it was when you came here. I would advise you to go down at once, see that the motor is running and that you have enough gas. I will give you some if you need it, and just as soon as morning comes and the day dawns, go back in a direct line to the capital. Start your steamer and go. I will tie myself up and tell my people that you took me unaware, beat me, and made your escape."

"That is mighty fine of you, Mr. Scheermann," commented Dr. Rock.

"Just the courtesy one white man owes others of his race. I never have gone completely native."

"If we are going to leave in a few hours, I ought to go down and see how the motor is," said Captain Lewellen. "Suppose we state our position plainly. We came of our own accord and we are leaving through the courtesy of this man. I do not recall that we have made any promises to him."

"No promises are necessary, Captain. I have always been able to care for myself. But I agree with you that no time is to be lost in preparing for the return trip. Suppose we go? Miss Brown, I will have to ask you to wear that wedding dress and take the jewels. It will make my story to the natives and Sakio more plausible."

Down at the shore they found the hydroplane exactly where they had left it. Apparently, it was unharmed. They reached it at once, but it was four before the Captain announced that he was ready. Even then some more gasoline had to be carried down. The three men and the two women made themselves comfortable, and then Scheermann started to say goodbye. He thanked them for the kindly way that they had acted. He shook hands with the ladies and then, just as he was shaking hands with the Professor, Captain Lewellen hit him on the head with the butt of a revolver, dragged his unconscious form over the side, hog-tied him with a rope, and started the engine. As the dawn came over the lake, the hydroplane rose from the water and started on a direct line over the forests to Sandakan.

No one said a word on the return trip. The capital was sighted, the steamer located in the harbor. By a fine piece of landing, Lewellen brought the hydroplane alongside the steamer and shouted for O'Malley. That startled individual came on deck with a tin of coffee and a sea biscuit in his hand.

"I swear!" he yelled, dropping the coffee and the biscuit. "Here are the folks come home alive and another one with them!"

At the captain's orders, a rope was lowered and the unconscious Scheermann hauled on deck.

"A job for you, O'Malley," said the captain. "Keep this bird safe."

CHAPTER EIGHTEEN
A Conference with the Governor

WITHOUT the loss of a minute, Captain Lewellen had the sailors row him to shore. He made a direct line to the governor's mansion and nearly had a fight with the butler who refused him admission, because the governor saw no one till ten. However, the matter finally reached the right person, and word was sent down to have the captain stay to breakfast.

The captain could hardly wait till coffee was served. Then he blurted out, "General Wood! We had rather a bad time of it, but we are all back, and I brought with me the biggest criminal you ever saw. He is the head of that gang of criminals up there and I think that just as soon as you can do so, you had better go up there and clean them out. It is a long story to tell you, and I do not want to spoil your breakfast; but we have enough on this man to hang him a dozen times. He came within an ace of having us killed and eaten, but for some reason lost his nerve. At the last moment I hit him on the head and brought him along with us."

"Well, anyhow, I am glad you are all back. It was a foolish thing to do, captain, especially to take the women with you. I told you that it was next door to hell, but you would not believe me. Finish your coffee and then I will go right back with you to the steamer. I want to see this man. Scheermann, you say? No doubt I have seen him a hundred times and not known who he was. Are you through? Suppose we go?"

Two hours after he had left the steamer, the captain was back again, and with him General Wood. The ladies were congratulated on their escape and the men mildly scolded for going into such danger. Then the governor asked to be taken to see the prisoner. He found him in one of the cabins, conscious, but still tied, with O'Malley watching over him with a revolver.

"So, you are Scheermann?" asked the governor.

"At least I am still alive. If that blow had landed on my scalp instead of on my turban, it would not make any difference now what my name is or was or will be. Glory!

How my head swims—and a bump there as large as an egg. Who hit me? Was it Dr. Rock?"

"No...I hit you," answered Lewellen. "You are either a criminal or an insane man. In either case, you had to be delivered to the authorities. This is the governor of North Borneo, General Wood. I am going to place you in his care."

"Anything to say, Mr. Scheermann?" asked the governor.

"Yes. Are you going to prefer charges against me?"

"Not personally. I do not know anything about you. But I will give full credit to anything this gentleman may prefer to say."

"Well, am I under arrest?"

"You are."

"Then, please take me to land and put me in a safe place. There are people, even on this ship, that would kill me if they had a chance. You do not want to see me murdered, do you, Governor? You do not want to see a dagger in the heart of an old sick man, do you?"

The governor turned to the captain.

"Take those ropes off him. I will take him back with me and be responsible for him."

"Be careful, General. He is a desperate man."

The governor laughed.

"I am accustomed to danger. I used to be heavyweight champion at Oxford. Do you think I am afraid of a little old man? Come now, liberate him. When you are ready to prefer charges, you will find him in my care."

"I will be over right after dinner."

"Fine! This man and I will be in my office at that time. Suppose we say two o'clock? Perhaps you better bring the whole party so the prosecuting attorney can hear every side of the story."

As the boat neared the shore, Scheermann whispered to the governor, "Can I see you alone for a few minutes?"

"See here, man. No rough stuff. I am armed and will shoot at the first false move."

"Oh, I know that," moaned Scheermann," and it's not bribery, either. My head is aching so I can hardly think, but there is something I want to show you. I think you ought to know it at once. Make it awkward if you wait too long. I cannot talk much with this headache, but you can see for yourself."

They went into the governor's office and that worthy dismissed his secretary. Scheermann opened his white coat, took some papers out of a pocket, handed them to General Wood, and collapsed on the floor.

AT two that afternoon the party of explorers arrived at the stately mansion of the governor. They were shown, with great ceremony, into the executive offices, and punch was served to the men and tea to the ladies. After some informal chatting, the governor proposed that they start with the business of the meeting, the preferring of charges against Scheermann. Stenographers were brought in, the prosecuting attorney and several other lawyers were called and finally Scheermann himself, a little pale, but almost recovered from the blow that had so nearly cost him his life.

While the stenographers rapidly took complete notes, one after the other of the five companions in this expedition that had so nearly cost them their lives gave statements of the incidents of the days while they were away from Sandakan. Dr. Rock was especially careful to give full details in regard to the silkworm industry, the breeding of the giant dragonflies and the threat that these enormous creatures had for the human race.

"Fortunately," she concluded, "we have secured Scheermann, but his chief helper, Sakio, is still at large, and there are thousands of eggs that can be dropped into the swamps and rivers by anyone. I feel that these facts should be given careful consideration and no time lost in sending a large air force to these caves to destroy the eggs, kill the living dragonflies, and, for all eternity, rid the human race of this flying threat."

"I think that is a very good suggestion," agreed the governor, heartily. "I will put it in force and will ask Captain Lewellen to be good enough to serve as the guide. I think that we have sufficient details to make a satisfactory charge against Scheermann and Sakio. Unfortunately, the Sakio is not here and I cannot proceed against this man whom you call Scheermann. He showed me some papers this morning that put a new light on the matter."

Captain Lewellen jumped up from his chair and threw his right hand into the air, as he cried, "I do not care what he told you, General Wood! Whatever he said was a lie! He is the most clever criminal I ever met. If there is any chance of his pulling the wool over your eyes, I will kill him myself, right here and now. Damned if I don't!"

"Now, Captain, calm yourself," urged the governor. "I am willing to admit that you had a hard time and were nervous and all that sort of thing, but let me tell you what the right of this is. This man is not Scheermann."

"Not Scheermann?" cried Dr. Rock.

"No. He is not Scheermann. He is just dressed in Scheermann's clothes, and he has on a beard to make him look like Scheermann. He showed me his papers and established his identity, as far as I am concerned. He is attached to the British Foreign Office and was assigned, by special request, to the clearing up of certain matters connected with North Borneo. I was not notified of it because it was thought by the Secretary of Colonial Affairs that the fewer who were in on the thing the better it would be. I want to introduce to you Major Percy King of the

Foreign Office. Major, perhaps if you took off your beard and wig and put on your glass, you would convince them of the difference between you and Mr. Scheermann. Suppose you retire to my inner office and make the change?"

In a few minutes the mystery man came out. He was no longer the old German, but a rather youthful, good-looking chap, with a smooth face, black hair, no beard and a monocle screwed into his left eye. He stood rather bashfully by the door, as he remarked, "Happy to meet all of you. Sorry we had such a mess of it, but I was all on my own and had to go slow. Good we got out alive."

Captain Lewellen walked over to him and looked at the bump on his head, and then the flyer showed his real manhood.

"Sorry I biffed you one, King, my lad," he said, holding out his hand.

"That is all right. Stop thinking about it. Had to be done. All in the game," replied Major King, as he took the professor's hand and shook it heartily.

"And now, Major King," said the governor, "tell your story. I know our friends are anxious to hear it."

"Not much to tell, General. I went up there and looked around and found out that Scheermann was in the habit of talking out of the fossil dragon's head the night of the full moon. I had studied the old fellow a lot; so, up I went into the cave, right back of the fossil head, and when the German came to do his mumbo-jumbo work, I had an argument with him. After that, I did the talking. I put on his clothes and some false hair, and you know the rest. I knew Scheermann had spies here; so I wanted to represent him as long as possible. I want Sakio to think Scheermann is a prisoner. That is all. I am sorry you men had such a hard time, but it is all over now."

"Just one question, Major King," interrupted Sterling Powers. "You have not told us where Scheermann is?"

The major dropped his eyeglass, put it back on, stroked his little mustache, and looked peculiarly inane.

"By Jove! I overlooked that. The German? Why, after the argument I left him in the cave. You see, he was dead. I had to get rough. He would not be safe otherwise."

He scratched his head.

"Peculiar. Never thought of it till you asked me the question. Glad you did. Might have failed to put it in my report. Been a bad blunder. Kill a man and then forget it. Must have been the blow on the head."

There being nothing more to do the Americans started to go back to their steamer. The governor insisted that they return that night for supper with him. They did so. All dressed in their best, and Miss Helen Brown, because she had nothing prettier, wore the dress that she was to have been married in; also the jewels that had been given to her. At the table, she had Major King on her right and Captain Lewellen on her left. The conversation was mainly on the left. The major seemed to be lost in thought. After supper, the party walked through the governor's gardens. Major King asked Miss Helen Brown to walk with him. They had hardly started when they met Sterling Powers and Dr. Rock, who were announcing their engagement and receiving the hearty congratulations of everyone.

At last Miss Brown sat down on a marble bench. The major stood in back of her. He dropped his monocle.

"I am glad it is all over, Miss Brown. This is the last piece of work I am going to do of this kind. I am wealthy and I think that I should go into some less dangerous business."

"Have you anything in mind?" asked the lady.

"Yes. I thought that if I could be appointed a manager of an A. and P. store I would be happy in the work. Selling hose is cleaner, but I like to see the little children run in the store for bananas and the old women come in for pig liver and butter substitute."

The woman almost jumped in the air as she shook the man by the shoulders and cried, "Timothy Jones!"

"Yes, Miss Brown, always Timothy Jones to you. And now there is something I want to tell you, but I am afraid."

"Why are you afraid, Timothy?"

"I feel that you would not believe me. So many things I told you, you never did believe."

"Why not take a chance and tell me anyway? Why not try it?"

"By Jove! A sporting proposition! I will. *I LOVE YOU!*"

"I believe *that,*" said Miss Helen Brown, slowly, falling into his arms.

THE END

If you've enjoyed this book, you will not want to miss these terrific titles…

ARMCHAIR SCI-FI & HORROR DOUBLE NOVELS, $12.95 each

D-171   **REGAN'S PLANET** by Robert Silverberg
SOMEONE TO WATCH OVER ME by H. L. Gold and Floyd Gale

D-172   **PEOPLE MINUS X** by Raymond Z. Gallun
THE SAVAGE MACHINE by Randall Garrett

D-173   **THE FACE BEYOND THE VEIL** by Rog Phillips
REST IN AGONY by Paul W. Fairman

D-174   **VIRGIN OF VALKARION** by Poul Anderson
EARTH ALERT by Kris Neville

D-175   **WHEN THE ATOMS FAILED** by John W. Campbell, Jr.
DRAGONS OF SPACE by Aladra Septama

D-176   **THE TATTOOED MAN** by Edmond Hamilton
A RESCUE FROM JUPITER by Gawain Edwards

D-177   **THE FLYING THREAT** by David H. Keller, M. D.
THE FIFTH-DIMENSION TUBE by Murray Leinster

D-178   **LAST DAYS OF THRONAS** by S. J. Byrne
GODDESS OF WORLD 21 by Henry Slesar

D-179   **THE MOTHER WORLD** by B. Wallis & George C. Wallis
BEYOND THE VANISHING POINT by Ray Cummings

D-180   **DARK DESTINY** by Dwight V. Swain
SECRET OF PLANETOID 88 by Ed Earl Repp

ARMCHAIR SCIENCE FICTION CLASSICS, $12.95 each

C-69   **EXILES OF THE MOON**
by Nathan Schachner & Arthur Leo Zagut

C-70   **SKYLARK OF SPACE**
by E. E. "Doc' Smith

ARMCHAIR MYSTERY-CRIME DOUBLE NOVELS, $12.95 each

B-11   **THE BABY DOLL MURDERS** by James O. Causey
DEATH HITCHES A RIDE by Martin L. Weiss

B-12   **THE DOVE** by Milton Ozaki
THE GLASS LADDER by Paul W. Fairman

B-13   **THE NAKED STORM** by C. M. Kornbluth
THE MAN OUTSIDE by Alexander Blade

If you've enjoyed this book, you will not want to miss these terrific titles...

ARMCHAIR SCI-FI & HORROR DOUBLE NOVELS, $12.95 each

D-31   **A HOAX IN TIME** by Keith Laumer
        INSIDE EARTH by Poul Anderson

D-32   **TERROR STATION** by Dwight V. Swain
        THE WEAPON FROM ETERNITY by Dwight V. Swain

D-33   **THE SHIP FROM INFINITY** by Edmond Hamilton
        TAKEOFF by C. M. Kornbluth

D-34   **THE METAL DOOM** by David H. Keller
        TWELVE TIMES ZERO by Howard Browne

D-35   **HUNTERS OUT OF SPACE** by Joseph Kelleam
        INVASION FROM THE DEEP by Paul W. Fairman,

D-36   **THE BEES OF DEATH** by Robert Moore Williams
        A PLAGUE OF PYTHONS by Frederik Pohl

D-37   **THE LORDS OF QUARMALL** by Fritz Leiber and Harry Fischer
        BEACON TO ELSEWHERE by James H. Schmitz

D-38   **BEYOND PLUTO** by John S. Campbell
        ARTERY OF FIRE by Thomas N. Scortia

D-39   **SPECIAL DELIVERY** by Kris Neville
        NO TIME FOR TOFFEE by Charles F. Meyers

D-40   **RECALLED TO LIFE** by Robert Silverberg
        JUNGLE IN THE SKY by Milton Lesser

ARMCHAIR SCIENCE FICTION CLASSICS, $12.95 each

C-10   **MARS IS MY DESTINATION**
        by Frank Belknap Long

C-11   **SPACE PLAGUE**
        by George O. Smith

C-12   **SO SHALL YE REAP**
        by Rog Phillips

ARMCHAIR SCI-FI & HORROR GEMS SERIES, $12.95 each

G-3   **SCIENCE FICTION GEMS, Vol. Two**
        James Blish and others

G-4   **HORROR GEMS, Vol. Two**
        Joseph Payne Brennan and others

If you've enjoyed this book, you will not want to miss these terrific titles…

ARMCHAIR SCI-FI & HORROR DOUBLE NOVELS, $12.95 each

D-61   **THE MAN WHO STOPPED AT NOTHING** by Paul W. Fairman
TEN FROM INFINITY by Ivar Jorgensen

D-62   **WORLDS WITHIN** by Rog Phillips
THE SLAVE by C.M. Kornbluth

D-63   **SECRET OF THE BLACK PLANET** by Milton Lesser
THE OUTCASTS OF SOLAR III by Emmett McDowell

D-64   **WEB OF THE WORLDS** by Harry Harrison and Katherine MacLean
RULE GOLDEN by Damon Knight

D-65   **TEN TO THE STARS** by Raymond Z. Gallun
THE CONQUERORS by David H. Keller, M. D.

D-66   **THE HORDE FROM INFINITY** by Dwight V. Swain
THE DAY THE EARTH FROZE by Gerald Hatch

D-67   **THE WAR OF THE WORLDS** by H. G. Wells
THE TIME MACHINE by H. G. Wells

D-68   **STARCOMBERS** by Edmond Hamilton
THE YEAR WHEN STARDUST FELL by Raymond F. Jones

D-69   **HOCUS-POCUS UNIVERSE** by Jack Williamson
QUEEN OF THE PANTHER WORLD by Berkeley Livingston

D-70   **BATTERING RAMS OF SPACE** by Don Wilcox
DOOMSDAY WING by George H. Smith

ARMCHAIR SCIENCE FICTION CLASSICS, $12.95 each

C-19   **EMPIRE OF JEGGA**
by David V. Reed

C-20   **THE TOMORROW PEOPLE**
by Judith Merril

C-21   **THE MAN FROM YESTERDAY**
by Howard Browne as by Lee Francis

C-22   **THE TIME TRADERS**
by Andre Norton

C-23   **ISLANDS OF SPACE**
by John W. Campbell

C-24   **THE GALAXY PRIMES**
by E. E. "Doc" Smith

ABOUT MURRAY LEINSTER

Murray Leinster...

...was born William F. Jenkins on June 16th, 1896 in Norfolk, Va. His writing career began in 1916 with the publishing of his first story, "The Foreigner" in *The Smart Set* magazine. Although he is considered one of the great writers of the science fiction genre, in his early years Leinster wrote many tales i n other genres: jungle, m ystery, horror, and western. Leinster broke into the science fiction field with his story, "The Runaway Skyscraper," which appeared i n a 1919 issue of *Argosy* magazine. Duri ng the '30s, '40s, ' 50s, and '60s Leinster was a regul ar contributor to well-known pulp and digest m agazines such as *Astounding Stories, Amazing Stories,* and *Weird Tales*. Leinster is considered the father of "parallel universe" stories wi th the publication of his 1934 story, "Sidewise in Time." During hi s long career Lei nster was nominated for many writing awards, including the coveted Hugo Award, which he won in 1956 for his novelette, "Exploration Team." During his science fiction career, Leinster published over 30 nov els and over 170 short stories. He passed away on June 8th, 1975.

AUTHOR PORTRAIT

MURRAY LEINSTER, 1896-1975

THE FIFTH-
DIMENSION
TUBE

By
MURRAY LEINSTER

ARMCHAIR FICTION
PO Box 4369, Medford, Oregon 97504

*For more information about Armchair Books and products, visit our
website at…*

www.armchairfiction.com

Or email us at…

armchairfiction@yahoo.com

CHAPTER ONE
The Tube

THE generator rumbled and roared, building up to its maximum speed. The whole laboratory quivered from its vibration. The dynamo hummed and whined and the night silence outside seemed to make the noises within more deafening. Tommy Reames ran his eyes again over the power-leads to the monstrous, misshapen coils. Professor Denham bent over one of them, straightened, and nodded. Tommy Reames nodded to Evelyn, and she threw the heavy multiple-pole switch.

There was a flash of jumping current. The masses of metal on the floor seemed to leap into ungainly life. The whine of the dynamo rose to a scream and its brushes streaked blue flame. The metal things on the floor flicked together and were a tube, three feet and more in diameter. That tube writhed and twisted. It began to form itself into an awkward and seemingly impossible shape, while metal surfaces sliding on each other produced screams that cut through the din of the motor and dynamo. The writhing tube strained and wriggled. Then there was a queer, inaudible *snap* and something gave. A part of the tube quivered into nothingness. Another part hurt the eyes that looked upon it.

And then there was the smell of burned insulation and a wire was arcing somewhere, while thick rubbery smoke arose. A fuse blew out with a thunderous report, and Tommy Reames leaped to the suddenly racing motor-generator. The motor died amid gasps and rumblings. And Tommy Reames looked anxiously at the Fifth-Dimension Tube.

It was important, that Tube. Through it, Tommy Reames and Professor Denham had reason to believe they could travel to another universe, of which other men had only dreamed.

139

And it was important in other ways, too. At the moment Evelyn Denham threw the switch, last-edition newspapers in Chicago were showing headlines about "King" Jacaro's forfeiture of two hundred thousand dollars' bail by failing to appear in court. King Jacaro was a lord of racketeerdom.

Evelyn swayed...and the thing moved!

Illustration by H. W. Wesso

While Tommy inspected the Tube anxiously, a certain chief of police in a small town upstate was telling feverishly over the telephone of a posse having killed a monster lizard by torchlight, having discovered it in the act of devouring a cow. The lizard was eight feet high, walked on its hind legs, and had a collar of solid gold about its neck. And jewel importers, in New York, were in anxious conference about a flood of untraced jewels upon the market. Their origin was unknown. The Fifth-Dimension Tube ultimately affected all of those affairs, and the Death Mist as well. And—though it was not considered dangerous then—everybody remembers the Death Mist now.

But at the moment Professor Denham stared at the Tube concernedly, his daughter Evelyn shivered from pure excitement as she looked at it, and a red-headed man named Smithers looked impassively from the Tube to Tommy Reames and back again. He'd done most of the mechanical work on the Tube's parts, and he was as anxious as the rest. But nobody thought of the world outside the laboratory.

Professor Denham moved suddenly. He was nearest to the open end of the Tube. He sniffed curiously and seemed to listen. Within seconds the others became aware of a new smell in the laboratory. It seemed to come from the Tube itself, and it was a warm, damp smell that could only be imagined as coming from a jungle in the tropics. There were the rich odors of feverishly growing things; the heavy fragrance of unknown tropic blossoms, and a background of some curious blend of scents and smells which was alien and luring, and exotic. The whole was like the smell of another planet of the jungles of a strange world which men had never trod. And then, definitely coming out of the Tube, there was a hollow, booming noise.

IT had been echoed and re-echoed amid the twistings of the Tube, but only an animal could have made it. It grew louder, a monstrous roar. Then yells sounded suddenly above it—human yells, wild yells, insane, half-gibbering yells of hysterical excitement and blood lust. The beast-thing bellowed and an ululating chorus of joyous screams arose. The laboratory reverberated with the thunderous noise. Then there was the sound of crashing and of paddings, and abruptly the noise was diminishing as if its source were moving farther away. The beast-thing roared and bellowed as if in agony, and the yelling noise seemed to show that men were following close upon its flanks.

Those in the laboratory seemed to awaken as if from a bad dream. Denham was kneeling before the mouth of the Tube, an automatic rifle in his hands. Tommy Reames stood grimly before Evelyn. He'd snatched up a pair of automatic pistols. Smithers clutched a spanner and watched the mouth of the Tube with a strained attention. Evelyn stood shivering behind Tommy.

Tommy said with a hint of grim humor:

"I don't think there's any doubt about the Tube having gotten through. That's the Fifth Dimension planet, all right."

He smiled at Evelyn. She was deathly pale.

"I—remember—hearing noises like that…"

Denham stood up. He painstakingly slipped on the safety of his rifle and laid it on a bench with the other guns. There was a small arsenal on a bench at one side of the laboratory. The array looked much more like arms for in expedition into dangerous territory than a normal part of apparatus for an experiment in rather abstruse mathematical physics. There were even gas masks on the bench, and some of those converted brass Very pistols now used only for discharging tear- and sternutatory-gas bombs.

"The Tube wasn't seen, anyhow," said Professor Denham briskly. "Who's going through first?"

Tommy slung a cartridge belt about his waist and a gas mask about his neck.

"I am," he said shortly. "We'll want to camouflage the mouth of the Tube. I'll watch a bit before I get out."

He crawled into the mouth of the twisted pipe.

THE Tube was nearly three feet across, each section was five feet long, and there were gigantic solenoids at each end of each section.

It was not an experiment made at random, nor was the world to which it reached an unknown one to Tommy or to Denham. Months before, Denham had built an instrument which would bend a ray of light into the Fifth Dimension and had found that he could fix a telescope to the device and look into a new and wholly strange cosmos. He had seen tree-fern jungles and a monstrous red sun, and all the flora and fauna of a planet in the carboniferous period of development. More, by the accident of its placing he had seen the towers and the pinnacles of a city whose walls and towers seemed plated with gold.

Having gone so far, he had devised a catapult which literally flung objects to the surface of that incredible world. Insects, birds, and at last a cat had made the journey unharmed, and he had built a steel globe in which to attempt the journey in person. His daughter Evelyn had demanded to accompany him, and he believed it safe. The trip had been made in security, but return was another matter. A laboratory assistant, Von Holtz, had sent them into the Fifth Dimension, only to betray them. One King Jacaro, lord of Chicago racketeers, was convinced by him of the existence of the golden city of that other world, and that it was full of delectable loot. He offered a bribe past envy for the secret of Denham's apparatus. And Von Holtz had removed the apparatus for Denham's return before working the catapult to send him on his strange journey. He wanted to be free to sell full privileges of rapine and murder to Jacaro.

The result was unexpected. Von Holtz could not unravel the secret of the catapult he himself had operated. He could not sell the secret for which he had committed a crime. In desperation he called in Tommy Reames—rather more than an amateur in mathematical physics—showed him Evelyn and her father marooned in a tree-fern jungle, and hypocritically asked for aid.

Tommy's enthusiastic efforts soon became more than merely enthusiastic. The men of the Golden City remained invisible, but there were strange, half-mad outlaws of the jungles who hated the city. Tommy Reames had watched helplessly as they hunted for the occupants of the steel globe. He had worked frenziedly to achieve a rescue. In the course of his labor he discovered the treachery of Von Holtz as well as the secret of the catapult, and with the aid of Smithers—who had helped to build the original catapult—he made a new small device to achieve the original end.

THE whole affair came to an end on one mad afternoon when the Ragged Men captured first an inhabitant of the Golden City, and then Denham and Evelyn in a forlorn attempt at rescue. Tommy Reames went mad. He used a tiny sub-machine gun upon the Ragged Men through the model magnetic catapult he had made, and contrived communication with Denham afterward. Instructed by Denham, he brought about the return of father and daughter to Earth just before Ragged Men and Earthling alike would have perished in a vengeful gas cloud from the Golden City. Even then, though, his triumph was incomplete because Von Holtz had gotten word to Jacaro, and nattily-dressed gunmen raided the laboratory and made off with the model catapult, leaving three bullets in Tommy and one in Smithers as souvenirs.

Now, using the principle developed in the catapult, Tommy and Denham had built a large Tube, and as Tommy climbed along its corrugated interior he knew a good part of what he should expect at the other end. A steady current of air blew past him. It was laden with a myriad unfamiliar scents. The Tube was a tunnel from one set of dimensions to another, a permanent way from Earth to a strange, carboniferous-period planet on which a monstrous dull-red sun shone hotly. Tommy should come out into a tree-fern forest whose lush vegetation would hide the sky, and which furnished a lurking place not only for strange reptilian monsters akin to those of the long-dead past of Earth, but for the bands of ragged, half-mad human beings who were outlaws from the civilization of which Denham and Evelyn had seen proofs.

TOMMY reached the third bend in the Tube. By now he had lost all sense of orientation. An object may be bent through one right angle only in two dimensions, and a second perfect right angle—at ninety degrees to all former paths—only in three dimensions. It follows that a third perfect right angle requires four dimensions for existence, and four perfect right angles five. The Tube bent itself through four perfect right angles, and since no human-being can ever have experience of more than three dimensions, plus time, it followed that Tommy was experiencing other dimensions than those of Earth as soon as he passed the third bend. In short, he was in another cosmos.

There was a moment of awful sickness as he passed the third bend. He was hideously dizzy when he passed the fourth. For a time he felt as if he had no weight at all. But then, quite abruptly, he was climbing vertically upward and the soughing of tree-fern fronds was loud in his ears, and suddenly the end of the Tube was under his fingers and he stared out into the world of the Fifth Dimension.

Now a gentle wind blew in his face. Tree-ferns rose to incredible heights above his head, and now and again by the movements of their fronds he caught stray glimpses of unfamiliar stars. There were red stars, and blue ones, and once he caught sight of a clearly distinguishable double star, of which each component was visible to the naked eye. And very, very far away he heard the beastly yellings he knew must be the outlaws, the Ragged Men, feasting horribly on half-scorched flesh torn from the quivering, yet-living flanks of a monstrous reptile.

Something moved, whimpered—and fled suddenly. It sounded like a human being. And Tommy Reames was struck with the utterly impossible conviction that he had heard just that sound before. It was not dangerous, in any case, and he watched, and listened, and presently he slipped from the mouth of the Tube and by the glow of a flashlight stripped foliage from nearby growths and piled it about the Tube's mouth. And then, because the purpose of the Tube was not adventure but science, he went back down into the laboratory.

THE three men, with Evelyn, worked until dawn at the rest of their preparations for the use of the Tube. All that time the laboratory was filled with the heavy fragrance of a tree-fern jungle upon an unknown planet. The heavy, sickly-sweet scents of closed jungle blossoms filled their nostrils. The reek of feverishly growing green things saturated the air. A steady wind blew down the Tube, and it bore innumerable unfamiliar odors into the laboratory. Once a gigantic moth bumped and blundered into the Tube, and finally crawled heavily out into the light. It was scaled, and terrible because of its monstrous size, but it had broken a wing and could not fly. So it crawled with feverish haste toward a brilliant electric light. Its eyes were especially horrible because they were not compound like the moths of Earth. They were single, like those of a man, and were fixed in an expression of utter, fascinated hypnosis. The thing looked horribly human with those eyes staring from an insect's head, and Smithers killed it in a flash of nerve-racked horror. None of them were able to go on with their work until the thing and its fascinated, staring eyes had been put out of sight. Then they labored on with the smell of the jungles of that unnamed planet thick about them, and noises now and then coming down the Tube. There were roars, and growlings, and once there was a thin high sound which seemed like the far-distant, death-startled scream of a man.

CHAPTER TWO
The Death Mist

TOMMY REAMES saw the red sun rise while he was on guard at the mouth of the Tube. The tree-ferns above him came into view as vague gray outlines. The many-colored stars grew pale. And presently a bit of crimson light peeped through the jungle somewhere. It moved along the horizon and very slowly grew higher. For a moment, Tommy saw the huge, dull-red ball that was the sun of this alien planet. Queer mosses took form and color in the daylight, displaying colors never seen on Earth. He saw flying things dart among the tree-fern fronds, and some were scaled and some were not, but none of them were feathered.

Then a tiny buzzing noise. The telephone that now rested below the lip of the Tube was being used from the laboratory.

"Smithers will relieve you," said Denham's voice in the receiver. "Come on down. We're not the only people experimenting with the Fifth Dimension. Jacaro's been working, and all hell's loose!"

Tommy slid down the Tube in an instant. The four right-angled turns made him sick and dizzy again, but he came out with his jaw set grimly. There was good reason for Tommy's interest in Jacaro. Besides sides three bullet wounds, Tommy owed Jacaro something for stealing the first model Tube.

He emerged in the laboratory on his hands and knees as the size of the Tube made necessary. Smithers smiled placidly at him and crawled in to take his place.

"What the devil happened?" demanded Tommy.

Denham was bitter. He held a newspaper before him. Evelyn had brought coffee and the morning paper to the laboratory. She seemed rather pale.

"Jacaro's gotten through too!" snapped Denham. "He's gotten in a pack of trouble. And he's loosed the devil on Earth. Here—look!" He jabbed his finger at one headline. "And here—and here!" He thrust at others. "Here's proof."

The first headline read: "KING JACARO FORFEITS BOND." Smaller headings beneath it read: "Racketeer Missing for Income Tax Trial. $200,000 Bail Forfeited." The second headline was in smaller type: "Monster Lizard Killed! Giant Meat Eater Brought Down by Rifleman. Akin to Ancient Dinosaurs, Say Scientists."

"JACARO'S missing," said Denham harshly. "This article says he's vanished, and with him a dozen of his most prominent gunmen. You know he had a model catapult to duplicate—the one he got from you. Von Holtz could arrange the construction of a big Tube for him. And he knew about the Golden City. Look!"

His finger, trembling, tapped on the flashlight picture of the giant lizard of which the story told. And it was a giant. A rope had upheld a colossal, leering, reptilian head while men with rifles posed self-consciously beside the dead creature. It was as big as a horse, and at first glance its kinship to the extinct dinosaurs of Earth was plain. Huge teeth in sharklike rows. A long, trailing tail. But there was a collar about the beast-thing's neck.

"It had killed and was devouring a cow when they shot it," said Denham bitterly. "There've been reports of these creatures for days—so the news story says. They weren't printed because nobody believed them. But there are a couple of people missing. A searching party was hunting for them. They found this!"

Tommy Reames stared at the picture. His face went grimmer still. He thought of sounds he had heard beyond the Tube, not long since.

"There's no question where they came from. The Fifth Dimension. But if Jacaro brought them back, he's a fool."

"Jacaro's missing," said Denham savagely. "Don't you understand? He could get through to the Golden City. These beast-things are proof somebody did. And these things came down the Tube that somebody travelled through. Jacaro wouldn't send them, but somebody did. They've got collars around their necks! Who sent them? And why?"

TOMMY'S eyes narrowed.

"If civilized men found the mouth of a Tube, it would seem like the mouth of an artificial tunnel or a cave—"

"And if annoying vermin, like Jacaro's gunmen..." Denham's voice was brittle, "...had come out of it, why, intelligent men might send something living and deadly down it, as men on Earth will send ferrets down a rat-hole! To wipe out the breed! That's what's happened! Jacaro's gone through and attacked the Golden City. They've found his Tube. And they've sent these things down..."

"If *we* found rats coming from a rat-hole," said Tommy very quietly, "and ferrets went down and didn't come up, we'd gas them."

"And so," Denham told him, "so would the Golden City."

He pointed to a boxed double paragraph news story under leaded twenty-point headline: "Poisonous Fog Kills Wild Life."

The story was not alarming. It said merely that state game wardens had found numerous dead game animals in a thinly-settled district near Coltsville, N.Y., and on investigation had found a bank of mist, all of half a mile across, which seemed to have caused the trouble. State chemists and biologists were investigating the phenomenon. Curiously, the bank of mist seemed not to dissipate in a normal fashion. Samples of the fog were being analyzed. It was probably akin to the Belgian fogs which on several occasions had caused much loss of life. The mist was especially interesting because in sunlight it displayed prismatic colorings. State troopers were warning the inhabitants of the neighborhood.

"The gassing's started," said Denham savagely. "I know a gas that shows rainbow colors. The Golden City uses it. So we've got to find Jacaro's Tube and seal it, or only God knows what will come out of it next. I'm going off, Tommy. You and Smithers guard our Tube. Blow it up, if necessary. It's dangerous. I'll get some authority in Albany, and we'll find Jacaro's Tube and blast it shut."

Tommy nodded, his eyes keen and thoughtful. Denham hurried out.

MINUTES later, only, they heard the roar of a car motor going down the long lane away from the laboratory. Evelyn tried to smile at Tommy.

"It seems terrible, dangerous."

Tommy considered and shrugged.

"This news is old," he observed. "This paper was printed last night. I think I'll make a couple of long-distance calls. If the Golden City's had trouble with Jacaro, it's going to make things bad for us."

He swept his eyes about and frowningly loaded a light rifle. He put it convenient to Evelyn's hand and made for the dwelling-house and the telephone. It was odd that as he emerged into the open air, the familiar smells of Earth struck his nostrils as strange and unaccustomed. The laboratory was redolent of the tree-fern forest into which the Tube extended. And Smithers was watching amid those dank, incredible carboniferous-period growths now.

Tommy put through calls, seeing all his and Denham's plans for a peaceful exploration party and amicable contact with the civilization of that other planet, utterly shattered by presumed outrages by Jacaro. He made call after call, and his demands for information grew more urgent as he got closer to the source of trouble. His cause for worry was verified long before he had finished. Even as he made the first call, New York newspapers had crowded a second-grade murder off their front pages to make room for the white mist upstate.

THE early-morning editions had termed it a "poisonous fog." The breakfast editions spoke of it as a "poison fog." But it grew and moved and by the time Tommy had a clear line to get actual information about it, a tabloid had christened it the "Death Mist" and there were three chartered planes circling about it for the benefit of their newspapers. State troopers were being reinforced. At ten o'clock it was necessary to post extra traffic police to take care of the cars headed upstate to look at the mystery. At eleven it began to move! Sluggishly, to be sure, and rather raggedly, but it undoubtedly moved, and as undoubtedly it moved independently of the wind.

It was at twelve-thirty that the first casualty occurred. Before that time, the police had frantically demanded that the flood of sightseers be stopped. The Death Mist covered a square mile or more. It clung to the ground, nowhere more than fifty or sixty feet high, and glittered with all the colors of the rainbow. It moved with a velocity of anywhere from ten to twenty miles an hour. In its path were a myriad small tragedies—nesting birds stiff and still, and rabbits and other small furry bodies contorted in queer agonized postures. But until twelve-thirty no human beings were known to be its victims.

Then, though, it was moving blindly across the wind with a thin trailing edge behind it and a rolling billow of descending mist as its forefront. It rolled up to and across a concrete highway, watched by perspiring motor cops who had performed miracles in clearing a path for it among the horde of sightseeing cars. It swept on into a spindling pine wood. Behind it lay a thinning sheet of vapor—thick white mist which seemed to rise and move more swiftly to overtake the main body. It lay across the highway in a sheet which was ten feet deep, then thinned to six, to three…

THE mist was no more than a foot thick, when a party of motorists essayed to drive through it as through a sheet of water. They dodged a swearing motorcycle cop and, yelling hilariously, plunged forward. It happened that they had not more than a hundred yards to go, so the whole thing was plainly seen.

The car was ten yards across the sheet of mist before the effect of its motion was apparent. Then the mist, torn by the car-eddy, swirled madly in their wake. The motorists yelled delightedly. There is a picture extant, taken at just this moment. It shows the driver with a foolish grin on his face, clutching the wheel and very obviously stepping on the accelerator. A pandemonium of triumphant, hilarious shouting—and then a very sudden silence.

The car roared on. The road curved slightly. The car did not. It went off the road, turned over, and its engine shrieked itself into silence. The Death Mist went on, draining from the roadway to follow the tall, prismatically-colored cloud. It moved swiftly and blindly. To the circling planes above it, it seemed like a blind thing imagining itself confined, and searching for the edges of its prison. It gave an uncanny impression of being directed by intelligence. But the Death Mist, itself, was not alive.

Neither were the occupants of the motor car.

When Tommy got back to the laboratory after his last call for news, he found Evelyn in the act of starting to fetch him.

"Smithers called," she said uneasily. "He says something's moving about—" The buzzer of the telephone was humming stridently. Tommy answered quickly.

"Just want you handy," said Smithers' calm voice. "I might have to duck. Some Ragged Men are chasin' something. Get set, will ya?"

"Ready for anything," Tommy assured him.

Then he made it true: rifles handy, a sub-machine gun, grenades, gas masks. He handed one to Evelyn. Smithers had one already. Then Tommy waited, grimly ready by the Tube-mouth.

THE warm, scent-laden breeze blew upon him. Straining his ears, he could hear the sound of tree-fern fronds clashing in the wind. He heard the louder sounds made by Smithers, stirring ever so slightly in the Tube. And then he caught a vague, distant uproar. It would have been faint and confused at best but the Tube was partly blocked by Smithers' body, and there were the multiple bends further to complicate the echoes. It was no more than a formless tumult through which faint yells came occasionally. It drew nearer and nearer. Tommy heard Smithers stir suddenly, almost as if he had jumped. Then there were scrapings which could only mean one thing: Smithers was climbing out of the Tube into the jungle of the Fifth-Dimension world.

The noise rose abruptly to a roar as the muffling effect of Smithers' body was removed. The yells were sharp and savage and half mad. There was a sudden crackling sound and a voice screamed:

"*Gott!*"

The hair rose at the back of Tommy's neck. Then there came the deafening report of an automatic pistol roaring itself empty above the end of the Tube. Smithers' voice, vastly calm:

"It's a'right, Mr. Reames. Don't worry."

A second pistol took up the fusillade. Yells and howls and screams arose. Men fled. Something came crashing to the mouth of the Tube. Smithers' voice again, with purring note in it: "Get down there. I'll hold 'em off." Then single deliberately spaced shots, while something came stumbling, fumbling, squirming down through the Tube, so filling it that Smithers' shooting was muted.

THEN came the subtly different explosions of the Very pistols, discharging gas bombs. And Tommy drew back, his jaw set, and he stood with his weapons very ready indeed, and a scratched, bleeding, exhausted, panting, terror-stricken human being in the tattered costume of Earth crawled from the Tube and groveled on the floor before him.

Evelyn gave a little exclamation, partly of disgust and partly of horror. Because this man, who had had come from the world of the Fifth Dimension, was wholly familiar. He was tall, and he was lean, emaciated now; he wept sobbingly behind thick-lensed spectacles, and his lips were far too full and red. His name was Von Holtz; he had once been laboratory assistant to Professor Denham, and he had betrayed Evelyn and her father to the most ghastly of possible fates for a bribe offered him by Jacaro. Now he groveled. He was horrible to look at. Where he was not scratched and torn his flesh was reddened as if by fire. He was exhausted, and trembling with an awful terror, and he gasped out abject, placatory ejaculations and suddenly collapsed into a sobbing mass on the floor.

Smithers emerged from the Tube with a look of unpleasant satisfaction on his face.

"I chased off the Ragged Men with sneeze gas," he observed with a vast calmness. "They ain't comin' back for a while. An' I always wanted to break this guy's neck. I think I'll do it now."

"Not till I've questioned him," said Tommy savagely. "He and Jacaro have started hell to popping, with that Tube design they stole from me. He's got to stay alive and tell us how to stop it. Von Holtz, talk! And talk quick, or back you go through the Tube for the Ragged Men to work on!"

CHAPTER THREE
The Tree-Fern Jungle

TOMMY watched Smithers drive away. The sun was sinking low toward the west, and the car stirred up a cloud of light-encarmined dust as it sped down the long, narrow lane to the main road. The laboratory had intentionally been built in an isolated spot, but at the moment Tommy would have given a good deal for a few men nearby. Smithers was taking Von Holtz to Albany to add his information to Denham's pleas. Denham had ordered it, when they reached him by phone after hours of effort. Smithers had to go, to guard against Von Holtz's escape, even sick and ill as he was. And Evelyn had refused to go with him.

"If I stay in the laboratory," she insisted fiercely, "you can slip down and I can blow up the Tube after you, if the Ragged Men don't stay away. But by yourself..."

Tommy did not consent, but he was helpless. There was danger from the Tube. Not only from ghastly animals which might come through, but from men. Smithers had fought the Ragged Men above it. He had chased them off, but they would come back. Perhaps they would come very soon, perhaps not until Denham and Smithers had returned. If they could be held off, the as yet unknown dangers from the other Tube—of which only the lizards and the Death Mist were certainties—might be counteracted. In any case, the Tube must not be destroyed until its defense was hopeless.

Tommy made up a grim bundle to go through the Tube with him: the sub-machine gun, extra drums of shells, more gas bombs and half a dozen grenades. He hung the various objects about himself. Evelyn watched him miserably.

"You—you'll be careful, Tommy?"

"Nothing else but," said Tommy. He grinned reassuringly. "There's nothing to it, really. Just sitting still, listening. If I pop off some fireworks I'll just have to sit down and watch them run."

HE settled his gas mask about his neck and started to enter the Tube. Evelyn touched his arm.

"I'm—frightened, Tommy."

"Shucks!" said Tommy. "Also a couple of tut-tuts." He stood up, put his arms about her, and kissed her until she smiled. "Feel better now?" he asked interestedly.

"Y-yes..."

"Fine!" said Tommy, and grinned again. "When you feel scared again, ring me on the phone and I'll give you another treatment."

But her smile faded as, beaming at her, he crawled into the first section of the Tube. And his own expression grew serious enough when she could see him no longer. The situation was not comfortable. Evelyn intended to marry him and he had to keep her cheerful, but he wished she were well away from here.

He tried to move cautiously through the Tube, but his bundles bumped and rattled. It seemed hours before he was climbing up the last section into the tree-fern jungle. He was caution itself as he peered over the edge. It was already night upon Earth, but here the monstrous, dull-red sun was barely sinking. It moved slowly along the horizon as it dipped, but presently a gray cast come over the colorings in the forest. Flying things came clattering homeward through the masses of fern-fronds overhead. He saw a projectile-like thing with a lizard's head and jaws go darting through an incredibly small opening. It seemed to have no wings at all. But then, in one instant, a vast wing-surface flashed out, made a single gigantic flap—and the thing was a projectile again, darting through a *cheraux-de-frise* of interlaced fronds without a sign of wings to support it.

TOMMY inspected his surroundings with an infinite care. As the darkness deepened he meditatively taped a flashlight below the barrel of the sub-machine gun. Turned on, it would cast a pitiless light upon his target, and the sights would be silhouetted against the thing to be killed. He hung his grenades in a handy row just inside the mouth of the Tube and set his gas bombs conveniently in place, then settled down to watch.

155

It was assuredly necessary. Von Holtz's story confirmed his own and Denham's guesses and made their worst fears seem optimistic. Von Holtz had made a Tube for Jacaro, working from the model of Tommy's own construction. It had been completed nearly a month before. But no jungle odors had seeped through that other Tube on its completion. It opened in a sub-cellar of a structure in the Golden City itself, the city of towers and soaring spires Denham had glimpsed long months before. By sheer fortune it opened upon a rarely used storeroom where improbable small animals—the equivalent of rats—played obscenely in the light of ever-glowing panels in the wall.

For two days of the Fifth-Dimension world Jacaro and his gunmen lay quiet. During two nights they made infinitely cautious reconnaissance. The second night it was necessary to kill two men who sighted the tiny exploring party. But the killing was done with silenced automatics, and there was no alarm. The third night they lay still, fearing an ambush. The fourth night Jacaro struck.

HE and his men fled back to their Tube with plunder and precious gems. Their loot was vast even beyond their hopes, though they had killed other men in gathering it. The Golden City was rich beyond belief. The very crust of the Fifth-Dimension world seemed to be composed of other substances than those of Earth. The common metals of Earth were rare or even unknown. The rarer metals of Earth were the commonplace ones in the Golden City. Even the roofs seemed plated with gold, but Jacaro's gunmen saw not one particle of iron save in a ring they took from a dead man's finger. There, an acid-etched plate of steel was set as if to be used for a signet.

Von Holtz had accompanied the raiders perforce on every journey. Jeweled bearings for motors; objects of commonest use, made of gold beat thin for lightness; huge ingots of silver for industry; once a queer-shaped spool of platinum wire that it took two men to carry—these things made up the loot they scurried back to their rathole with. Five raids they made, and twenty men they shot down before they came upon disaster. On the sixth raid an outcry rose and an ambush fell upon them.

Flashes of incredibly vivid actinic flame leaped from queer engines that opened upon them. Curious small truncheonlike weapons spat paralyzing electric shocks upon them. The twelve gangsters fought with the desperation of cornered rats, with notched and explosive bullets and with streams of lead from tommy-guns.

A CHANCE bullet blew something up. One of the flame weapons flew to bits, spouting what seemed to be liquid thermit upon friend and foe alike. The way of the gangsters back to their Tube was barred. The route they knew was a chaos of scorched bodies and melting metal. The thermit flowed in all directions, seeming to grow in volume as it flamed. Jacaro and his gangsters fled. They broke through the shaken remnants of the ambush. The six of them who survived the fighting found a man somnolently driving a ground vehicle with two wheels. They burst upon him and, with their scared faces constituting threats in themselves, forced him to drive them out of the Golden City. They fled along aluminum roads into the tree-fern forests, while the sky behind them seemed to flame as the city woke to the tumult in its ways.

They killed the driver of their vehicle when he refused to take them farther, and it was that murder which saved their lives. It was seen by Ragged Men, the outlaws of the jungle, and it proved their enmity to the Golden City. The Ragged Men greeted them joyously and fed them, and enlisted their aid in a savage attack on a land-convoy on the way to the city. Their weapons carried the convoy, and they watched wounded prisoners killed with excruciating tortures…

They were with the Ragged Men now, Von Holtz believed. He had fled a week or more before, when Jacaro—already learning the language of his half-mad allies—began to plan a grandiose attack upon the Golden City. Von Holtz was born a coward, and he knew where Tommy Reames and Denham would shortly thrust a Tube through. It would come out just where the catapult had flung Evelyn and Denham, months before, the same spot where he had marooned them. He searched desperately for that Tube, and failed to find it. He was chased by carnivores, scratched by thorns, and at last pursued by a yelling horde of human devils who were fired into by Smithers from the mouth of the just-finished Tube.

TOMMY debated the story grimly as he stood guard in the Tube in the humid jungle night. Many-colored stars winked fitfully through the thatch of giant ferns overhead. The wind soughed unsteadily above the jungle. There were queer creakings, and once or twice there were distant cries, and when the wind died down there was a deep-toned croaking audible somewhere which sounded rather like the croaking of unthinkably, monstrous frogs. But it could not be that, of course. And once there was the sound of dainty movement and something passed nearby. Tommy Reames saw the shadowy outline of a bulk so vast that it turned him cold to think about it, and it did not seem fair for any creature as huge as that to move so quietly.

Then there was a little scuffling noise beneath him. A hand touched his foot.

"It's—it's me, Tommy." Evelyn crowded up beside him and whispered shakenly: "It—it was so lonesome down there, so quiet."

Tommy frowned unhappily in the darkness. If he sent her back, she would know it was because he knew danger lurked here. Then she would worry. If he did not send her back...

"I'll go back the minute you tell me," she insisted forlornly. "Honestly. But—I was lonesome."

Tommy slipped his arm about her.

"Woman," he said sternly. "I'm going to let you stay ten minutes, so you can brag to our grandchildren that you were the first Earth-girl ever to be kissed in the Fifth Dimension. But I want you down in the laboratory so you won't be in my way if I start running!"

His tone was the right one. She even laughed a little, softly, as he pressed her to him. Then she clung to his hand and tried eagerly to pierce the darkness all about them.

"You'll be able to see something presently," he assured her in a low tone. "Just keep quiet, now."

SHE gazed up at the stars, then around in the so-nearly complete obscurity. Tommy answered her comments abstractedly, after a little. He was not quite sure that certain irregular sounds, yet far distant, were not actually quite regular ones. The Ragged Men Smithers had shot into had run away. But they would come back and they might come with Jacaro and his gunmen as allies. If those distant sounds were men...

She withdrew her hand from his. Her back was toward him then, as she tried to pierce the darkness with her eyes. Tommy listened uneasily to the distant sound. Suddenly he felt Evelyn bump against his shoulder. He turned sharply—and she was out of the Tube! She was walking steadily off into the darkness!

"Evelyn! Evelyn!"

She did not falter or turn. He switched on the flashlight beneath his gun barrel and leaped out of the Tube himself. The light swept about. Evelyn's lithe figure kept moving away from him. Then his heart stood still. There were eyes beyond her in the darkness, huge, monstrous, steady eyes, half a yard apart in a head like something out of hell. And he could not fire because Evelyn was between the Thing and himself. Its eyes glowed unholily—fascinating, hypnotic, insane...

EVELYN swayed ... and the Thing moved! Tommy leaped like a madman shouting. As his feet struck the ground a mass of sold-seeming fungus gave way beneath him. He fell sprawling, but clutching the gun fast. The spreading beam of the flashlight showed him Evelyn turning, her face filled with a

159

wakening horror—the horror of one released from the fascination of a snake. She screamed his name.

Then a huge lizard paw swept forward and seized her body. A second gripped her as she screamed again. And Tommy Reames was deathly, terribly cool. The whole thing had happened in seconds only. He was submerged in slimy, sticky ooze which was the crushed fungus that had tripped him. But he cleared the gun. The flashlight limned a ghastly, obscenely fat body and a long tapering tail. Tommy aimed at the base of that tail and pulled the trigger, praying frenziedly.

A stream of flame leaped from the gun-muzzle. Explosive bullets uttered their queer cracking noise. The thing screamed horribly. Its cry was hoarsely shrill. The flashlight showed it swinging ponderously about, with Evelyn held fast against its body in a fashion horribly reminiscent of a child holding a doll.

Tommy was scrambling upright. Jaws clamped, cold horror filling him, he aimed again, at the sharp-toothed head above Evelyn's body. He could not try a heart shot with her in the way. Again the gun spat out a burst of explosive lead. And Tommy should have been sickened by the effect of detonating missiles. The thing's lower jaw was shattered, half severed, made useless. It should have been killed a dozen times over.

But it screamed again until the jungle rang with the uproar, and then it fled, still screaming and still holding Evelyn clutched fast against its scaly breast.

CHAPTER FOUR
The Fifth-Dimension World

TOMMY flung himself in pursuit, despairing. Evelyn cried out once more as the lumbering thing fled with her, giving utterance to shrieking outcries at which the tree-fern jungle shook. It leaped once, upon monstrous hind legs, but came crashing heavily to the ground. Tommy's explosive bullets had shattered the bones which supported the balancing tail. Now that huge fleshy member dragged uselessly. The thing could not progress in its normal fashion of leaps covering many yards. It began to waddle clumsily, shrieking, with Evelyn clasped close. Its jaw was a shattered horror. It went marching insanely through the blackness of the jungle, and with it went the unholy din of its anguish, and behind it Tommy Reames came flinging himself frenziedly in pursuit.

Normally, the thing should have distanced him in seconds. Even crippled as it was, it moved swiftly. The scaly, duck-shaped head reared a good twenty feet above the fallen tree-fern fronds which carpeted the jungle. The monstrous splayed feet stretched a good yard and a half from front to rear upon the ground. Even its waddling footprints were yards apart, and it moved in terror.

Tommy tripped, fell, and got to his feet again, and the shrieking tumult was farther away. He raced madly toward the sound, the flashlight beam cutting swordlike through the blackness. He caught sight of the warty, scaly bulk of the monster at the extreme limit of the rays. It was moving faster than he could travel. He sobbed helpless curses at the thing and put forth superhuman exertions. He leaped fallen tree-fern trunks, he splashed through shallow ponds—later, when he knew something of the inhabitants of such pools, Tommy would turn cold at that memory—and raced on, gasping for breath while the shrieking of the thing that bore Evelyn grew more and more distant.

IN five minutes he was almost strangling and the thing was half a mile ahead of him. In ten, he was exhausted, and the shrieking noise it made as it waddled away was distinctly fainter. In fifteen minutes he only heard its hooting scream between the harsh laboring rasps of his own breath as he drew it into tortured lungs. But he ran on. He leaped and climbed and ran in a terrible obliviousness to all dangers the jungle might hold.

He leaped down from one toppled tree-trunk upon what seemed be another. But the thing he landed upon gave beneath his boots in the unmistakable fashion of yielding flesh.

Something vast and angry stirred and hissed furiously. Something—a head, perhaps—whipped toward him among the fallen fern-fronds. But he was racing on, sobbing, cursing, praying all at once.

Then suddenly he broke out into a profuse sweat. His breathing became easier, and then he was running lightly. His second wind had come to him. He was no longer exhausted. He felt as if he could run forever, and ran on more swiftly still. Suddenly the flashlight beam showed him a deep furrow in the rotting vegetation underfoot, and something glistened. A musky reek filled his nostrils. The thing's trail—the furrow left by its dragging tail! That musky reek was the thing's blood. It was bleeding from the wounds the explosive bullets had made. It was spouting whatever filthy fluid ran in its veins even as it waddled onward, screaming.

Five minutes more, and he felt that he was gaining on it. Then, and he was sure of it. But it was half an hour before he actually overtook the injured monster marching like a mad machine. Its mutilated ducklike head held high, its colossal feet lifting one after the other in a heavy, slowing waddle, and its hoarse screams re-echoing in a senseless uproar of agony.

TOMMY'S hands were shaking, but his brain was cool with a vast coolness. He raced past the shrieking monster, and halted in its path. He saw Evelyn, a huddled bundle, clasped still to the creature's scaly breast. And Tommy sent a burst of explosive bullets into a gigantic, foot thick ankle-joint.

The monster toppled, and flung out its prehensile lizard claws in an instinctive effort to catch itself. Evelyn was thrown clear. And Tommy, standing alone in the blackness of a carboniferous jungle upon an alien planet, sent bullet after bullet into the shaking, obscenely flabby body of the thing. The bullets penetrated, and exploded. Great masses of flesh upheaved and fell away. Great gouts of awful smelling fluid were flung out and blown to mist by the explosions. The thing did not so much die as disintegrate under the storm of detonating missiles.

Then Tommy went to Evelyn. He was wild with grief. He had no faintest hope that she could still be living. But as he picked her up she moaned softly, and when he cried her name she clung to him, pressing close in an agony of thankfulness almost as devastating as her fear had been.

It was minutes before either of them could think of anything other than her safety and the fact that they were together again. But then Tommy said, in a shaken effort to be himself again:

"I—I'd have done better if—if I'd had roller skates, maybe." His grin was wholly unconvincing. "Why'd you get out of the Tube?"

"Its eyes!" Evelyn shuddered, her own eyes hidden against Tommy's shoulder. "I saw them suddenly, looking at me. And I—hadn't any will. I felt myself getting out of the Tube and walking toward it. It was like the way a snake fascinates—hypnotizes—a bird..."

A vagrant wind-eddy submerged them in the foul reek of the dead thing's flesh. Tommy stirred.

"Ugh! Let's get out of this. There'll be things coming to feed on that carcass. They'll smell it."

Evelyn tried to stand, and succeeded. She clung to his hand.

"Do you think you can find the Tube again?"

Tommy was already thinking of that. He grimaced.

"Probably. Back-trail the damned thing. If the flashlight battery holds out. Its tail left plenty of sign for us to follow."

THEY started. And Evelyn had literally been forgotten in its agony by the monster which had carried her. Its body, though scaled and warty, was flabby and soft. Pressed against its breast she had been half strangled, but had no injuries beyond huge, purple bruises which had not yet reached the point of stiffness. She followed Tommy gamely, and the need for action kept her from yielding to the reaction from her terror.

For a long, long time they back-trailed. Less than fifteen minutes after leaving the carcass of the thing Tommy had killed, they heard beast-roarings and the sound of fighting. But that noise died away as they traveled. Presently they reached the spot where Tommy had leaped upon a huge living thing. It was gone now, but the impress of a body the thickness of a barrel remained upon the rotted vegetation of the jungle floor. Evelyn shivered when Tommy pointed it out.

"It was large," said Tommy ruefully. "I didn't even get a good look it the thing. Probably just as well, though. I might have been—er—delayed. Good Lord! What's that?"

A light had sprung into being somewhere. It was bright. It was blinding in its brilliance. Coming through the tangled jungle growth, it seemed as if spears of flame shot through the air, irradiating stray patches of scabrous tree-trunk with unbearable light. For an instant the illumination held. Then there was a distant, cracking detonation. The unmistakable explosion of gun-cotton split the air, and its echoes rolled and reverberated through the jungle. The light went out. Then came a thin, high yelling sound which, faint as it was, had something of the quality of hysterical glee. That crazy ululation kept up for several minutes. Evelyn shivered.

"The Ragged Men," said Tommy very quietly. "They sneaked up on the Tube. They flung blazing thermit, or something like it, with a weapon captured from the Golden City. That explosion was the grenades going off. I'm afraid the Tube's blown up, Evelyn."

She caught her breath, looking mutely up at him.

"Here's a pistol," he said briefly, "and shells. There's no use our going to the Tube to-night. It would be dangerous. We'll do our investigating at dawn."

HE found a crevice where tree-fern trunks grew close together and closed in three sides of a sort of roofless cave. He seated himself grimly at the opening to wait for daybreak. He was not easy in his mind. There had been two Tubes to the Fifth-Dimension world. One had been made by Jacaro for his gunmen. That was now held by the men of the Golden City, as was proved by carnivorous lizards and the Death Mist that had come down it. The other was now blown up or, worse, in the hands of the Ragged Men. In any case Tommy and Evelyn were isolated upon a strange planet in a strange universe. To fall into the hands of the Ragged Men was to die horribly, and the Golden City would not now welcome inhabitants of the world Jacaro and his men had come from. To the civilized men of this world, Jacaro's raids would seem invasion. They would seem acts of war on the part of the people of Earth. And the people of Earth, all of them, would seem enemies. Jacaro would never be identified as an unauthorized invader. He would seem to be a scout, an advance guard, a spy, for hordes of other invaders yet to come.

As the long night wore away, Tommy's grim hopelessness intensified. The Ragged Men would hunt them for sport and out of hatred for all sane human beings. The men of the Golden City would be merciless to compatriots of Jacaro's gunmen. And Tommy had Evelyn to look out for.

WHEN dawn came, his face was drawn and lined. Evelyn woke with a little gasp, staring affrightedly about her. Then she tried gamely to smile.

"Morning, Tommy," she said shakily. She added in a brave attempt at levity: "Where do we go from here?"

"We look at the Tube," said Tommy heavily. "There's a bare chance…"

He led the way as on the night before, with his gun held ready. They traveled for half an hour through the awakening jungle. Then for long, long minutes Tommy searched for a sign of living men before he ventured forth to look at the wreckage of the Tube. He found no live men, and only two dead ones. But a glimpse of their bestial, vice-ridden faces was enough to remove any regret for their deaths.

The Tube was shattered. Its mouth had belled out and broken by the explosion of the grenades hung within it. A part of the metal was molten—from the thermit, past question. There was a veritable crater fifteen feet across where the Tube had come through, and there were only shattered shreds of metal where the first bend had been. Tommy regarded the wreckage grimly. A pair of oxidized copper wires, their insulation burnt off, stung his eyes as he traced them to where they vanished in torn-up earth. He took them in his bare hands. The tingling sting of a low-voltage current made his heart leap. Then he smiled grimly. He touched them to each other. Dot-dot-dot—dash-dash-dash—dot-dot-dot. S O S! If there was anybody in the laboratory, that would tell them.

His hands stung sharply. Someone was there, ringing the phone! Evelyn came toward him, her face resolutely cheerful.

"No hope, Tommy?" she asked. "I just saw the telephone, all battered up. I guess we're pretty badly off."

"Get it!" said Tommy feverishly. "For Heaven's sake, get it! The phone wires weren't broken. If we can make it work…"

THE instrument was a wreck. It was crumpled and torn and apparently useless. The diaphragm of the receiver was punctured. The transmitter seemed to have been crushed. But Tommy worked desperately over them, and twisted the earth-wires into place.

"Hello, hello, hello!"

The voice that answered was Smithers', strained and fearful:

"Mr. Reames! Thank Gawd! What's happened? Is Miss Evelyn all right?"

"So far," said Tommy. "Listen!" He told curtly just what had happened. "Now, what's happened on Earth?"

"Hell!" panted Smithers bitterly. "Hell's been poppin'! The Death Mist's two miles across an' still growin an' movin'. Four townships under martial law an' movin' out the people. It got thirty of 'em this morning. An' they think the professor's crazy an' nobody'll listen to him!"

"Damn!" said Tommy. He considered, grimly. "Look here, Von Holtz ought to convince them."

"He caved in, outa his head, before I got to Albany. He's in hospital now, ravin'. He's got some kinda fever the doctors don't know nothin' about. Sick as hell!"

Tommy compressed his lips. Matters were more desperate even than he had believed. He informed his helper measuredly:

"Evelyn and I can't stay around here, Smithers. The Ragged Men may come back, and it'll be weeks before you and the professor can get another Tube through. I'm going to make for the Golden City and work on them there to cut off the Death Mist."

There was an inarticulate sound from Smithers.

"Tell the professor. If he can find Jacaro's Tube, he'll work out some way to communicate through it. We've got to stop that Death Mist somehow. And we don't know what else they may try."

Smithers tried to speak, and could not. He merely made grief-stricken noises. He worshiped Evelyn and she was isolated in a hostile world which was vastly more unreachable than could be measured by millions or trillions of miles. But at last he said unsteadily:

"We'll be comin', Mr. Reames. We'll come, if we have t' blow half the world apart!"

Tommy said grimly: "Then hunt up the Golden City and bring extra ammunition. Mostly explosive bullets. Good-by."

HE untwisted the wires from the shattered phone units and thrust them in his pocket. Evelyn was picking up stray small objects from the ground.

"I've found some cartridges, Tommy," she said constrainedly, "and a pistol I think will work."

"Then listen for visitors," commanded Tommy, "while I look for more."

For half in hour he scoured the area around the shattered Tube. He found where some clumsy-wheeled thing had been pushed to a spot near the Tube—undoubtedly the machine which had sprayed the flaming stuff upon it. He found two pockets full of shells. He found an extra magazine, for the sub-machine gun. It was nearly full and only a little bent. That was all.

"Now," he said briskly, "we'll start. I've got a hunch the jungle thins out over that way. We'll find a clearing, try to locate the Golden City either by seeing it or by watching for aircraft flying to it, and then make for it. They're making war on Earth there. They don't understand. We've got to make them understand. Okay?"

Evelyn nodded. She put out her hand suddenly, a brave slender figure amid the incredible growths about her.

"I'm glad, Tommy," she said slowly, "that if—if anything happens, it will be the—the two of us. Funny, isn't it?"

Tommy kissed the twisted little smile from her face.

"And now that that's over," he observed, ashamed of his own emotion, "let's go!"

THEY went. Tommy watched the sun and kept approximately a straight line. They traveled three miles, and the jungle broke abruptly. Before them was a spongy surface neither solid earth or marsh. It shelved gently down to a vast and steaming morass upon which the dull-red sun shone hotly. It was vast, that marsh, and a steaming haze hung over it, and it seemed to reach to the world's end. But vaguely, through the attenuating upper layers of the steamy haze, they saw the outlines of a city beyond: tall towers and soaring spires, buildings of a grace and perfection of outline unknown upon the Earth. And faint golden flashes came from the walls and pinnacles of that city. They were reflections of this planet's monster sun, upon walls and roofs of plated gold.

"The Golden City," said Tommy heavily. He looked at the horrible marsh between. His heart sank.

And then there was a sudden screaming ululation nearby. A half-naked man was running out of sight. Two others danced and capered and yelled in insane glee, pointing at Tommy and at Evelyn. The running man's outcry was echoed from far away. Then it was taken up and repeated here and there in the jungle.

"They saw our tracks near the Tube," snapped Tommy bitterly. "Oh, what a fool I am! Now they'll ring us in."

He seized Evelyn's hand and began to run. There was a little rise in the ground a hundred yards away, with a clump of leafy ferns to shade it. They reached it as other half-naked, wholly mad human forms burst out of the jungle to yell and caper and make derisive and horrible gestures at the fugitives.

"Here we fight," said Tommy grimly. "The ground's open, anyhow. We fight here, and very probably we die here. But first…"

He knelt down and drew the finest of fine beads upon a bearded man who carried a glittering truncheonlike club which, by the way it was carried, was more than merely a bludgeon. He pulled the trigger for a single shot.

The bullet struck the capering Ragged Man fairly in the chest. And it exploded.

CHAPTER FIVE
The Fight in the Marsh

TWICE, within the next two hours, the Ragged Men mustered the courage to charge. They came racing across the semi-solid ooze like the madmen they were. Their yells and shouts were maniacal howls of blood-lust or worse. And twice Tommy broke their rush with a savage ruthlessness. The sub-machine-gun's first magazine was nearly empty. It was an unhandy weapon for single-shot work but it was loaded with explosive shells. The second rush he stopped with an automatic pistol. There were half-naked bodies partly buried in the ooze all the way from the jungle's edge to within ten yards of the hillock on which he and Evelyn had taken refuge.

It was hot there, terribly hot. The air was stifling. It fairly reeked of moisture and the smells from the swamp behind them were sickening. Tommy began to transfer the shells from the spare bent magazine to the one he had carried with the gun.

"We've a couple of reasons to be thankful," he observed. "One is that there's a bit of shade overhead. The other is that we had the big magazines for this gun. We still have nearly ninety shells, besides the ones for the pistols."

Evelyn said soberly:

"We're going to be killed, don't you think, Tommy?"

Tommy frowned.

"I'm rather afraid we are," he said irritably. "Confound it, and I'd thought of such excellent arguments to use in the City back yonder! Smithers said the Death Mist was two miles across, to-day, and still growing. The people in the city are still pouring the stuff down through Jacaro's Tube."

Evelyn smiled faintly. She touched his hand.

"Trying to keep me from worrying? Tommy..." She hesitated until he growled a question. "Please—remember that when Daddy and I were in the jungle before, we saw what these Ragged Men do to prisoners they take. I just want you to promise that—well, you won't wait too long, in hopes of somehow saving me."

Tommy stared at her. Then he decisively reached forward and put his hand over her mouth.

"Keep quiet," he said gently. "They shan't capture you. I promise that. Now keep quiet."

THERE was only silence for a long time. Now and again a hidden figure screamed in rage at them. Now and again some flapping thing sped toward the jungle's edge. Once a naked arm thrust one of the golden truncheons from behind its cover, pointing at a flying thing a few yards overhead. The flying thing suddenly toppled, turning over and over before it crashed to the ground. There were howls of glee.

"They seem mad," said Tommy meditatively, "and they act like lunatics, but I've got a hunch of some sort about them. But what?"

Sunlight gleamed on something golden beyond the jungle's edge. Naked figures went running to the spot. An exultant tumult arose.

"Now they try another trick," Tommy observed dispassionately. "I remember that at the Tube they had pushed something on wheels…"

The sub-machine gun was unhandy for accurate single shots, and no pistol can be used to effect at long ranges. To conserve ammunition, Tommy had been shooting only at relatively close targets, allowing the Ragged Men immunity at over two hundred yards. But now he flung over the continuous-fire stud. He watched grimly.

The foliage at the edge of the jungle parted. A crude wagon appeared. Its axles were lesser tree-trunks. Its wheels were clumsy and crude beyond belief. But mounted upon it there was a queer mass of golden metal which looked strangely beautiful and strangely deadly.

"That's the thing," said Tommy dispassionately, "which made the flare of light last night. It blew up the Tube. And Von Holtz told me—hm—his friends, in the City…"

He sighted carefully. The wagon and its contents were surrounded by a leaping, capering mob. They shook their fists in an insane hatred.

A storm of bullets burst upon them. Tommy was traversing the little gun with the trigger pressed down. His lips were set tightly. And suddenly it seemed as if the solid earth burst asunder! There had been an instant in which the bullet-bursts were visible. They tore and shattered the howling mob of Ragged Men. But then they struck the golden weapon. A sheet of blue-white flame leaped skyward and round about. A blast of blistering, horrible heat smote upon the beleaguered pair. The moisture of the ooze between them and the jungle flashed into steam. A section of the jungle itself, a hundred yards across, shriveled and died.

STEAM shot upward in a monstrous cloud—miles high, it seemed. Then, almost instantly, there was nothing left of the Ragged Men about the golden weapon, or of the weapon itself, but an unbearable blue-white light which poured away and trickled here and there and seemed to grow in volume as it flamed.

From the rest of the jungle a howl arose. It was a howl of such loss, and of such unspeakable rage, that the hair at the back of Tommy's neck lifted, as a dog's hackles lift at sight of an enemy.

"Keep your head down, Evelyn," said Tommy composedly. "I have an idea that the burning stuff gives off a lot of ultra-violet. Von Holtz was badly burned, you remember."

Naked figures flashed forward from the jungle beyond the burned area. Tommy shot them down grimly. He discarded the sub-machine gun with its explosive shells for the automatics. Some of his targets were only wounded. Those wounded men dragged themselves forward, screaming their rage. Tommy felt sickened, as if he were shooting down madmen. A voice roared a rage-thickened order from the jungle. The assault slackened.

Five minutes later it began again, and this time the attackers waded out into the softer ooze and flung themselves down, and then began a half-swimming, half-crawling progress behind bits of tree-fern stump, or merely pushing walls of the jellylike mud before them. The white light expanded and grew huge—but it dulled as it expanded, and presently seemed no hotter than molten steel, and later still it was no more than a dull-red heat, and later yet...

Tommy shot savagely. Some of the Ragged Men died. More did not.

"I'm afraid," he said coolly, "they're going to get us. It seems rather purposeless, but I'm afraid they're going to win."

Evelyn thrust a shaking hand skyward. "There, Tommy!"

A STRANGE, angular flying thing was moving steadily across the marsh, barely above the steamlike haze that hung in thinning layers about its foulness. The flying thing moved with a machinelike steadiness, and the sun twinkled upon something bright and shining before it.

"A flying machine," said Tommy shortly. His mind leaped ahead and his lips parted in a mirthless smile. "Get your gas mask ready, Evelyn. The explosion of that thermit-thrower made them curious in the City. They sent a ship to see."

The flying thing grew closer, grew distinct. A wail arose from the Ragged Men. Some of them leaped to their feet and fled. A man came out into the open and shook his fists at the angular thing in the air. He screamed at it, and such ghastly hatred was in the sound that Evelyn shuddered.

Tommy could see it plainly, now. Its single wing was thick and queerly unlike the air-foils of Earth. A framework hung below it, but it had no balancing tail. And there was a glittering something before it that obviously was its propelling mechanism, but as obviously was not a screw propeller. It swept overhead, with a man in it looking downward. Tommy watched coolly. It was past him, sweeping toward the jungle. It swung sharply to the right, banking steeply. Smoking things dropped from it, which expanded into columns of swiftly-descending vapor. They reached the jungle and blotted it out. The flying machine swung again and swept back to the left. More smoking things dropped. Ragged Men erupted from the jungle's edge in screaming groups, only to writhe and fall and lie still. But a group of five of them sped toward Tommy, shrieking their rage upon him as the cause of disaster. Tommy held his fire, looking upward. A hundred yards, fifty yards, twenty-five...

THE flying machine soared in easy, effortless circles. The man in it was watching, making no effort to interfere.

Tommy shot down the five men, one after the other, with a curiously detached feeling that their vice-brutalized faces would haunt him forever. Then he stood up.

The flying machine banked, turned, and swept toward him, and a smoking thing dropped toward the earth. It was a gas bomb like those that had wiped out the Ragged Men. It would strike not ten yards away.

"Your mask!" snapped Tommy.

He helped Evelyn adjust it. The billowing white cloud rolled around him. He held his breath, clapped on his mask, exhaled until his lungs ached, and was breathing comfortably. The mask was effective protection. And then he held Evelyn comfortably close.

For what seemed a long, long while they were surrounded by the white mist. The cloud was so dense, indeed, that the light about them faded to a gray twilight. But gradually, bit by bit, the mist grew thinner. Then it moved aside. It drifted before the wind toward the tree-fern forest and was lost to sight.

The flying machine was circling and soaring silently overhead. As the mist drew aside, the pilot dived down and down. And Tommy emptied his automatic at the glittering thing which drew it. There was a crashing bolt of blue light. The machine canted, spun about with one wing almost vertical, that wing-tip struck the marsh, and it settled with a monstrous splashing of mud. All was still.

Tommy reloaded, watching it keenly.

"The framework isn't smashed up, anyhow," he observed grimly. "The pilot thinks we're some of Jacaro's gang. My guns were proof, to him. So, since the Ragged Men didn't get us, he gassed us." He watched again, his eyes narrow. The pilot was utterly still. "He may be knocked out. I hope so! I'm going to see."

AUTOMATIC held ready, Tommy moved toward the crashed machine. It had splashed into the ooze less than a hundred yards away. Tommy moved cautiously. Twenty yards away, the pilot moved feebly. He had knocked his head against some part of his machine. A moment later he opened his eyes and stared about. The next instant he had seen Tommy and moved convulsively. A glittering thing appeared in his hand—and Tommy fired. The glittering thing flew to one side and the pilot clapped his hand to a punctured forearm. He went white, but his jaw set. He stared at Tommy, waiting for death.

"For the love of Pete," said Tommy irritably, "I'm not going to kill you! You tried to kill me, and it was very annoying, but I have some things I want to tell you."

He stopped and felt foolish because his words were, of course, unintelligible. The pilot was staring amazedly at him. Tommy's tone had been irritated, certainly, but there was neither hatred nor triumph in it. He waved his hand.

"Come on and I'll bandage you up and see if we can make you understand a few things."

Evelyn came running through the muck.

"He didn't hurt you, Tommy?" she gasped. "I saw you shoot—"

The pilot fairly jumped. At first glance he had recognized her as a woman. Tommy growled that he'd had to "shoot the damn fool through the arm." The pilot spoke, curiously. Evelyn looked at his arm and exclaimed. He was holding it above the wound to stop the bleeding. Evelyn looked about helplessly for something with which to bandage it.

"Make pads with your handkerchief," grunted Tommy. "Take my tie to hold them in place."

The prisoner looked curiously from one to the other. His color was returning. As Evelyn worked on his arm he seemed to grow excited at some inner thought. He spoke again, and looked at once puzzled and confirmed in some conviction when they were unable to comprehend. When Evelyn finished her first-aid task he smiled suddenly, flashing white teeth at them. He even made a little speech which was humorously apologetic, to judge by its tone. When they turned to go back to their fortress he went with them without a trace of hesitation.

"Now what?" asked Evelyn.

"They'll be looking for him in a little while," said Tommy curtly. "If we can convince him we're not enemies, he'll keep them from giving us more gas."

THE pilot was fumbling at a belt about the curious tunic he wore. Tommy watched him warily. But a pad of what seemed to be black metal came out, with a silvery-white stylus attached to it. The pilot sat down the instant they stopped and began to draw in white lines on the black surface. He drew a picture of a man and an angular flying machine, and then a sketchy, impressionistic outline of a city's towers. He drew a circle to enclose all three drawings and indicated himself, the machine, and the distant city. Tommy nodded comprehension as the pilot looked up. Then came a picture of a half-naked man shaking his fists at the three encircled sketches. The half-naked man stood beneath a roughly indicated tree-fern.

"Clever," said Tommy, as a larger circle enclosed that with the city and the machine. "He's identifying himself, and saying the Ragged Men are enemies of himself and his Golden City, too. That much is not hard to get."

He nodded vigorously as the pilot looked up again. And then he watched as a lively, tiny sketch grew on the black slab, showing half a dozen men, garbed almost as Tommy was, using weapons which could only be sub-machine guns and automatic pistols. They were obviously Jacaro's gangsters. The pilot handed over the plate and watched absorbedly as Tommy fumbled with the stylus. He drew, not well but well enough, an outline of the towers of New York. The difference in architecture was striking. There followed tiny figures of himself and Evelyn—with a drily murmured, "This isn't a flattering portrait of you, Evelyn…!" And a circle enclosing them with the towers of New York.

The pilot nodded in his turn. And then Tommy encircled the previously drawn figures of the gangsters with New York, just as the Ragged Men had been linked with the other city. And a second circle linked gangsters and Ragged Men together.

"I'M saying," observed Tommy, "that Jacaro and his mob are the Ragged Men of our world, which may not be wrong, at that."

There was no question but that the pilot took his meaning. He grinned in a friendly fashion, and winced as his wounded arm hurt him. Ruefully, he looked down at his bandage. Then he pressed a tiny stud at the top of the black-metal pad and all the white lines vanished instantly. He drew a new circle, with tree-ferns scattered about its upper third—a tiny sketch of a city's towers. He pointed to that and to the city visible through the mist—a second city, and a third, in other places. He waved his hand vaguely about, then impatiently scribbled over the middle third of the circle and handed it back to Tommy.

Tommy grinned ruefully.

"A map," he said amusedly. "He's pointed out his own city and a couple of others, and he wants us to tell him where we come from. Evelyn—er—how are we going to explain a trip through five dimensions in a sketch?"

Evelyn shook her head. But a shadow passed over their heads. The pilot leaped to his feet and shouted. There were three planes soaring above them, and the pilot in the first was in the act of releasing a smoking object over the side. At the grounded pilot's shout, he flung his ship into a frantic dive, while behind him the smoking thing billowed out a thicker and thicker cloud. His plane was nearly hidden by the vapor when he released it. It fell two hundred yards and more away, and the white mist spread and spread. But it fell short of the little hillock.

"QUICK thinking," said Tommy coolly. "He thought he had this man a prisoner, and he'd be better off dead. But—"

Their captive was shouting again. His head thrown back, he called sentence after sentence aloft while the three ships soared back and forth above their heads, soundless as bats. One of the three rose steeply and soared away toward the city. Their captive, grinning, turned and nodded his head satisfiedly. Then he sat down to wait.

Twenty minutes later a monstrous machine with ungainly flapping wings came heavily over the swamp. It checked and settled with a terrific flapping and an even more terrific din. Half a dozen armed men waited warily for the three to approach. The golden weapons lifted alertly as they drew near. The wounded man explained at some length. His explanation was dismissed brusquely. A man advanced and held out his hands for Tommy's weapons.

"I don't like it," growled Tommy, "but we've got to think of Earth. If you get a chance hide your gun, Evelyn."

He pushed on the safety catches and passed over his guns. The pilot he had shot down led them onto the fenced-in deck of the monstrous ornithopter. Machinery roared. The wings began to beat. They were nearly invisible from the speed of their flapping when the ship lifted vertically from the ground. It rose straight up for fifty feet, the motion of the wings changed subtly, and it swept forward.

It swung in a vast half circle and headed back across the marsh for the Golden City. Five minutes of noisy flight during which the machine flapped its way higher and higher above the marsh—which seemed more noisome and horrible still from above—and then the golden towers of the city were below. Strange and tapering and beautiful, they were. No single line was perfectly straight, nor was any form ungraceful. These towers sprang upward in clean-soaring curves toward the sky. Bridges between them were gossamerlike things that seemed lace spun out in metal. And as Tommy looked keenly and saw the jungle crowding close against the city's metal walls, the flapping of the ornithopter's wings changed again and it seemed to plunge downward like a stone toward a narrow landing place amid the great city's towering buildings.

CHAPTER SIX
The Golden City

THE thing that struck Tommy first of all was the scarcity of men in the city, compared to its size. The next thing was the entire absence of women. The roar of machines smote upon his consciousness as a bad third, though they made din enough. Perhaps he ignored the machine noises because the ornithopter on which they had arrived made such a racket itself.

They landed on a paved space perhaps a hundred yards by two hundred, three sides of which were walled off by soaring towers. The fourth gave off on empty space, and he realized that he was still at least a hundred feet above the ground. The ornithopter landed with a certain skilful precision and its wings ceased to beat. Behind it, the two fixed-wing machines soared down, leveled, hovered, and settled upon amazingly inadequate wheels. Their pilots got out and began to push them toward one side of the landing area. Tommy noticed it, of course. He was noticing everything, just now. He said amazedly:

"Evelyn! They launch these planes with catapults like those our battleships use! They don't take off under their own power!"

The six men on the ornithopter put their shoulders to their machine and trundled it out of the way. Tommy blinked at the sight.

"No field attendants!" He gazed out across the open portion of the land area and saw an elevated thoroughfare below. Some sort of vehicle, gleaming like gold, moved swiftly on two wheels. There was a walkway in the center of the street with room for a multitude. But only two men were in sight upon it. "Lord!" said Tommy. "Where are the people?"

There was brief talk among the crew of the ornithopter. Two of them picked up Tommy's weapons, and the pilot he had wounded made a gesture indicating that he should follow. He led the way to an arched door in the nearest tower. A little two-wheeled car was waiting. They got into it and the pilot fumbled with the controls. As he worked at it—rather clumsily on account of his arm—the rest of the ornithopter's crew came in. They wheeled out another vehicle, climbed into it, and shot away down a sloping passage.

THEIR own vehicle followed and emerged upon the paved and nearly empty thoroughfare. Tall buildings rose all about them, with curved walls soaring dizzily skyward. There was every sign of a populous city, including the dull drumming roar of many machines, but the streets were empty. The little machine moved swiftly for minutes. Twice it swung aside and entered a sloping incline. Once it went up. The other time it dived down seventy feet on a four-hundred-foot ramp. Then it swung sharply to the right, meandered into a street-level way leading into the heart of a monster building, and stopped. And in all its travel it had not passed fifty people.

The pilot-turned-chauffeur turned and grinned amiably, and led the way again. Steps—twenty or thirty of them. Then they emerged suddenly into a vast room. It must have been a hundred and fifty feet long, fifty wide, and nearly as high. It was floored with alternate blocks of what seemed to be an iron-hard black wood and the omnipresent golden metal. Columns and pilasters about the place gave forth the same subdued deep golden glow. Light streamed from panels inset in the wall and ceiling—a curious saffron-red light. There was a massive table of the hard black wood. Chairs with curiously designed backs were ranged about it. They were benches, really, but they served the purpose of chairs. Each was too narrow to hold more than one person. The room was empty.

They waited. After a long time a man in a blue tunic came into the room and sat down on one of the benches. A long time later, another man came in, in red; and another and another, until there were a dozen in all. They regarded Tommy and

Evelyn with a weary suspicion. One of them—an old man with a white beard—asked questions. The pilot answered them. At a word, the two men with Tommy's weapons placed them on the table. They were inspected casually, as familiar things. They probably were, since some of Jacaro's gunmen had been killed in a fight in this city. Another question.

The pilot explained briefly and offered Tommy the black-metal pad again. It still contained the incomplete map of a hemisphere, and was obviously a repetition of the question of where he came from.

TOMMY took it, frowning thoughtfully. Then an idea struck him. He found the little stud which, pressed by the pad's owner, had erased the previous drawings. He pressed it and the lines disappeared. And Tommy drew, crudely enough, that complicated diagram which is supposed to represent a cube which is a cube in four dimensions: a tesseract. Upon one surface of the cube he indicated the curving towers of the Golden City. Upon a surface representing a plane beyond the three dimensions of normal experience, he repeated the angular tower structures of New York. He shrugged rather hopelessly as he passed it over, but to his amazement it was understood at once.

The little black pad passed from hand to hand and an animated discussion took place. One rather hard-faced man was the most animated of all. The bearded old man demurred. The hard-faced man insisted. Tommy could see that his pilot's expression was becoming uneasy. But then a compromise seemed to be arrived at. The bearded man spoke a single, ceremonial phrase and the twelve men rose. They moved toward various doors and one by one left, until the room was empty.

But the pilot looked relieved. He grinned cheerfully at Tommy and led the way back to the two-wheeled vehicle. The two men with Tommy's weapons vanished. And again there was a swift, cyclonelike passage along empty ways with the throbbing of machinery audible everywhere. Into the base of a second building, up endless stairs, past innumerable doors. It seemed to Tommy that he heard voices behind some of them, and they were women's voices.

At a private, triple knock a door opened wide, and the pilot led the way into a room, closed and locked the door behind him, and called. A woman's voice cried out in astonishment. Through an inner arch a woman came running eagerly. Her face went blank at sight of Tommy and Evelyn, and her hand flew to a tiny golden object at her waist. Then, at the pilot's chuckle, she flushed vividly.

HOURS later, Tommy and Evelyn were able to talk it over. They were alone then, and could look out an oval window upon the Golden City all about them. It was dark, but saffron-red panels glowed in building walls all along the thoroughfares, and tiny glowing dots in the soaring spires of gold told of people within other dwellings like this.

"As I see it," said Tommy restlessly, "the Council—and it must have been that in the big room to-day—put us in our friend's hands to learn the language. He's been working with me four hours, drawing pictures, and I've been writing down words I've learned. I must have several hundred of them. But we do our best talking with pictures. And Evelyn, this city's in a bad fix."

Evelyn said irrelevantly: "Her name is Ahnya, Tommy, and she's a dear. We got along beautifully. I'll bet I found out things you don't even guess at."

"You probably have," admitted Tommy, frowning. "Check up on this: our friend's name is Aten, and he's an air-pilot and also has something to do with growing foodstuffs in some special towers where they grow crops by artificial light only. Some of the plants he sketched look amazingly like wheat, by the way. The name of the town is…" He looked at his notes. "…Yugna. There are some other towns, ten or twelve of them. Rahn is the nearest, and it's worse off than this one."

"Of course," said Evelyn, smiling. "They use *cuyal* openly, there!"

"How'd you learn all that?" demanded Tommy.

"Ahnya told me. We made gestures and smiled at each other. We understood perfectly. She's crazy about her husband, and I—well she knows I'm going to marry you, so..."

Tommy grunted.

"I suppose she explained with a smile and gestures just how much of a strain it is, simply keeping the city going?"

"Of course," said Evelyn calmly. "The city's fighting against the jungle, which grows worse all the time. They used to grow their foodstuffs in the open fields. Then within the city. Now they use empty towers and artificial light. I don't know why."

TOMMY grunted again.

"This planet's just had, or is having, a change of geologic period," he explained, frowning. "The plants people need to live on aren't adapted to the new climate and new plants fit for food are scarce. They have to grow food under shelter, now, and their machines take an abnormal amount of supervision—I don't know why. The air-conditions for the food plants; the machines that fight back the jungle creepers which thrive in the new climate and try to crawl into the city to smother it; the power machines; the clothing machines—a million machines have to be kept going to keep back the jungle and fight off starvation and just hold on doggedly to the bare fact of civilization. And they're short-handed. The law of diminishing returns seems to operate. They're trying to maintain a civilization higher than their environment will support. They work until they're ready to drop, just to stay in the same place. And the monotony and the strain makes some of them take to *cuyal* for relief."

He surveyed the city from the oval window, frowning in thought.

"It's a drug which grows wild," he added slowly. "It peps them up. It makes the monotony and the weariness bearable.

And then, suddenly, they break. They hate the machines and the city and everything they ever knew or did. It's a sort of delayed-action psychosis which goes off with a bang. Some of them go amuck in the city, using their belt-weapons until they're killed. More of them bolt for the jungle. The city loses better than one per cent of its population a year to the jungle. And then they're Ragged Men, half mad at all times and wholly mad as far as the city and its machines are concerned."

Evelyn linked her arm in his.

"Somehow," she told him, smiling, "I think one Thomas Reames is working out ways and means to help a city named Yugna."

"Not yet," said Tommy grimly. "We have to think of Earth. Not everybody in the Council approved of us. Aten told me one chap argued that we ought to be shoved out into the jungle again as compatriots of Jacaro. And the machines were especially short-handed to-day because of a diversion of labor to get ready something monstrous and really deadly to send down the Tube to Earth. We've got to find out what that is, and stop it."

BUT on the second day afterward, when he and Evelyn were summoned before the Council again, he still had not found out. During those two days he learned many other things, to be sure: that Aten for instance, was relieved from duty at the machines only because he was wounded; that the power of the main machines came from a deep bore which brought up superheated steam from the source of boiling springs long since built over; that iron was a rare metal, and consequently there was no dynamo in the city and magnetism was practically an unknown force; that electrokinetics was a laboratory puzzle—or had been, when there was leisure for research—while the science of electrostatics had progressed far past its state on Earth. The little truncheonlike weapons carried a stored-up static charge measurable only in hundreds of thousands of volts, which could be released in flashes which were effective up to a hundred feet or more.

And he learned that the thermit-throwers actually spat out in normal operation tiny droplets of matter Aten could not describe clearly, but which seemed to be radioactive with a period of five minutes or less; that in Rahn, the nearest other city, *cuyal* was taken openly, and the jungle was growing into the town with no one to hold it back; that two generations since there had been twenty cities like this one, but that a bare dozen still survived; that there was a tradition that human beings had come upon this planet from another world where other human beings had harried them, and that in that other world there were divers races of humanity, of different colors, whereas in the world of the Golden City all mankind was one race; that Tommy's declaration that he came from another group of dimensions had been debated and, on re-examination of Jacaro's Tube, accepted, and that there was keen argument going on as to the measures to be taken concerning it.

THESE things Tommy had learned, and he and Evelyn went to their second interrogation by the city's Council armed with written vocabularies of nearly a thousand words, which they had sorted out and made ready for use. But they were still ignorant of the weapons the Golden City might use against Earth.

The Council meeting took place in the same hall, with its alternating black-and-gold flooring and the saffron-red lighting panels casting a soft light everywhere. This was a scheduled meeting, foreseen and arranged for. The twelve chairs above the heavy table were all occupied from the first. But Tommy realized that the table had been intended to seat a large number of councilors. There were guards stationed formally behind the chairs. There were spectators, auditors of the deliberations of the Council. They were dressed in a myriad colors, and they talked quietly among themselves; but it seemed to Tommy that nowhere had he seen weariness, as an ingrained expression, upon so many faces.

Tommy and Evelyn were led to the foot of the Council table. The bearded old man in blue began the questioning. As Keeper of Foodstuffs—according to Aten—he was a sort of presiding officer.

Tommy answered the questions crisply. He had known what they would be, and he had developed a vocabulary to answer them. He told them of Earth, of Professor Denham, of his and the professor's experiments. He outlined the first experiment with the Fifth-Dimension catapult and the result of it—when the Golden City had sent the Death Mist to wipe out a band of Ragged Men who had captured a citizen, and after him Evelyn and her father.

THIS they remembered. Nods went around the table. Tommy told them of Jacaro, stressing the fact that Jacaro was an outlaw, a criminal upon Earth. He explained the theft of the model Tube, and how it was that their first contact with Earth had been with the dregs of Earth humanity. On behalf of his countrymen he offered reparation for all the damage Jacaro and his men had done. He proposed a peaceful commerce between worlds, to the infinite benefit of both.

There was silence until he finished. The faces before him were immobile. But a hawk-faced man in brown asked dry questions. Were there more races than one upon Earth? Were they of diverse colors? Did they ever war among themselves? At Tommy's answers the atmosphere seemed to change. And the hawk-faced man rose to speak.

Tommy and Evelyn, he conceded caustically, had certainly come from another world. Their own most ancient legends described just such a world as his: a world of many races of many colors, who fought many wars among themselves. Their ancestors had fled from such a world, according to legend through a twisting cavern which they had sealed behind them. The conditions Tommy described had been the cause of their ancestors' flight. They, the people of Yugna, would do well to follow the example of their forebears: strip these Earth folk of their weapons, exile them to the jungles, destroy the Tube through which the Mist of Many Colors had been sent. All should be as in past ages.

TOMMY opened his mouth to answer, but another man sprang to his feet. His face alone was not weary and worn. As he stood up, Aten murmured "*Cuyal!*" and Tommy understood that this man used the drug which was destroying the city's citizens, but gave a transient energy to its victims. He spoke in fiery phrases, urging action which would be drastic and certain. He spoke confidently, persuasively. There was a rustling among those who watched and listened to the debate. He had caught at their imagination.

Evelyn, exerting every faculty to understand, saw Tommy's lips set grimly.

"What—what is it?" she whispered. "II don't understand…"

Tommy spoke in a savage growl.

"He says," he told her bitterly, "that in one blow they can defeat both the jungle and the invaders from Earth. In past ages their ancestors were faced by enemies they could not defeat. They fled to this world. Now they are faced by jungles they cannot defeat. He proposes that they flee to our world. The Death Mist is a toy, he reminds them, compared with gases they know. There is a gas of which one part in ten hundred million is fatal! In a hundred of their days they can make and send through the Tube enough of it to kill every living thing on Earth. They've figures on the Earth's size and atmosphere from me, damn 'em! And he reminds them that that deadly gas changes of itself into a harmless substance. He urges them to gas Earth humanity out of existence, call upon the other cities of this world, and presently move through the Tube to Earth. They'll carry their food-plants, rebuild their cities, and abandon this planet to the jungles and the Ragged Men. And the hell of it is, they can do it!"

A sudden approving buzz went through the Council hall.

CHAPTER SEVEN
The Fleet from Rahn

THE approval of the citizens of Yugna was not enthusiastic. It was desperate. Their faces were weary. Their lives were warped. They had been fighting since birth against the encroachment of the jungle, which until the days of their grandparents had been no menace at all. But for two generations these people had been foredoomed, and they knew it. Nearly half the cities of their race were overwhelmed and their inhabitants reduced to savage hunters in the victorious jungles. Now the people of Yugna saw a chance to escape from the jungle. They were offered rest. Peace. Relaxation from the desperate need to serve insatiable machines. Sheer desperation impelled them. In their situation, the people of Earth would annihilate a solar system for relief, let alone the inhabitants of a single planet.

Shouts began to be heard above the uproar in the Council hall—approving shouts, demands that one be appointed to conduct the operation which was to give them a new planet on which to live, where their food-plants would thrive in the open, where jungles would no longer press on them.

Tommy's face went savage and desperate, itself. He clenched and unclenched his hands, struggling among his meagre supply of words for promises of help from Earth, which promises would tip the scales for peace again. He raised his voice in a shout for attention. He was unheard. The Council hall was in an uproar of desperate approval. The orator stood flushed and triumphant. The Council members looked from eye to eye, and slowly the old, white-bearded Keeper of Foodstuffs placed a golden box upon the table. He touched it in a certain fashion, and handed it to the next man. That second man touched it, and passed it to a third. And that man...

A HUSH fell instantly. Tommy understood. The measure was being decided by solemn vote. The voting device had reached the fifth man when there was a frantic clatter of footsteps, a door burst in, and babbling men stood in the opening, white-faced and stammering and overwhelmed, but trying to make a report.

Consternation reigned, incredulous, amazed consternation. The bearded old man rose dazedly and strode from the hall with the rest of the Council following him. A pause of stunned stupefaction, and the spectators in the hall rushed for other doors.

"Stick to Aten," snapped Tommy. "Something's broken, and it has to be our way. Let's see what it is."

He clung alike to Evelyn and to Aten as the air-pilot fought to clear a way. The doors were jammed. It was minutes before they could make their way through and plunge up the interminable steps Aten mounted, only to fling himself out to the open air. Then they were upon a flying bridge between two of the towers of the city. All about the city human figures were massing, staring upward.

And above the city swirled a swarm of aircraft. Tommy counted three of the clumsy ornithopters, high and motelike. There were twenty or thirty of the small, one-man craft. There were a dozen or more two-man planes. And there were at least forty giant single-wing ships which looked as if they had been made for carrying freight. They soared and circled above the city in soundless confusion. Before each of them glittered something silvery, like glass, which was not a screw propeller but somehow drew them on.

The Council was massed two hundred yards away. A single-seater dived downward, soared and circled noiselessly fifty yards overhead, and its pilot shouted a message. Then he climbed swiftly and rejoined his fellows. The men about Tommy looked stunned, as if they could not believe their ears. Aten seemed stricken beyond the passability of reaction.

"I GOT part of it," snapped Tommy, to Evelyn's whispered question. "I think I know the rest. Aten!" He snapped question after question in his inadequate phrasing of the city's tongue. Evelyn saw Aten answer dully, then bitterly, and then, as Tommy caught his arm and whispered savagely to him, Aten's eyes caught fire. He nodded violently and turned on his heel.

"Come on!" And Tommy seized Evelyn's arm again.

They followed closely as Aten wormed his way through the crowd. They raced behind him downstairs and through a door into a dusty and unvisited room. It was a museum. Aten pointed grimly.

Here were the automatic pistols taken from those of Jacaro's men who had been killed, a nasty sub-machine gun which had been Tommy's, and grenades—Jacaro's. Tommy checked shell calibres and carried off a ninety-shot magazine full of explosive bullets, and a repeating rifle.

"I can do more accurate work with this than the machine gun," he said cryptically. "Let's go!"

It was not until they were racing away from the Council building in one of the two-wheeled vehicles that Evelyn spoke again.

"I—understand part," she said unsteadily. "Those planes overhead are from Rahn. And they're threatening—"

"Blackmail," said Tommy between clenched teeth. "It sounds like a perfectly normal Earth racket. A fleet from Rahn is over Yugna, loaded with the Death Mist. Yugna pays food and goods and women or it's wiped out by gas. Further, it surrenders its aircraft to make further collections easier. Rahn refuses to die, though it's let in the jungle. It's turned pirate stronghold. Fed and clothed by a few other cities like this one, it should be able to hold out. It's a racket, Evelyn. A stick-up. A hijacking of a civilised city. Sounds like Jacaro."

THE little vehicle darted madly through empty highways, passing groups of men staring dazedly upward at the soaring motes overhead. It darted down this inclined way, up that one.

It shot into a building and around a winding ramp. It stopped with a jerk and Aten was climbing out. He ran through a doorway, Tommy and Evelyn following. Planes of all sizes, still and lifeless, filled a vast hall. And Aten struggled with a door mechanism and a monster valve swung wide. Then Tommy threw his weight with Aten's to roll out the plane he had selected. It was a small, triangular ship, with seats for three, but it was heavy. The two men moved it with desperate exertion. Aten pointed, panting, to slide-rail and it took them five minutes to get the plane about that rail and engage a curious contrivance in a slot in the ship's fuselage.

"Tommy," said Evelyn, "you're not going to—"

"Run away? Hardly!" said Tommy. "We're going up. I'm going to fight the fleet with bullets. They don't have missile-weapons here, and Aten will know the range of their electric-charge outfits."

"I'm coming too," said Evelyn desperately.

Tommy hesitated, then agreed.

"If we fail they'll gas the city anyway. One way or the other..."

There was a sudden rumble as Evelyn took her place. The plane shot forward with a swift smooth acceleration. There was no sound of any motor. There was no movement of the glittering thing at the forepart of the plane. But the ship reached the end of the slide and lifted, and then was in mid-air, fifty feet above the vehicular way, a hundred feet above the ground.

TOMMY spoke urgently. Aten nodded. The ship had started to climb. He leveled it out and darted straight forward. He swung madly to dodge a soaring tower. He swept upward a little to avoid a flying bridge. The ship was travelling with an enormous speed, and the golden walls of the city flashed past below them and they sped away across feathery jungle.

"If we climbed at once," observed Tommy shortly, "they'd think we meant to fight. They might start their gassing. As it is, we look like we're running away."

Evelyn said nothing. For five miles the plane fled as if in panic. Evelyn clung to the filigree side of the cockpit. The city dwindled behind them. Then Aten climbed steeply. Tommy was looking keenly at the glittering thing which propelled the ship. It seemed like a crystal gridwork, like angular lace contrived of glass. But a cold blue flame burned in it and Tommy was obscurely reminded of a neon tube, though the color was wholly unlike. A blast of air poured back through the grid. Somehow, by some development of electro-statics, the "static jet" which is merely a toy in Earth laboratories had become usable as a means of propelling aircraft.

Back they swept toward the Golden City, five thousand feet or more aloft. The ground was partly obscured by the hazy, humid atmosphere, but glinting sun-reflections from the city guided them. Soaring things took shape before them and grew swiftly nearer. Tommy spoke again, busily loading the automatic rifle with explosive shells.

Aten swung to follow a vast dark shape in its circular soaring, a hundred feet above it and a hundred yards behind. Wind whistled, rising to a shriek. Tommy fired painstakingly.

THE other plane zoomed suddenly as a flash of blue flame spouted before it. It dived, then, fluttering and swooping, began to drift helplessly toward the spires of the city below it.

"Good!" snapped Tommy. "Another one, Aten."

Aten made no reply. He flung his ship sidewise and dived steeply before a monstrous freight carrier. Tommy fired deliberately as they swept past. The propelling grid flashed blue flame in a vast, crashing flame. It, too, began to flutter down.

Tommy did not miss until the fifth time, and Aten turned with a grimace of disappointment. Tommy's second shot burst in a freight compartment and a man screamed. His voice carried horribly in the silence of these heights. But Tommy shot again, and, again, and there was a satisfying blue flash as a fifth big ship went fluttering helplessly down.

Aten began to circle for height Tommy refilled the magazine.

"I'm bringing 'em down," he explained unnecessarily to Evelyn, "by smashing their propellers. They have to land, and when they land they're hostages—I hope!"

Confusion became apparent among the hostile planes. The one Yugna ship was identified as the source of disaster. Tommy worked his rifle in cold fury. He aimed at no man, but the propelling grids were large. For a one-man ship they were five feet in diameter, and for the big freight ships, they were circles fifteen feet across. They were perfect targets, and Aten seemed to grasp the necessary tactics almost instantly. Dead ahead or from straight astern, Tommy could not miss a shot. The fleet of Rahn went fluttering downward. Fifteen of the biggest were down, and six of the two-man planes. A sixteenth and seventeenth flashed at their bows and drifted helplessly...

THEN the one-man ships attacked. Six of them at once. Aten grinned and dived for all of them. One by one, Tommy smashed their crystal grids and watched them sinking unsteadily toward the towers of the city. As his own ship drove over them, little golden flashes licked out. Electric-charge weapons. One flash struck the wingtip of their plane, and flame burst out, but Aten flung the ship into a mad whirl in which the blaze was blown out.

Another freight ship helpless—and another. Then the air fleet of Rahn turned and fled. The ornithopters winged away in heavy, creaking terror. The others dived for speed and flattened out hardly above the tree-fern jungle. They streaked away in ignominious panic. Aten darted and circled above them and, as Tommy failed to fire, turned and went racing back toward the city.

"After the first ones went down," observed Tommy, "they knew that if they gassed the city we'd shoot them down into their own gas cloud. So they ran away. I hope this gives us a pull."

The city's towers loomed before them. The lacy bridges swarmed with human figures. Somewhere a fight was in progress about a grounded plane from Rahn. Others seemed to have surrendered sullenly on alighting. For the first time Tommy saw the city as a thronging mass of humanity, and for the first time he realized how terrible must be the strain upon the city if with so large a population so few could be free for leisure in normal times.

The little plane settled down and landed lightly. There were a dozen men on the landing platform now, and they were herding disarmed men from Rahn away from a big ship Tommy had brought down. Tommy looked curiously at the prisoners. They seemed freer than the inhabitants of Yugna. Their faces showed no such signs of strain. But they did not seem well-fed, nor did they appear as capable or as resolute.

"*Cuyal*," said Aten in an explanatory tone, seeing Tommy's expression. He put his shoulder to the big ship, to wheel it back into its shed.

"You son of a gun," grunted Tommy, "it's all in the day's work to you, fighting an invading fleet!"

A messenger came panting through the doorway. Tommy grinned.

"The Council wants us, Evelyn. Now maybe they'll listen."

THE atmosphere of the resumed Council meeting was, as a matter of fact, considerably changed. The white-bearded Keeper of Foodstuffs thanked them with dignity. He invited Tommy to offer advice, since his services had proved so useful.

"Advice?" said Tommy, in the halting, fumbling phrases he had slaved to acquire. "I would put the prisoners from Rahn to work at the machines, releasing citizens." There was a buzz of approval, and he added drily in English: "I'm playing politics, Evelyn." Again in the speech of Yugna he added: "And I would have the fleet of Yugna soar above Rahn, not to demand tribute as that city did, but to disable all its aircraft, so that such piracy as to-day may not be tried again!" There was a second buzz of approval. "And third," said Tommy earnestly, "I would communicate with Earth, rather than assassinate it. I would require the science of Earth for the benefit of this world, rather than use the science of this world to annihilate that! I—"

For the second time the Council meeting was interrupted. An armed messenger came pounding into the room. He reported swiftly. Tommy grasped Evelyn's wrist in what was almost a painful grip.

"Noises in the Tube!" he told her sharply. "Earth-folk doing something in the Tube Jacaro came through. Your father..."

There was an alert silence in the Council hall. The white-bearded old man had listened to the messenger. Now he asked a grim question of Tommy.

"They may be my friends, or your enemies," said Tommy briefly. "Mass thermit-throwers and let me find out!"

IT was the only possible thing to do. Tommy and Evelyn went with the Council, in a body, in a huge wheeled vehicle that raced across the city. Lingering groups still searched the sky above them, now blessedly empty again. But the Council's vehicle dived down and down to ground level, where the rumble of machines was loud indeed, and then turned into a tunnel which went down still farther. There was feverish activity ahead, where it stopped, and a golden thermit-thrower came into sight upon a dull-colored truck.

Questions. Feverish replies. The white-bearded man touched Tommy on the shoulder, regarding him with a peculiarly noncommittal gaze, and pointed to a doorway that someone was just opening. The door swung wide. There was a confusion of prismatically-colored mist within it, and Tommy noticed that tanks upon tanks were massed outside the metal wall of that compartment, and seemingly had been pouring something into the room.

The mist drew back from the door. Saffron-red lighting panels appeared dimly, then grew distinct. There were small, collapsed bundles of fur upon the floor of the storeroom being exposed to view. They were, probably, the equivalent of rats. And then the last remnant of mist vanished with a curiously wraithlike abruptness, and the end of Jacaro's Tube came into view.

Tommy advanced, Evelyn clinging to his sleeve. There were clanking noises audible in this room even above the dull rumble of the city's machines. The noises came from the Tube's mouth. It was four feet and more across, and it projected at a crazy angle out of a previously solid wall.

"Hello!" shouted Tommy. "Down the Tube!"

THE clattering noise stopped, then continued at a faster rate.

"The gas is cut off!" shouted Tommy again. "Who's there?"

A voice gasped from the Tube's depths:

"It's him!" The tone was made metallic by echoing and reechoing in the bends of the Tube, but it was Smithers. "We're comin', Mr. Reames."

"Is—is Daddy there?" called Evelyn eagerly. "Daddy!"

"Coming," said a grim voice.

The clattering grew nearer. A goggled, gas-masked head appeared, and a body followed it out of the Tube, laden with a multitude of burdens. A second climbed still more heavily after the first. The brightly-colored citizens of the Golden City reached quietly to the weapons at their waists. A third voice came up the Tube, distant and nearly unintelligible. It roared a question.

Smithers ripped off his gas mask and said distinctly:

"Sure we're through. Go ahead. An' go to hell!"

Then there was a thunderous detonation somewhere down in the Tube's depths. The visible part of it jerked spasmodically and cracked across. A wisp of brownish smoke puffed out of it, and the stinging reek of high explosive tainted the air. Then Evelyn was clinging close to her father, and he was patting her comfortingly, and Smithers was pumping both of Tommy's hands, his normal calmness torn from him for once. But after a bare moment he had gripped himself again. He unloaded an impressive number of parcels from about his person. Then he regarded the citizens of the Golden City with an impersonal, estimating gaze, ignoring twenty weapons trained upon him.

"Those damn fools back on Earth," he observed impassively, "decided the professor an' me was better off of it. So they let us come through the Tube before they blew it up. We brought the explosive bullets, Mr. Reames. I hope we brought enough."

And Tommy grinned elatedly as Denham turned to crush his hands in his own.

CHAPTER EIGHT
"Those Devils have got Evelyn!"

THAT night the three of them talked, on a high terrace with most of the Golden City spread out below them. Over their heads, lights of many colors moved and shifted slowly in the sky. There were a myriad glowing specks of saffron-red about the ways of the city, and the air was full of fragrant odors. The breath of the jungle reached them even a thousand feet above ground. And the dull, persistent roar of the machines reached them too. There were five people on the terrace: Tommy, Denham, Smithers, Aten and the white-bearded old Keeper of Foodstuffs. He looked on as the Earthmen talked.

"We're marooned," Tommy was saying crisply, "and for the time being we've got to throw in with these people. I believe they came from Earth originally. Four, five thousand years ago, perhaps. Their tale is of a cave they sealed up behind them. It might have been a primitive Tube, if such a thing can be imagined."

Denham filled his pipe and lighted it meditatively.

"Half the American Indian tribes," he observed drily, "had legends of coming originally from an underworld. I wonder if Tubes are less your own invention than we thought?"

Tommy shrugged.

"In any case, Earth is safe."

"Is it?" insisted Denham. "You say they understood at once when you talked of dimension-travel. Ask the old chap there."

TOMMY frowned, then labored with the question. The bearded old man spoke gravely. At his answer, Tommy grimaced.

"Datl's gone looking for the cave their legends tell of," he said reluctantly. "He's the lad who wanted the city to gas Earth with some ghastly stuff they know of, and move over when the gas was harmless again. But the cave has been lost for centuries, and it's in the torrid zone—which *is* torrid! We're near the North Pole of this planet, and it's tropic here. It must be mighty hot at the equator. Datl took a ship and supplies and sailed off. He may be killed. In any case it'll be some time before he's dangerous. Meanwhile, as I said, we're marooned."

"And more," said Denham deliberately. "By the time the authorities halfway believed me, and Von Holtz could talk, there were more deaths from the Death Mist. It wiped out a village, clean. So when it was realized that I'd caused it—or that was their interpretation—and was the only man who could cause it again, why, the authorities thought it a splendid idea for me to come through the Tube. They invited me to commit suicide. My knowledge was too dangerous for a man to have. So," he added grimly, "I have committed suicide. We will not be welcomed back on Earth, Tommy."

Tommy made an impatient gesture.

"Worry about that later," he said impatiently. "Right now there's a war on. Rahn's desperate, and the prisoners we took this morning say Jacaro and his gunmen are there, advising them. Ragged Men have joined in to help kill civilized humans. And they've still got aircraft."

"Which can still bombard this city," observed Denham. "Can't they?"

Tommy pointed to the many-colored beams of light playing through the sky overhead.

"No. Those lights were invented to guide night-flying planes back home. They're static lights—cold lights, by the way—and they register powerfully when a static-discharge propeller comes within range of them. If Rahn tries a night attack, Aten and I take off and shoot them down again. That's that. But we've got to design gas masks for these people, and I think I can persuade the Council to send over and take all Rahn's aircraft away to-morrow. But the real emergency is the jungle."

HE expounded the situation of the city as he understood it. He labored painstakingly to make his meaning clear while Denham blew meditative smoke rings and Smithers listened quietly. But when Tommy had finished, Smithers said in a vast calm:

"Say, Mr. Reames, y'know I asked you to get somebody to take me through some o' these engine rooms. That's kinda my specialty. An' these folks are good, no question! There's engines—even steam engines—we couldn't build on Earth. But, my Gawd, they're dumb! There ain't a piece of automatic machinery on the place. There's one man to every motor, handlin' the controls or the throttle. They got stuff we couldn't come near, but they never thought of a steam governor."

Tommy turned kindling eyes upon him. "Go on!"

"Hell," said Smithers, "gimme some tools an' I'll go through one shop an' cut the workin' force in half, just slammin' governors, reducin' valves, an' automatic cut-offs on the machines I understand!"

Tommy jumped to his feet. He paced up and down, then halted and began to spout at Aten and the Keeper of Foodstuffs. He gesticulated, fumbling for words, and hunted absurdly for the ones he wanted among his written lists, and finally was drawing excitedly on Aten's black-metal tablet. Smithers got up and looked over his shoulder.

"That ain't it, Mr. Reames," he said slowly. "Maybe I…"

TOMMY pressed the stud that erased the page. Smithers took the tablet and began to draw painstakingly. Aten, watching, exclaimed suddenly. Smithers was drawing an actual machine, actually used in the Golden City, and he was making a working sketch of a governor so that it would operate without supervision while the steam pressure continued. Aten began to talk excitedly. The Keeper of Foodstuffs took the tablet and examined it. He looked blank, then amazed, and as the utterly foreign idea of a machine which controlled itself struck home, his hands shook and color deepened in his cheeks.

He gave an order to Aten, who dashed away. In ten minutes other men began to arrive. They bent over the drawing. Excited comments, discussions and disputes began. A dawning enthusiasm manifested itself. Two of them approached Smithers respectfully, with shining eyes. They drew their tablets from their belts, rather skilfully drew the governor he had indicated in larger scale, and by gestures asked for more detailed plans. Smithers stood up to go with them.

"You're a hero, now, Smithers," Tommy informed him exultantly. "They'll work you to death and call you blessed!"

"Yes, sir," said Smithers. "These fellas are right good mechanics. They just happened to miss this trick." He paused. "Uh—where's Miss Evelyn?"

"With Aten's—wife," said Tommy. This was no time to discuss the marital system of Yugna. "We were prisoners until this morning. Now we're guests of honor. Evelyn's talking to a lot of women and trying to boost our prestige."

SMITHERS went over to the gesticulating group of draftsmen. He settled down to explain by drawings, since he had not a word of their language. In a few minutes a group went rushing away with the sketch tablets held jealously to their breasts, bound for workshops. Other men appeared to present new problems. A wave of sheer enthusiasm was in being. A new idea which would lessen the demands of the machines was a godsend to these folk.

Then Denham blew a smoke ring and said meditatively:

"I think I've got something too, Tommy. Ultra-sonic vibrations. Sound waves at two to three hundred thousand per second. Air won't carry them. Liquids will. They use 'em to sterilize milk, killing the germs by sound waves carried through the fluid. I think we can start some ultra-sonic generators out there that will go through the wet soil and kill all vegetation within a given range. We might clear away the jungle for half a mile or so and then use ultra-sonic beams to help it clear while new food-plants are tried out."

Tommy's eyes glowed.

"You've given yourself a job! We'll turn this planet upside down."

"We'll have to," said Denham drily. "This city may believe in you, but there are others, and these folk are a little too clever. There's no reason why some other city shouldn't attack Earth, if they seriously attack the problem of building a Tube."

Tommy ground his teeth, frowning. Then he started up. There was a new noise down in the city. A sudden flare of intolerable illumination broke out. There was an explosion, many screams, then the yelling tumult of men in deadly battle.

EVERY man on the tower terrace was facing toward the noise, staring. The white-bearded man gave an order, deliberately. Men rushed. But as they swarmed toward an exit, a green beam of light appeared near the uproar. It streaked upward, wavering from side to side and making the golden walls visible in a ghostly fashion. It shivered in a hasty rhythm.

Aten groaned, almost sobbed. There was another flash of that unbearable actinic flame. A thermit-thrower was in action. Then a third flash. This was farther away. The tumult died suddenly, but the green light-beam continued its motion.

Tommy was snapping questions. Aten spoke, and choked upon his words. Tommy swore in a sudden raging passion and then turned a chalky face toward the other two men from Earth.

"The prisoners!" he said in a hoarse voice. "The men from Rahn! They broke loose. They rushed an arsenal. With hand weapons and a thermit-thrower they fought their way to a place where the big vehicles are kept. They raided a dwelling-tower on the way and seized women. They've gone off on the metal roads through the jungle!" He tried to ease his collar. Aten, still watching the green beam, croaked another sentence. "Those devils have got Evelyn!" cried Tommy hoarsely. "My God! Aten's wife, and his..." He jerked a hand toward the Councilor. "Fifty women—gone through the jungle with them, toward Rahn! Those devils have got Evelyn!"

He whirled upon Aten, seizing his shoulder, shaking the man as he roared questions.

"No chance of catching them." Far away, in the jungle, the infinitely vivid actinic flame blazed for several seconds. "They've sprayed thermit on the road. It's melted and ruined. It'd take hours to haul the ground vehicles past the gap. They're got arms and lights. They can fight off the beasts and Ragged Men. They'll make Rahn. And then..." He shook with the rage that possessed him. "...Jacaro's there with those gunmen of his and his friends the Ragged Men!"

HE seemed to control himself with a terrific effort. He turned to the white-bearded Councilor, whose bearing was that of a man stunned by disaster. Tommy spoke measuredly, choosing words with a painstaking care, clipping the words crisply as he spoke.

The Councilor stiffened. Old as he was, an undeniable fighting light came into his eyes. He barked orders right and left. Men woke from the paralysis of shock and fled upon errands of his command. And Tommy turned to Denham and Smithers.

"The women will be safe until dawn," he said evenly. "Our late prisoners can't lose the way—aluminum roads that are no longer much used lead between all the cities—but they won't dare stop in the jungles. They'll go straight on through. They should reach Rahn at dawn or a little before. And at dawn our air fleet will be over the city and they'll give back the women, unharmed, or we'll turn their own trick on them, by God! It'd be better for Evelyn to die of gas than as—as the Ragged Men would kill her!"

His hands were clenched and he breathed noisily for an instant. Then he swallowed, and went on in the same unnatural calm:

"Smithers, you're going to stay behind, with part of the air fleet. You'll get aloft before dawn and shoot down any strange aircraft. They might try to stalemate us by repeating their threat, with our guns over Rahn. I'll give orders."

He turned again to the Councilor, who nodded, glanced at Smithers, and repeated the command.

"You, sir," he spoke to Denham, "you'll come with me. It's your right, I suppose. And we'll go down and get ready."

He led the way steadily toward a door. But he reached up to his collar, once, as if he were choking, and ripped away collar and coat and all, unconscious of the resistance of the cloth.

THAT night the Golden City made savage preparation for war. Ships were loaded and ranged in order. Crews armed themselves, and helped in the loading and arming of other ships. Oddly enough, it was to Tommy that men came to ask if the directing apparatus for the Death Mist should be carried. The Death Mist could, of course, be used as a gas alone, drifting with the wind, or it could be directed from a distance. This had been done on Earth, with the directional impulses sent blindly down the Tube merely to keep the Mist moving always. The controlling apparatus could be carried in a monster freight plane. Tommy ordered it done. Also he had the captured planes from Rahn refitted for flight by replacing their smashed propelling grids. Fresh crews of men for these ships organized themselves.

When the fleet took off there was only darkness in all the world. The unfamiliar stars above shone bright and very near as

Tommy's ship, leading, winged noiselessly up and down and straight away from the play of prismatic lights above the city. Behind him, silhouetted against that many-colored glow, were the angular shapes of many other noiseless shadows. The ornithopters with their racket would start later, so the planes would be soaring above Rahn before their presence was even suspected. The rest of the fleet flew in darkness.

THE flight above the jungle would have been awe-inspiring at another time. There were the stars above, nearer and brighter than those of Earth. There was no Milky Way in the firmament of this universe. The stars were separate and fewer in number. There was no moon. And below there was only utter, unrelieved darkness, from which now and again beast-sounds arose. They were clearly audible on board the silent air fleet. Roarings, bellowings, and hoarse screamings. Once the ships passed above a tumult as of unthinkable monsters in deadly battle, when for an instant the very clashing of monstrous jaws was audible and a hissing sound which seemed filled with deadly hate.

Then lights—few of them, and dim ones. Then blazing fires—Ragged Men, camped without the walls of Rahn or in some gold-walled courtyard where the jungle thrust greedy, invading green tentacles. The air fleet circled noiselessly in a huge batlike cloud. Then things came racing from the darkness, down below, and there was a tumult and a shouting, and presently the hilarious, insanely gleeful uproar of the Ragged Men. Tommy's face went gray. These were the escaped prisoners, arrived actually after the air fleet which was to demand the return of their captives.

Tommy wet his lips and spoke grimly to his pilot. There were six men and many Death-Mist bombs in his ship. He was asking if communication could be had with the other ships. It was wise to let Rahn know at once that avengers lurked overhead for the captives just delivered there.

For answer, a green signal-beam shot out. It wavered here and there. Tommy commanded again. And as the signal-beam flickered, he somehow sensed the obedience of the invisible ships about him. They were sweeping off to right and left. Bombs of the Death Mist were dropping in the darkness. Even in the starlight, Tommy could see great walls of pale vapor building themselves up above the jungle. And a sudden confused noise of yapping defiance and raging hatred came up from the city of Rahn. But before dawn came there was no other sign that their presence was known.

THE ornithopters came squeaking and rattling in their heavy flight just as the dull-red sun of this world peered above the horizon. The tree-fern fronds waved languidly in the morning breeze. The walls and towers of Rahn gleamed bright gold, in parts, and in parts they seemed dull and scabrous with some creeping fungus stuff, and on one side of the city the wall was overwhelmed by a triumphant tide of green. There the jungle had crawled over the ramparts and surged into the city. Three of the towers had their bases in the welter of growing things, and creepers had climbed incredibly and were still climbing to enter and then destroy the man-made structures.

But about the city there now reared a new rampart, rising above the tree-fern tops: there was a wall of the Death Mist encompassing the city. No living thing could enter or leave the city without passing through that cloud. And at Tommy's order it moved forward to the very encampments of the Ragged Men.

He spoke, beginning his ultimatum. But a movement below checked him. On a landing stage that was spotted with molds and lichens, women were being herded into clear view. They were the women of the Golden City. Tommy saw a tiny figure in khaki—Evelyn! Then there was a sudden uproar from an encampment of the Ragged Men. His eyes flicked there, and he saw the Ragged Men running into and out of the tall wall of Death Mist. And they laughed uproariously and ran into and out of the Mist again.

His pilot dived down. The Ragged Men yelled and capered and howled derisively at him. He saw that they removed masklike things from their faces in order to shout, and donned them again before running again into the Mist. At once he understood. The Ragged Men had gas masks!

Then, a sudden cracking noise. Three men had opened fire with rifles from below. Their garments were drab-colored, in contrast to the vivid tints of the clothing of the inhabitants of Rahn. They were Jacaro's gunmen. And a great freight carrier from Yugna veered suddenly, and a bluish flash burst out before it, and it began to flutter helplessly down into the city beneath.

The weapons of Tommy's fleet were useless, since the citizens of Rahn were protected by gas masks. And Tommy's fighting ships were subject to the same rifle fire against their propelling grids that had defeated the fleet from Rahn. The only thing the avenging fleet could now accomplish was the death of the women it could not save.

CHAPTER NINE
War!

A HUGE ornithopter came heavily out on the landing stage in the city of Rahn. Its crew took their places. With a creaking and rattling noise it rose toward the invading fleet. From its filigree cockpit sides, men waved green branches. A green light wavered from the big plane that carried the bearded Council man and Denham. That plane swept forward and hovered above the ornithopter. The two flying things seemed almost fastened together, so closely did their pilots maintain that same speed and course. A snaky rope went coiling down into the lower ship's cockpit. A burly figure began to climb it hand over hand. A second figure followed. A third figure, in the drab clothing that distinguished Jacaro's men from all others, wrapped the rope about himself and was hauled up bodily. And Tommy had seen Jacaro but once, yet he was suddenly grimly convinced that this was Jacaro himself.

The two planes swept apart. The ornithopter descended toward the landing stage of Rahn. The freight plane swept toward the ship that carried Tommy. Again the snaky rope coiled down. And Tommy swung up the fifteen feet that alone separated the two soaring planes, and looked into the hard, amused eyes of Jacaro where he sat between two other emissaries of Rahn. One of them was half naked and savage, with the light of madness in his eyes. A Ragged Man. The other was lean and desperate, despite the colored tunic of a civilized man that he wore.

"HELLO," said Jacaro blandly. "We come up to talk things over."

Tommy gave him the briefest of nods. He looked at Denham—who was deathly white and grim—and the bearded Councilor.

"I' been givin' 'em the dope," said Jacaro easily. "We got the whip hand now. We got gas masks, we got guns just the same as you have, an' we got the women."

"You haven't ammunition," said Tommy evenly, "or damned little. Your men brought down one ship, and stopped. If you had enough shells would you have stopped there?"

Jacaro grinned.

"You got arithmetic, Reames," he conceded. "That's so. But—I'm sayin' it again—we got the women. Your girl, for one! Now, how about throwin' in with me, you an' the professor?"

"No," said Tommy.

"In a coupla months, Rahn'll be runnin' this planet," said Jacaro blandly, "and I'm runnin' Rahn! I didn't know how easy the racket'd be, or I'd 've let Yugna alone. I'd 've come here first. Now get it! Rahn runnin' the planet, with a couple guys runnin' Rahn an' passin' down through a Tube any little thing we want, like a few million bucks in solid gold. An' Rahn an' the other cities for kinda country homes for us an' our friends. All the women we want, good liquor, an' a swell time!"

"Talk sense," said Tommy, without even contempt in his tone.

JACARO snarled.

"No sense actin' too big!" But the snarl encouraged Tommy, because it proved Jacaro less confidant than he tried to seem. His next change of tone proved it. "Aw, hell!" he said placatingly. "This is what I'm figurin' on. These guys ain't used to fighting, but they got the stuff. They got gases that are hell-roarin'. They got ships can beat any we got back home. Figure out the racket. A couple big Tubes, that'll let a ship—maybe folded—go through. A fleet of 'em floatin' over N'York, loaded with gas—that white stuff y' can steer wherever y' want it. Figure the shake-down. We could pull a hundred million from Chicago! We c'd take over the whole United States! Try that on y' piano! Me, King Jacaro, King of America!" His dark eyes flashed. "I'll give y' Canada or Mexico, whichever y' want. Name y' price, guy. A coupla months organizin' here, buildin' a big Tube, then…"

Tommy's expression did not change.

"If it were that easy," he said drily, "you wouldn't be bargaining. I'm not altogether a fool, Jacaro. We want those women back. You want something we've got, and you want it badly. Cut out the oratory and tell me the real price for the return of the women, unharmed."

Jacaro burst into a flood of profanity.

"I'd rather Evelyn died from gas," said Tommy, "than as your filthy Ragged Men would kill her. And you know I mean it." He switched to the language of the cities to go on coldly: "If one woman is harmed, Rahn dies. We will shoot down every ship that rises from her stages. We will spray burning thermit through her streets. We will cover her towers with gas until her people starve in the gas masks they've made!"

The lean man in the tunic of Rahn snarled bitterly: "What matter? We starve now!"

Tommy turned upon him as Jacaro whirled and cursed him bitterly for the revealing outburst.

"We will ransom the women with food," said Tommy coldly—and then his eyes flamed, "and thrash you afterwards for fools!"

HE made a gesture to the Keeper of Foodstuffs. It was unconsciously an authoritative gesture, though the Keeper of Foodstuffs was in the state of affairs in Yugna the head of the Council. But that old man spoke deliberately. The man from Rahn snarled his reply. And Tommy turned aside as the bargaining went on. He could see Evelyn down below, a tiny speck of khaki amid the rainbow-colored robes of the other women. This had been a savage expedition, to rescue or to avenge. It had deteriorated into a bargain. Tommy heard, dully, amounts of unfamiliar weights and measures of foodstuffs he did not recognize. He heard the time and place of payment named: the gate of Yugna, the third dawn hence. He hardly looked up as at some signal one of their own ornithopters slid below and the three ambassadors of Rahn prepared to go over the side. But Jacaro snarled out of one corner of his mouth.

"These guys are takin' each other's words. Maybe that's all right, but I'm warnin' you, if there's any double-crossin'...."

He was gone. The Keeper of Foodstuffs touched Tommy's shoulder.

"Our flier," he said slowly, "will make sure our women are as yet unharmed. We are to deliver the foods at our own city gate, and after the women have been returned. Rahn dares not keep them or harm them. We of Yugna keep our word. Even in Rahn they know it."

"But they won't keep theirs," said Tommy heavily. "Not with a man of Earth to lead them."

HE watched with his heart in his mouth as the ornithopter alighted near the assembled women of Yugna. As the three ambassadors climbed out, he could hear the faint murmur of voices. The men of Yugna, under truce, called across the landing stage to the women of their own city, and the women replied to them. Then the crew of the one grounded freighter arrived on the landing stage and the flapping flier rose slowly and rejoined the fleet. Its crew shouted a shamefaced reassurance to the flagship.

"I suppose," said Tommy bitterly, "we'd better go back—if you're sure the women are safe."

"I am sure," said the old man unhappily, "or I had not agreed to pay half the foodstuffs in Yugna for their return."

He withdrew into a troubled silence as the fleet swept far from triumphantly for him. Denham had not spoken at all, though his eyes had blazed savagely upon the men of Rahn. Now he spoke, dry-throatedly:

"Tommy—Evelyn—"

"She is all right so far," said Tommy bitterly. "She's to be ransomed by foodstuffs, paid at the gates of Yugna. And Jacaro bragged he's running Rahn—and they've got gas masks. We'd better be ready for trouble after the women are returned."

Denham nodded grimly. Tommy reached out and took one of the black tablets from the man beside him. He began to draw carefully, his eyes savage.

"What's that?"

"There's high-pressure steam in Yugna," said Tommy coldly. "I'm designing steam guns. Gravity feed of spherical projectiles. A jet of steam instead of gunpowder. They'll be low-velocity, but we can use big-calibre balls for shock effect, and with long barrels they ought to serve for a hundred yards or better. Smooth bore, of course."

Denham stirred. His lips were pinched.

"I'll design a gas mask," he said restlessly, "and Smithers and I, between us, will do what we can."

THE air fleet went on over the waving tree-fern jungle in an unvarying monotony of bitterness. Presently Tommy wearily explained his design to the bearded Councilor who, with the quick comprehension of mechanical design apparently instinctive in these folk, grasped it immediately. He selected three of the six-man crew and passed Tommy's drawings to them. While the jungle flowed beneath the fleet they studied the sketches, made other drawings, and showed them eagerly to Tommy. When the fleet soared down to the scattered landing stages, not only was the design understood but apparently plans for production had been made. It did not take the men of the Golden City long to respond.

Tommy flung himself savagely into the work he had taken upon himself. It did not occur to him to ask for authority. He knew what had to be done and he set to work to do it, commanding men and materials as if there could be no question of disobedience. As a matter of fact, he yielded impatiently to an order of the Council that he should present himself in the Council hall, and, since no questions were asked him, continued his organizing in the very presence of the Council, sending for information and giving orders in a low tone while the Council deliberated. A vote was taken by the voting machine. At its end, he was solemnly informed that, though not a native of Yugna, he was entrusted with the command of the defense forces of the city. His skill in arms—as evidenced by his defeat of the fleet of Rahn—and his ability in command—when he met the gas-mask defense of Rahn with a threat of starvation—moved the Council to that action. He accepted the command almost abstractedly, and hurried away to pick gun emplacements.

WITHIN four hours after the return of the fleet, the first steam gun was ready for trial. Smithers appeared, sweat-streaked and vastly calm, to announce that others could be turned out in quantity.

"These guys have got the stuff," he said steadily. "Instead o' castin' their stuff, they shoot it on a core in a melted spray. They ain't got steel, an' copper's scarce, but they got some alloys that are good an' tough. One's part tungsten or I'm crazy."

Tommy nodded.

"Turn out all the guns you can," he said. "I look for fighting."

"Yeah," said Smithers. "Miss Evelyn's still all right?"

"Up to three hours ago," said Tommy grimly. "Every three hours one of our ships lands in Rahn and reports. We give the Rahnians their stuff at our own city gates. I've warned Jacaro that we've mounted thermit-throwers on our food stores. If he manages to gas us by surprise, nevertheless our foodstuffs can't be captured. They've got to turn over Evelyn and cart off their food before they dare to fight, else they'll starve."

"But—uh—there're other cities they could stick up, ain't there?"

"We've warned them," said Tommy curtly. "They've got thermit-throwers mounted on their food supplies, too. And they're desperate enough to keep Rahn off. They're willing enough to let Yugna do the fighting, but they know what Rahn's winning will mean."

Smithers turned away, then turned back.

"Uh—Mr. Reames," he said heavily, "these fellas've gone near crazy about governors an' reducing valves an' such. They're inventin' ways to use 'em on machines I don't make head or tail of. We got three-four hundred men loose from machines already, an' they're turnin' out these steam guns as soon as you check up. There'll be more loose by night. I had 'em spray some castin's for another Tube, too. Workin' like they do, an' with the tools they got, they make speed."

Tommy responded impatiently: "There's no steel, no iron for magnets."

"I know," admitted Smithers. "I'm tryin' steam cylinders to—uh—energize the castin's, instead o' coils. It'll be ready by mornin'. I wish you'd look it over, Mr. Reames. If Miss Evelyn gets safe into the city, we could send her down the Tube to Earth until the fightin's over."

"I'll try to see it," said Tommy impatiently. "I'll try!"

HE turned back to the set-up steam gun. A flexible pipe from a heavily insulated cylinder ran to it. A hopper dropped metallic balls down into a bored-out barrel, where they were sucked into the blast of superheated steam from the storage cylinder. At a touch of the trigger a monstrous cloud of steam poured out. It was six feet from the gun muzzle before it condensed enough to be visible. Then a huge white cloud developed; but the metal pellets went on with deadly force. Half an inch in diameter, they carried seven hundred yards at extreme elevation. Point-blank range was seventy-five yards. They would kill at three hundred, and stun or disable beyond that. At a hundred yards they would tear through a man's body.

Tommy was promised a hundred of the weapons, with their boilers, in two days. He selected their emplacements. He directed that a disabling device be inserted, so if rushed they could not be turned against their owners. He inspected the gas masks being turned out by the women, who in this emergency worked like the men. Though helpless before machinery, it seemed, they could contrive a fabric device like a gas mask.

The second day the work went on more desperately still. But Smithers' work in releasing men was telling. There were fifteen hundred governors, or reducing valves, or autocratic cut-outs in operation now. And fifteen hundred men were released from the machines, which had to be kept going to keep the city alive. With that many men, intelligent mechanics all, Tommy and Smithers worked wonders. Smithers drove them mercilessly, using profanity and mechanical drawings instead of speech. Denham withdrew twenty men and labored on top of one of the towers. Toward sunset of the second day, vast clouds of steam bellied out from it at odd, irregular intervals. Nothing else manifested itself. Those irregular belchings of steam continued until dark, but Tommy paid no attention to them. He was driving the gunners of the machine guns to practice. He was planning patrols, devising a reserve, mounting thermit-throwers, and arranging for the delivery of the promised ransom at the specified city gate. So far, there was no sign of anything unusual in Rahn. Messengers from Yugna saw the captive women regularly, once every three hours. The last to leave had reported them being loaded into great ground vehicles under a defending escort, to travel through the dark jungle roads to Yugna. A vast concourse of empty vehicles was trailing into the jungle after them, to bring back the food which would keep Rahn from starving, for a while. It all seemed wholly regular.

AT dawn, the remaining ships of the air fleet of Rahn were soaring silently above the jungle about the Golden City. They made no threat. They offered no affront. But they soared, and soared...

A little after dawn, glitterings in the jungle announced the arrival of the convoy. Messengers, in advance, shouted the news. Men from Yugna went out to inspect. The atmosphere grew tense. The air fleet of Rahn drew closer.

Slowly, a great golden gateway yawned. Four ground vehicles rolled forward, and under escort of the Rahnians entered the city. Half the captive women from Yugna were within them. They alighted, weeping for joy, and were promptly whisked away. Evelyn was not among them. Tommy ground his teeth. An explanation came. When one half the promised ransom was paid, the others would be forthcoming.

Tommy gave grim orders. Half the foodstuffs were taken to the city gate—half, no more. At his direction, it was explained gently to the Rahnians that the rest of the ransom remained under guard of the thermit-throwers. It would not be exposed to capture until the last of the captives were released. There was argument, expostulation. The rest of the women appeared. Aten, at Tommy's express command, piled Evelyn and his own wife into a ground vehicle and came racing madly to the tower from which Tommy could see all the circuit of the city.

"You're all right?" asked Tommy. At Evelyn's speechless nod, he put his hand heavily on her shoulder. "I'm glad," he managed to say. "Put on that gas mask. Hell's going to pop in a minute."

He watched, every muscle tense. There was confusion about the city gate. Ground vehicles, loaded with foodstuffs, poured out of the gate and back toward the jungle. Other vehicles with improvised enlargements to their carrying platforms—making them into huge closed boxes—rolled up to the gate. The loaded vehicles rolled back and back and back, and ever more apparently empty ones crowded about the city gate waiting for admission.

Then there was a sudden flare of intolerable light. A wild yell arose. Clouds of steam shot up from the ready steam guns. But the circling air fleet turned as one ship and plunged for the city. The leaders began to drop smoking things that turned into monstrous pillars of prismatically-colored mist. A wave of deadly vapor rolled over the ramparts of the city. And then there was a long-continued ululation and the noise of battle. Ragged Men, hidden in the jungle, had swarmed upon the walls with ladders made of jungle reeds. They came over the parapet in a wave of howling madness. And they surged into the city, flinging gas bombs as they came.

CHAPTER TEN
The Fight

THE city was pandemonium. Tommy, looking down from his post of command, swore softly under his breath. The Death Mist was harmless to the defenders of Yugna as a gas, because of their gas masks. But it served as a screen. It blotted out the waves of attackers so the steam guns could not be aimed save at the shortest of short ranges. His precautions were taking effect, to be sure. Two thirds of the attackers were Ragged Men drawn from about half the surviving cities, and against such a horde Yugna could not have held out at all but for his preparations. Now the defenders took a heavy toll. Swarms of men came racing toward the open gate, their truncheons aglow in the sunlight. The ring of Death Mist was contracting as if to strangle the city, and it left the ramparts bare again. And from more than one point upon the battlements the roaring clouds of steam burst out again. A dozen guns concentrated on the racing men of Rahn, plunging from the jungle to enter by the gate. They were racing forward, without order but at top speed, to share in the fighting and loot. Then streams of metal balls tore into them. The front of the irregular column was wiped out utterly. Wide swathes were cut in the rest. The survivors ran wildly forward over a litter of dead and dying men. Electric-charge weapons sent crackling discharges among them. Their contorted figures reeled and fell or leaped convulsively to lie forever still where they struck. And then the steam guns turned about to fire into the rear of the men who had charged past them.

The steam guns had literally blasted away the line of Ragged Men where they stood. But the line went on, with great ragged gaps in it, to be sure, but still vastly outnumbering the defenders of the city. Here and there a steam gun was silent, its gun crew dead. And presently those that were left were useless, immobile upon the ramparts in the rear of the attack.

DOWN in the ways of the city the fight rose to a riotous clamor. At Tommy's order the women of the city had been concentrated into a few strong towers. The machines of the city were left undefended for a time. A few strong patrols of fighting men, strategically placed, flung themselves with irresistible force upon certain bands of maddened Ragged Men. But where a combat raged, there the Ragged Men swarmed howling. Their hatred impelled them to suicidal courage and to unspeakable atrocities. From his tower, Tommy saw a man of Yugna, evidently a prisoner. Four Ragged Men surrounded him, literally tearing him to pieces like the maniacs they were. Then he saw dust spurting up in a swift-advancing line, and all four Ragged Men twitched and collapsed on top of their victim. A steam gun had done that. A fighting patrol of the men of Yugna swept fiercely down a paved way in one of the Golden City's vehicles. There was the glint of gold from it. A solid, choked mass of invaders rushed upon it. Without slackening speed, without a pause, the vehicle raced ahead. Intolerable flashes of light appeared. A thermit-thrower was mounted on the machine. It drove forward like a flaming meteor, and as electric-charge weapons flashed upon it men screamed and died. It tore into a vast cloud of the Death Mist and the unbearable flames of its weapon could only be seen as illuminations of that deadly vapor.

A part of the city was free of defenders, save the isolated steam gunners left behind upon the walls. Ragged Men, drunk with success, ran through its ways, slashing at the walls, battering at the light-panels, pounding upon the doorways of the towers. Tommy saw them hacking at the great doorway of a tower. It gave. They rushed within. Almost instantly thereafter the opening spouted them forth again and after them, leaping upon them, snapping and biting and striking out with monstrous paws and teeth, were green lizard-things like the one that had been killed—years back, it seemed—on Earth. A deadly combat began instantly. But when the last of the fighting creatures was down, no more than a dozen were left of the three score who had begun the fight.

BUT this was not the main battle. The main battle was hidden under the Death-Mist cloud, concentrated in a vast thick mass in the very center of the city. Tommy watched that grimly. Perhaps eight thousand men had assailed the city. Certainly two thousand of them were represented by the still or twitching forms in queer attitudes here and there, in single dots or groups. There were seven hundred corpses before the city gate alone, where the steam guns had mowed down a reinforcing column. And there were others scattered all about. The defenders had lost heavily enough, but Tommy's defense behind the line of the ramparts was soundly concentrated in strong points, equipped with steam guns and mostly armed with thermit-throwers as well. From the center of the city there came only a vast, unorganized tumult of battle and death.

Then a huge winged thing came soaring down past Tommy's tower. It landed with a crash on the roofs below, spilling its men like ants. Tommy strained his eyes. There was a billowing outburst of steam from the tower where Denham had been working the night before. A big flier burst into the weird bright flame of the thermit fluid. It fell, splitting apart as it dropped. Again the billowing steam. No result—but beyond the city walls showed a flash of thermit flame.

"Denham!" muttered Tommy. "He's got a steam cannon; he's shooting shells loaded with thermit! They smash when they hit. Good!"

He dispatched a man with orders, but a messenger was panting his way up as the runner left. He thrust a scribbled bit of paper into Tommy's hand.

"I'm trying to bring down the ship that's controlling the Death Mist. I'll shell those devils in the middle of town as soon as our controls can handle the Mist.

Denham."

Tommy began to snap out his commands. He raced downward toward the street. Men seemed to spring up like magic about him. A ship with one wing aflame was tottering in mid-air, and another was dropping like a plummet.

Then Tommy uttered a roar of pure joy. The huge globe of beautiful, deadly vapor was lifting! Its control-ship was shattered, and men of the Golden City had found its setting. The Mist rose swiftly in a single vast globule of varicolored reflections. And the situation in the center of the city was clear. Two towers were besieged. Dense masses of the invaders crowded about them, battering at them. Steam guns opened from their windows. Thermit-throwers shot out flashes of deadly fire.

Tommy led five hundred men in savage assault, cleaving the mass of invaders like a wedge. He cut off a hundred men and wiped them out, while a rear guard poured electric charges into the main body of the enemy. More men of Yugna came leaping from a dozen doorways and joined them. Tommy found Smithers by his side, powder-stained and sweat-streaked.

"MISS Evelyn's all right?" Smithers asked in a great calm.

"She is," growled Tommy. "On the top floor of a tower, with a hundred men to guard her."

"You didn't look at the Tube I made," said Smithers impassively; "but I turned on the steam. Looks like it worked. It's ready to go through, anyways. It's the same place the other one was, down in that cellar. I'm tellin' you in case anything happens."

He opened fire with a magazine rifle into the thick of the mob that assailed the two towers. Tommy left him with fifty men to block a highway and led his men again into the mass of mingled Ragged Men and Rahnians. His followers saw his tactics now. They split off a section of the mob and fell upon it ferociously. There were sudden awful screams. Thermit flame was rising from two places in the very thick of the mob. It burst up from a third, and fourth, and fifth... Denham, atop his tower, had the range with his steam cannon, and was flinging heavy shells into the attackers of the two central buildings. And then there was a roaring of steam and a ground vehicle came to a stop not fifty feet away. A gun crew of Yugnans had shifted their unwieldy weapon and its insulated steam boiler to a freight-carrying vehicle. Now the gunner pulled trigger and traversed his weapon into the thick of the massed invaders, while his companions worked desperately to keep the hopper full of projectiles.

The invaders melted away. Steam guns in the towers, thermit projectiles from the cannon far away: now this... And the concealing cloud of Death Mist was rising still, headed straight up toward the zenith. It looked like a tiny, dwindling pearl.

THE assault upon Yugna had been a mad one, a frantic one. But the flight from Yugna was the flight of men trying to escape from hell. Wild panic characterized the fleeing men. They threw aside their weapons and ran with screams of terror no whit less horrible than their howls of triumph had been. And Tommy would have stopped the slaughter, but there was no way to send orders to the rampart gunners in time. As the fugitives swarmed toward the walls again, the storms of steam-propelled missiles mowed them down. Even those who scrambled down to the ground outside and fled sobbing for the jungle were pursued by hails of bullets. Of the eight thousand men who assailed Yugna, less than one in five escaped.

Pursuit was still in progress. Here and there, through the city, the sound of isolated combats still went on. Denham came down from his tower, looking rather sick as he saw the carnage about him. A strong escort brought Evelyn. Aten was grinning proudly, as though he had in person defeated the enemy. And as Evelyn shakingly put out her hand to touch Tommy's arm—it was only later that he realized he had been wounded in half a dozen minor ways—a shadow roared over their heads. The crackle of firearms came from it.

"Jacaro!" snarled Tommy. He leaped instinctively to pursue. But the flying thing was bound for a landing in an open square, the same one which not long since had seen the heaviest fighting. It alighted there and toppled askew on contact. Figures tumbled out of it, in torn and ragged garments fashioned in the style of the very best tailors of the Earth's underworld.

Men of Yugna raced to intercept them. Firearms spat and bellowed luridly. In a close-knit, flame-spitting group, the knot of men raced over fallen bodies and hurtled areas where the pavement had cooled to no more than a dull-red heat where a thermit shell had struck. One man, two, three men fell under the small-arms fire. The gangsters went racing on, firing desperately. They dived into a tunnel and disappeared.

"THE Tube!" roared Smithers. "They' goin' for the Tube!"
He plunged forward, and Tommy seized his arm.

"They'll go through your Tube," he said curtly. "It looks like the one they came through. They'll think it is. Let 'em!"

Smithers tried to tear free.

"But they'll get back to Earth!" he raged. "They'll get off clear!"

The sharp, cracking sound of a gun-cotton explosion came out of the doorway into which Jacaro and his men had dived. Tommy smiled very grimly indeed.

"They've gone through," he said drily, "and they've blown up the Tube behind them. But—I didn't tell you—I took a look at your castings. Your pupils were putting them together, ready for the steam to go in, in place of the coils I used. But—er—Smithers! You'd discarded one pair of castings. They didn't satisfy you. Your pupils forgot that. They hooked them all together."

Smithers gulped.

"Instead of four right-angled bends," said Tommy grimly, "you have six connected together. You turned on the steam in a hurry, not noticing. And I don't know how many series of dimensions there are in this universe of ours. We know of two. There may be any number. But Jacaro and his men didn't go back to Earth. God only knows where they landed, or what it's like. Maybe somewhere a million miles in space. Nobody knows. The main thing is that Earth is safe now. The Death Mist has faded out of the picture."

He turned and smiled warmly at Evelyn. He was a rather horrible sight just then, though he did not know it. He was bloody and burned and wounded. He ignored all matters but success, however.

"I think," he said drily, "we have won the confidence of the Golden City, Evelyn, and that there'll be no more talk of gassing Earth. As soon as the Council meets again, we'll make sure. And then—well, I think we can devote a certain amount of time to our personal affairs. You are the first Earth-girl to be kissed in the Fifth Dimension. We'll have to see if you can't distinguish yourself further."

AGAIN the Council hall in the tower of government in the Golden City of Yugna. Again the queer benches about the black wood table—though two of the seats that had been occupied were now empty. Again the guards behind the chairs, and the crowd of watchers—visitors, citizens of Yugna attending the deliberations of the Council. The audience was a queer one, this time. There were bandages here and there. There were men who were wounded, broken, bent and crippled in the fighting. But a warmly welcoming murmur spread through the hall as Tommy came in, himself rather extensively patched. He was wearing the tunic and breeches of the Golden City, because his own clothes were hopelessly beyond repair. The bearded old Councilor gathered the eyes of his fellows. They rose. This Council seated itself as one man.

Quiet, placid formalities. The Keeper of Foodstuffs murmured that the ransom paid to Rahn had been recaptured after the fight. The Keeper of Rolls reported with savage satisfaction the number of enemies who had been slain in battle. He added that the loss to Yugna was less than one man to ten of the enemy. And he added with still greater emphasis that the shops being fitted with automatic controls had released now—it had grown so much—two thousand men from the necessary day-and-night working force, and further releases were to be expected. The demands of the machines were lessened already beyond the memory of man. Eyes turned to Tommy. There was an expectant pause for his reply.

"I HAVE been Commander of Defense Forces," he told them slowly, "in this fighting. I have given you weapons. My two friends have done more. The machines will need fewer and fewer attendants as the hints they have given you are developed by yourselves. And there is some hope that one of my friends may show you, in ultra-sonic vibrations, a weapon against the jungle itself. My own work is finished. But I ask again for friendship for my planet Earth. I ask that no war be made on

222

my own people. I ask that what benefits you receive from us be passed to the other surviving cities on the same terms. And since there can be no further fighting on this scale, I give back my commission as Commander of Defense."

There was a little murmur among the men of Yugna, looking on. It rose to a protesting babble, to a shout of denial. The bearded old Keeper of Foodstuffs smiled.

"It is proposed that the appointment as Commander of Defense Forces be permanent," he said mildly.

He produced the queer black box and touched it in a certain fashion. He passed it to the next man, and the next and next. It went around the table. It passed a second time, but this time each man merely looked at the top.

"You command the defense forces of Yugna for always," said the bearded old man, gently. "Now give orders that your requests become laws."

TOMMY stared blankly. He was suddenly aware of Aten in the background, smiling triumphantly and very happily at him. There was something like a roar of approval from the men of Yugna, assembled.

"Just what," demanded Tommy, "does this mean?"

"For many years," said a hawk-faced man ungraciously, "we have had no Commander of Defense. We have had no wars. But we see it is needful. We have chosen you, with all agreeing. The Commander of Defense..." He sniffed a little, pugnaciously. "...has the authority the ancient kings once owned."

Tommy leaned back in the curious benchlike chair, his eyes narrow and thoughtful. This would simplify matters. No danger of trouble to Earth. A free hand for Denham and Smithers to help these folk, and for Denham to learn scientific facts—in the sciences they had developed—which would be of inestimable value to Earth. And it could be possible to open a peaceful trade with the nations of Earth without any danger of war. And maybe...

He smiled suddenly. It widened almost into a grin.

"All right. I'll settle down here for a while. But—er—just how does one set about getting married here?"

THE END

Made in the USA
Middletown, DE
22 November 2022

15364643R00135